MW01181386

Crystal Widow

By

Patricia A. Bremmer

"Put a little mystery in your life!"
Patricia A. Bremmer

Elusive Clue Series

Crystal Widow

Patricia A. Bremmer

ISBN# 978-0-9745884-3-8

For additional copies contact:

Windcall Publishing/
Windcall Enterprises
75345 RD. 317
Venango, Ne 69168

www.windcallenterprises.com

Acknowledgements

My thanks and acknowledgements to all who helped me create **“Crystal Widow”**.

Martin Bremmer, my husband, who took over my daily tasks so I could steal away to a private place to write.

Jamie Swayzee, for the hours and hours of grueling work on editing.

Detective Glen Karst, who lends his unending knowledge and experience to keep my crime scenes accurate. And for letting me build his fictional character into a larger than life Teddybear.

Jim Hayes, pharmacist extraordinaire who is a walking encyclopedia of information on drugs and their occasional sinister usage.

Debbie Karst, a dear friend, for allowing me to use her character in yet another book.

Kalli Weiss, for her assistance with insurance questions.

Brandenn Bremmer, for his outstanding photography skills on the cover.

Chapter 1

A strong breeze forced the sisters to huddle closer together on that cold April morning. Pouring rain from the previous night created a bog near the graveside. The soggy mud sucked the long stem of high-heeled shoes, holding fast, refusing to allow graceful walking. Paula, dressed more sensibly than her two older sisters, Carla and LeAnn, wore black slacks and flat shoes. Their mother, Anna, enforced strict rules for the girls to follow in every aspect of their lives. By the time Paula arrived, Anna's attentiveness to the rules eased. She allowed her to stray from the rigid tradition her sisters obediently followed.

With Paula's assistance, LeAnn maneuvered through the muddy grass while Carla, the favorite, guided their mother carefully to the dry grassy mat under the tent, where chairs were arranged in tidy rows for family members to be seated during the final ceremony.

Today, Lawrence, Anna's second husband and stepfather to the three girls, received his final blessing from the priest. The small family watched his casket being lowered. The somber setting remained silent. Sobbing and tears were not present, as Anna and the girls shed none. Anna repeatedly drilled the girls. Don't let anyone see you crying, that's a sign of weakness. Once someone knows you're a weak person that's when he or she will take advantage of you.

Lawrence's co-workers made up the remainder of the mourners. Although sad their co-worker died, not one of them had taken the opportunity to learn about this quiet little man.

Carla probably knew Lawrence better than her sisters. He had a two-fold role in her life being her stepfather as well as her boss at the insurance company.

When Charles, their real father, died, LeAnn was only thirteen, Carla eleven and the baby Paula, just nine. Lawrence, seven years younger than Anna, entered their lives five years after Charles' death. A quiet gentle man, he took on the responsibility of a wife and three teenage daughters. Anna, who ruled the household with an iron hand, simplified his job. The girls were well behaved and helpful around the house and the garden.

A small ray of sun shining over the grave exchanged places with dark rain-filled clouds. Suddenly, the rumble of thunder filled the silence followed by large raindrops spattering on the tent above the family. April in Omaha, Nebraska could burst into rain with little warning. A cold spring Nebraska rain produced heavy mud in the native clay soil. The torture of the bone chilling rain would quickly be forgotten when the most gorgeous array of spring flowers burst forth throughout the city in May.

Anna looked across the wet cemetery lawn to the parked cars waiting to drive them back to St. Mary's Church. If they were to reach the cars without being drenched to the skin they must hurry. Her blue eyes caught those of Father Patrick. He acknowledged the sense of urgency. He made his way through the people toward her, offering his condolences one last time thus bringing the service to an abrupt end.

Anna stood quickly, gathering her black trench coat around her short plump body. Her gesture made it obvious to the girls she intended a speedy departure. She trudged through the soggy sod without assistance, her blond hair pulled tightly into a bun. With plans for the remainder of the day, she anxiously wanted to leave the graveside. She walked quickly, making no attempt to visit with Lawrence's friends from his office. He had no family of his own. He grew up in an orphanage. At the young age of eighteen they released him to fend for himself.

He convinced the personnel office at Mutual of Omaha Insurance Company to hire him to work in the mailroom. The opening required someone more mature with work experience, but Lawrence, with his small frame and large sad brown eyes, was so convincing they took a chance. He did not disappoint the company. He remained a faithful employee for a record thirty-five years. As a model employee he never reported tardy for work, nor did he take his sick days even when he should have. Sometimes his supervisor urged him to return home when he arrived at the office under the weather to prevent the spread of his illness to the other employees.

He refused to take vacation time until he and Anna married. She insisted the company owed him that time and he should not allow them to take unfair advantage of him. Lawrence learned to take life in stride both at work and at home. When things were difficult somehow he managed to see his way through it without much grumbling. The years he spent married to Anna were far from happy.

Anna, from German decent and difficult to live with, made their marriage a prison for him. She felt it totally unnecessary for them to own two vehicles. Disposing of one of the vehicles would decrease the insurance as well as the annual tax and license payments. Lawrence worked hard to purchase a nice car by saving until he could pay cash. Shortly after his marriage to Anna she insisted they sell his car and keep hers. Desperate to be a good husband he reluctantly agreed. With her strange logic, she convinced him since he spent his entire day at work, her need for the car would supercede his, forcing Lawrence to take either the bus or rely on her to drive him to work. He preferred to take the bus. When Anna drove the lives of the passengers were at stake. She had no consideration for other drivers on the road. She darted in and out of the traffic, switching lanes without the use of her turn signal. She straddled the centerline more often than she stayed in her own lane. She made hair-raising turns when the light changed from yellow to red. On the days Anna insisted upon driving him he barely made it on time or arrived embarrassingly late. His co-workers pretended not to notice to save him the humiliation. The one trait they observed about him was his willingness to please. Possibly his marriage to Anna may have been easier on him if he would have stood up to her rather than allow her total control over every situation.

Without a family of his own for a role model he wanted to please Anna, please the girls, and please his co-workers. In doing so he gave no thought to pleasing himself. That changed one day. Lawrence finally found the strength within him to leave Anna. True to his quiet manner, he secretly set aside money over the years to hire an attorney to assist him with his desire for a divorce.

Anna stressed poverty in their marriage. She constantly reminded him of his shortcomings as a provider. She, however, did not feel the need to work outside their home even though the girls were grown and gone. She prepared terrible meals, scrimping and saving to keep the grocery bill down.

Lawrence refrained from complaining when she served him hotdogs and cooked cabbage for a week straight. Or when she discovered the ease of Hamburger Helper. That phase lasted nightly for a number of months. When she made breakfast omelets on Sunday morning she cut onion, ham and peppers in such large chunks he often wondered if she secretly hoped he would choke to death on them. She touted herself as a wonderful cook.

The unfortunate part of the story is Lawrence did bring in sufficient money. Anna, although wanting to complain about lack of funds, insisted Lawrence take her out to restaurants on a regular basis. When the girls were young and lived at home she lectured them before they entered the restaurant. They were instructed to order only from the children's portion of the menu and to find the least costly meal. They were also told to drink only water with the meal even if the waiter suggested alternative beverages.

Anna consistently ordered the most expensive item on the menu, multiple glasses of wine, a tasty dessert and coffee. Lawrence and the girls were forced to sit in the restaurant as long as Anna felt they needed to remain. Somehow being in public places with her family, spending money for others to see made her feel important. Not once did she allow the girls to bring games, books or toys into the restaurants for entertainment during the long wait.

She wanted other customers to notice her beautiful daughters. LeAnn, the oldest, resembled her father with his dark brown hair and gray eyes. Carla, the middle daughter, had the most gorgeous black hair falling to her waist, glistening under the bright lights at the restaurant. She also had her father's gray eyes. Finally, Paula's appearance mirrored that of her mother's. Her waist length hair, blond as butter, as her mother described it, carried the right amount of curl. Her eyes, the same shade of crystal blue as Anna's, had a warmth in them lacking in Anna's cold eyes.

Beautiful girls dressed in matching dresses did catch the eye of the other patrons. The girls despised dressing in the same clothes, but Anna wanted them to do so because it appealed to her. She never allowed the girls to go shopping with her for fabric. She bought only sale fabric but chose patterns no young girl would be happy in. She sewed the dresses, always making them a little too large for their tiny frames, explaining they would last longer by giving them room to grow.

The girls obediently wore the ghastly clothes. They were teased mercilessly at school but developed thick skins knowing Anna would not sympathize with them.

Frequently she invited neighbors, friends or other distant family members to join them for a meal at her favorite restaurant then expected Lawrence to pick up the tab for the entire group. During that period of her life Anna smoked. Whenever she went to a restaurant, whether it was with her family or larger crowds, she always insisted they sit in the smoking section. Many times her guests would cough and gag through their meal as Anna and those around them filled the area with smoke. She either secretly enjoyed making others suffer to be in her presence or she was totally oblivious to the needs of others.

After twenty years of living with Anna, Lawrence finally wanted out. He realized with each passing year life with her became more difficult. His future looked bleak. At his office he met, Dorothy, a widow who treated him with kindness. Dorothy kept up her slender appearance. Awareness of current fashion trends and make-up made her extremely attractive, still turning heads at her age. Unlike Anna, who assumed whatever she chose to wear no matter how ridiculous she looked, would cause envy in those around her.

Dorothy listened to his conversation over their sack lunches. Frequently, she brought an extra serving of dessert to share with him. He marveled at the taste of her home-cooked desserts, the likes of which he had never experienced in the orphanage, nor during his marriage to Anna, who thought burnt chocolate pudding could pass for a gourmet dish. His heart ached when she spoke of her loneliness since the death of her husband. Her life contained a void he wanted to fill.

Not quite sure how to break the news to Anna, he slowly and meticulously packed his things. He carried his belongings to work with him in white file folder boxes. Anna remained unaware of his secret move. Box by box he moved his things to a storage room.

He declared his love to Dorothy then explained his plan to leave his wife and marry her. She felt uncomfortable being the other woman but his constant reassurance that she was the best thing in his life put her at ease. She wanted to make him happy and she needed him. She kept his secret, helping him with his boxes whenever she could.

After he moved most of the personal belongings that held meaning to him, he filed for divorce. He knew Anna would cling to him. She made a big deal about how much she loved him, always snuggling up to him when others could watch. She longed for everyone to envy her perfect marriage. Anyone who knew Anna well felt sorry for Lawrence. Her transparent affections were real only to her. She had many pet names for him used only when within earshot of others.

He and Dorothy made plans to move him into her home as soon as Anna received her copy of the divorce papers. Lawrence knew, with her temper, living even one more day in the same house with her would be impossible.

He felt sad leaving the home he scrimped and paid for before he met her. A large older home located in a quiet neighborhood of south Omaha, while not a showplace, he loved it.

Paula called Carla.

"Hey Paula. What's up?"

"Are you free for lunch?" asked Paula.

"Today? Sure I guess so. Why?"

"I've got something I need to talk to you and LeAnn about. Do you think we can get her to join us?"

"Boy, I don't know. You know how she is about short notice. She's such an organizer."

"I know but this is really important. Can you call her? She's more apt to give in to you."

"I'll try."

Carla made the call to LeAnn.

"LeAnn, want to go to lunch with your two favorite sisters today?"

"Gee, I don't know. I've got a desk full of work and a meeting this afternoon."

LeAnn worked for Merrill Lynch as a stockbroker. She loved her job and performed it well, making loads of money for her clients. She managed to invest her own small sums of money to build a nest egg for her future. With her wide color assortment of business suits, short clean hairstyle and simple but elegant jewelry, she made her clients feel at ease allowing her to handle their money. She symbolized a wise successful businesswoman.

"All the more reason to take a break. Meet us at the Hunan Restaurant on Sixtieth and Center at eleven-thirty. I won't take no for an answer." Carla hung up the phone not allowing LeAnn the opportunity to refuse.

The girls met for lunch.

LeAnn studied Paula instead of her menu.

"You seem nervous. What's bugging you?"

Carla peered over her menu to look at Paula.

"There's something we need to talk about," answered Paula.

A young Oriental boy came to take their order. The girls ate there frequently, rarely straying from their favorite dishes. The small neighborhood restaurant filled to capacity each day for lunch and again during the dinner hour.

LeAnn, not wanting to be disturbed, blurted out, "Bring us the usual."

Both Carla and Paula looked at her, shocked by her statement.

"What? Did you want to order something different today?"

"No," said Carla, "but it might've been polite to ask first."

"I don't have much time, I need to get back to the office. Now spill it, Paula. What's on your mind?"

"I don't know if I should say anything," said Paula.

She scanned the restaurant as if there might be spies watching her every move. She fidgeted with the paper cover from her straw, tying it in one knot after the other, a habit she developed in childhood when they were forced to sit for hours in restaurants with their mother. Her finger traced the outline of the checkered tablecloth beneath the glass cover.

Carla noticed her stress.

"Is there a problem with you and Andy?" asked Carla.

"Oh, no. Nothing like that. Andy and I are just fine."

"Come on, sis, if you don't tell us we can't help you," said LeAnn.

"Okay, but make sure you don't tell anyone you heard it from me. I could lose my job."

"What job? You're a temp. You don't have a job to lose. You'd just work in a different office. You never stay anywhere much longer than a couple of days before they move you on," teased Carla.

"Okay, I'll tell you. Today..." the waiter returned with their food.

Paula sat quietly waiting until he served the others and finally left.

Paula picked through her lemon chicken while LeAnn ignored her shrimp lo mein. Carla listened as she devoured her almond chicken.

"Today at work I typed up a file on a new client. This client came in wanting to divorce his wife."

"That's pretty normal considering you worked for divorce attorneys today," said LeAnn.

"This is really hard and I'd appreciate it both of you would just let me get out what I'm trying to say without interrupting me."

Carla and LeAnn set their forks down to listen intently to what Paula had to tell them.

"The client who came in to file for divorce was Lawrence."

"Lawrence who? Not our Lawrence?" asked Carla.

"Yes, our Lawrence. Our step dad, Mom's husband, your boss."

"You've got to be kidding," said LeAnn.

"I wish I were. What should we do? Should we tell Mom?"

"I'm not sure what to do. I'm sure she's going to find out soon enough from Lawrence. Maybe we should stay out of this," suggested LeAnn.

LeAnn and Paula had a two-way conversation going when Paula realized Carla had not contributed one comment. She focused on her plate while she ate, hoping they would not notice.

"Why are you so quiet?" asked Paula.

"What do you mean?" responded Carla.

"Just what I said. Why are you so quiet?"

"You knew! You already knew, didn't you?" asked LeAnn.

Carla looked around the room to see if they were being stared at after LeAnn's outburst. Several of the customers looked up from their plates to watch the three sisters in their heated debate.

"Did you really know?" asked Paula.

"There's been gossip at work."

"Gossip about what?" asked Paula.

"Gossip about Lawrence."

"What kind of gossip?" asked LeAnn.

Carla set her fork down, took a drink from her glass of water then leaned back into her chair. She glanced around the room hoping the others had returned to their meals and no longer listened to their conversation.

"There's been talk at work about Lawrence and a woman named Dorothy. Her husband died a few years ago. She has lunch with Lawrence every day. Some of the women giggle and talk behind their backs. I didn't think too much of it. I was happy for Lawrence. I thought it was kinda cute that he has a lady friend on the side. Heaven knows Mom is not much of a friend to him. She never listens to what he has to say. Hell, she never listens to any of us. The only thing that matters to her is what she has to say or what she's interested in."

"Oh my God. Our little Lawrence has a girlfriend," giggled LeAnn.

"Seriously, I never said anything to you guys because I thought it was harmless. I never dreamed he'd file for divorce."

Financially minded LeAnn asked, "Did you get a chance to read through the file? Does he plan to split everything down the middle? Is Mom going to lose half of everything she has?"

"I suppose split. Fifty-fifty is pretty standard in Nebraska. She might have to get a job to help support herself," said Paula.

"You know, getting a job might be the best thing for her," commented LeAnn. "She might actually like it."

"Get real," said Carla. "She swore once she quit waiting tables to support us when Dad died, she'd never do it again."

"I know, but she's too young to collect Social Security."

"She'll probably have to move out of the house since it belongs to Lawrence," said Paula.

"I don't think he's planning to make her move," said Carla.

"What makes you think that?" asked Paula.

"If the rumor mill around work is right, which I didn't think they were, Lawrence's been moving his things into storage in our building one box at a time. I thought he was taking extra work back and forth."

"I, for one, think we should tell Mom what's happening," said Paula.

"I agree," said LeAnn.

"I don't want to," said Carla. "She's gonna be furious with me for not telling her sooner. Let's stay out of it. It's between her and Lawrence."

They finished their meal in silence.

Finally, LeAnn broke the silence. "I'm going to tell her."

Nothing more was mentioned about the day they discovered Lawrence's planned to leave their mother. Before he arranged for his attorney to finalize his plan to serve Anna with divorce papers, he died.

The girls saw no point in letting their mother know her husband had planned to leave her for another woman. They spared her the anguish of that knowledge.

Chapter 2

Anna wasted no time after Lawrence's funeral. She took Carla aside after the meal she served at her home inviting no one except the girls. They suffered through one of her terrible meatloaf dinners. The over-baked loaf stuffed with huge chunks of onion was drenched with cheap ketchup making it nearly impossible to choke down. She served lumpy undercooked mashed potatoes with no gravy. She dipped from the large economy-sized can of mixed vegetables she kept in her refrigerator to serve the four of them. Paula picked through them expecting to find mold while wondering how long the can had been open.

"How long will it take you to find out what kind of insurance Lawrence had on himself?"

"Mother, how can you think about something like that today? You just buried your husband."

"Don't you think I know that? I'm going to be alone now. I need to know how I'm going to pay bills. Do you think I'm going to have to sell the house?"

Anna now owned their home free and clear. Lawrence always made double mortgage payments each month to ensure the house would be paid off in a timely manner. Spending several years working for an insurance company he ran across thousands of hard luck stories. Insurance takes a bite out of the average family's budget. Many are tremendously under insured. Lawrence protected himself and his family.

"I'll look into it tomorrow," said Carla.

Anna looked at her watch.

"It's only three, can't you check yet today?"

"Today? You need to know today? Right this minute?"

"Need to know what right this minute?" asked Paula, as she walked into the kitchen to get a drink.

"Mom wants me to go to the office this very minute to check on Lawrence's insurance policy."

"What's the rush?" asked Paula.

"I just want to know now. Come on, we'll all go then I'll take you out to eat at your favorite Italian restaurant," insisted Anna.

The girls wondered how she could already be thinking of food after the meal she gobbled down only a few hours ago. Their stomachs were still suffering from the experience.

Whenever she got pushy about getting her own way, which actually happened all of the time, she used bribery.

Carla, Anna and Paula went to meet LeAnn in the living room. Paula and LeAnn were watching a movie.

"Mom wants us to go with her and Carla to the insurance company to find out where she stands with Lawrence's insurance," said Paula.

"Right now? Can't it wait another hour? What about our movie?"

"Oh, it's a stupid movie. I didn't like it when I watched it," said Anna.

"What do you mean a stupid movie? It won all kinds of awards," announced Paula.

"Yeah, well those critics wouldn't know a good movie if they saw one," complained Anna. "Now let's get going."

"Mom's promised to take us out to eat at Carla's choice," said Paula.

LeAnn shut off the television then followed the ladies outdoors.

"I'll drive," said Carla.

"No, I'll drive," said Anna.

"But Mom, your car's in the garage and LeAnn and Paula will have to move theirs out of the way before you can get yours out. It makes more sense to use my car."

She hoped explaining the confusion of moving all the vehicles would be one way to avoid having to ride in the car with Anna driving. The girls marveled that they managed to make it to adulthood without one accident. They each expected that phone call telling them their mother died in a car crash or killed some innocent family with her reckless ownership of the road.

"That's fine. They can move their cars, but I'm driving."

The girls rolled their eyes, but obeyed.

They hated to ride with Anna since the older she got the worse she drove. Not being flexible enough to turn properly around to check oncoming traffic, she developed the habit of gunning her engine and pulling out, hoping no one would hit her. There was the added annoyance of smelling the ridiculous pine air-freshener. The smell sent the girls into flashbacks of their earlier years driving around Omaha in a hot car because Anna did not want to use the air-conditioner. The scent of the air freshener mixed with her cigarette smoke made them carsick. More than once Paula, the youngest, forced to sit in the middle of the back seat without a window to breathe in fresh air, would vomit causing Anna to lose her temper.

Most of the way to the insurance office the girls either kept their eyes closed or prayed for their safety.

Carla led the way to her office. She pulled Lawrence's file from the cabinet.

Their suspicions were correct; Lawrence planned his insurance very carefully. He prepaid his funeral arrangements including a stone. Anna had nothing to concern herself with other than showing up on time for the service.

Carla thumbed through the papers. Anna became agitated about the amount of time it took to answer a few simple questions, like how much and when.

Carla glanced at LeAnn when Anna walked to the window. LeAnn stepped closer to Carla to read over her shoulder. Paula picked up on their lead. She joined Anna at the window pointing out cars or people on the sidewalks below to turn her attention from the paperwork.

"You know what Mom, this is going to take a while. Not all of the paperwork is here. It's probably on someone's desk being processed. I'll look into it tomorrow when I come to work. Sorry."

"Damn. Well, what do you expect from an insurance company. Crooks, that's all they are, crooks. Must be Republicans."

Anna stormed out of the door.

Carla quickly returned the file folder. Paula tried to hang back with them to find out what they learned. Carla shut off the light and locked her office door. She followed Anna and the girls down the dark hallway to the elevator. As they entered the elevator Paula gave a questioning look to Carla.

"Later," whispered Carla.

Unfortunately, for the girls, rush hour traffic hit its peak. Riding with Anna now took on a new form of danger.

Anna drove quickly, ducking and diving through traffic, cutting off other drivers then blaming them when they honked. She left the mainstream of traffic to weave around side roads and residential neighborhoods. This annoyed the girls because it added a half hour to their trip across town, forcing them to sit in the smelly car much longer.

Anna whipped out onto "L" Street.

"Where are we going? Did you forget where Caniglia's is? You're going the wrong way," Carla pointed out.

"No I'm not," said Anna. She executed a quick turn, throwing the passengers to the right side of the car.

"This is Village Inn," said Paula.

"I know," said Anna. "This is where I want to eat."

"But..." started Paula then decided it was no use.

The waitress arrived to take their orders.

"What'll you have girls, my treat," said Anna loud enough the nearby customers could hear her.

One by one they began to order.

Anna cut off the waitress, "These are my daughters. Aren't they beautiful?"

"Oh... um... yes, they're very beautiful."

She continued her conversation with Carla about her choices.

When the orders were placed, Anna added, "Oh, make sure you bring four pieces of blueberry pie with ice cream and four coffees."

The waitress turned as quickly as she could, returning to the kitchen before LeAnn had the opportunity to speak up.

"Mom, you know Carla and I don't like blueberry pie. Did you forget none of us drink coffee? We prefer tea."

"Everyone likes blueberry pie, don't be ridiculous. If you like tea then you'll be fine with the coffee here, it's so weak," said Anna.

Once the girls grew up and moved away they were spared multiple dinners with their mother. She tried to gather them for family lunches during the business week while they worked. They attempted it a couple of times but she would arrive just as they had finished eating. Many times they were already at the cashier paying their bill when she would walk in.

She acted hurt they finished without her then whined and begged for them to sit with her while she ate. Since she did not have a job she refused to understand they were busy and had commitments.

The waitress brought their meal but avoided polite chitchat with them, knowing Anna would drag her into an uncomfortable conversation. She had a reputation among the waitresses. They drew straws to see who would serve her.

When the dessert arrived, instead of explaining her error to the waitress, Anna ignored the fact two of her daughters disliked blueberry pie.

"Aren't you going to eat that?" she asked.

"No, help yourself," said Carla.

LeAnn slid her slice across the table to Anna as well.

Anna, although overweight and a borderline diabetic, devoured sweets at every opportunity. She believed if drugs could assist with a medical problem, why put yourself through the unpleasant task of exercising or watching what you eat and deprive yourself of life's pleasures.

She bored them through the meal with talk of her poodle. Although the girls were not allowed to have pets when they lived at home, Anna quickly purchased a little black poodle for herself and spoiled it in a way she would never have spoiled her girls.

She played hostess.

"Would anyone care for more coffee?" she asked as she filled her cup from the pot on the table.

The cups set in front of each girl remained filled to the top. Anna lived in her own make-believe world, totally oblivious to the full cups. The girls should be used to it, but living in the real world with sane people made them forget how strange their mother really was until they were reminded by spending time with her.

Once more she gave them a frightening ride back to her house.

"I'd better get going," said Paula. "Andy's waiting."

Anna curled her lip in disgust. "Let him wait. How often do I get my three girls together like this? Wait a minute. Let me get my camera. You all look so nice."

"I don't believe her," said LeAnn. "She just buried her husband and she wants to take pictures of us because we look nice. She's a certifiable idiot. I hope when we get older we don't end up like that."

Anna returned with her camera. She snapped shots of the girls. She never prepared them for the pictures, catching them straightening their hair or speaking so their mouths were distorted. Anna had the ability to make Miss America look like a poster child for the "before" pictures advertising a plastic surgeon. The strange thing was it did not happen occasionally; instead, occasionally she actually took a *good* shot.

The girls wanted to leave but Anna insisted on a long group hug. Her perfume nauseated the girls. She hoped the neighbors would be watching to see how much her girls adored her.

Finally LeAnn broke free. "I've really got to leave, I have plans with some friends tonight."

Anna bristled.

The other two sisters took advantage of the break to get to their cars.

Anna had no way of knowing the system worked out by the three. They drove off in different directions to join each other at Lola's Deli near One Hundred Forty-fourth and Dodge Street. They knew they were safe from Anna there, they vowed never to reveal the quaint little sandwich shop to her. Barbara, the owner, had moved into the new location, which previously housed a Godfather's Pizza. Her original location when the girls first discovered her was on Eighty-fourth and "F" Street. That spot was closer but they did not mind the extra drive, having fallen in love with the food, the atmosphere and, of course, the owner.

The first to arrive, Carla sat at a table with a cup of tea. Soon LeAnn and Paula joined her.

Paula asked, "What happened in your office, Carla?"

Carla dipped her teabag in the cup of hot water.

"Mom's gonna blow a gasket. Lawrence signed Dorothy as his beneficiary for all of his insurance polices. He must've accumulated over two million dollars worth of insurance. I'm not sure if Dorothy knows about it yet."

"Whew! That's a lot of money," said LeAnn. I could've made some great investments with that kind of money. Mom could've been set for life with plenty left over for us when she's gone."

"So now what?" asked Paula.

"I guess I'm gonna have to tell her," said Carla. "We know she has the house, the checking account, the savings account and I'm not sure what else."

"I know I've invested some money for Lawrence and Mom jointly. They have a small portfolio but I sure couldn't tell you how much it's worth at the moment," said LeAnn.

"At least she's in better shape than when Dad died," Paula pointed out.

Anna worked as a schoolteacher when she and Charles, her first husband, met. From the moment she laid eyes on him she knew they were to be married. She told him so on their first date. Anna's beautiful blonde hair, blue eyes and attractive figure convinced Charles he had found the perfect girl. They dated for a little over a year then they were married.

Charles moved his new bride to New Castle Air Force Base near Sacramento, California, where they planned to make their home for eternity. It offered them a chance to avoid the cold Nebraska winters compounded by icy roads and snow-packed highways.

On days when Charles did not have to report for duty the two of them explored California. Anna fell in love with the vegetation. She vowed never to live in a state without palm trees. They went to the ocean frequently. She adored the sound of the waves and the smell of salt and fish in the air. California became a new paradise and Nebraska a bad memory.

Anna chose to start their family rather than find a new teaching position. Charles, reluctant to agree at first, finally gave in to his persuasive wife.

Within one year of their arrival in California, Charles Junior arrived. Anna thought her baby boy was by far the smartest, most beautiful, most perfect baby ever born to mankind.

At every opportunity Anna found herself in a park or shopping center where she received lots of compliments on her baby boy. She knew everyone envied her. She shopped extensively for the little boy. Charles scolded her about not keeping to their budget but she could not resist temptation. Soon their home filled with stuffed animals and baby clothes. At that point in her life, Anna did not practice her later habit of buying or sewing clothes too large, allowing growing room. Instead, she bought outfits the exact size and sometimes too small just because they were cute. She loved the attention she got from the sales clerks, who knew an easy mark when they saw one.

Alone in their tiny apartment Charles Jr. did not receive the same attention he did in public. It became his father's job to care for the boy every minute he was home. Anna only seemed interested if she had an audience.

Charles Sr. did not seem to mind. He adored his son. He hoped for a son his entire life. He planned to entertain him when he grew older with ball games and guns.

Charles loved his guns and loved to target practice; a hobby Anna learned to love and appreciate. For Christmas one year Charles bought her a small handgun with white pearl grips. She adored her little pistol. She stored it in a drawer in the china cabinet, the one nice piece of furniture in the newlywed's apartment.

Anna's great grandmother lived in Germany. She collected Gregorian crystal. This particular pattern was called Newcastle. This rare and beautiful antique crystal passed from generation to generation with great care. The firstborn daughter of each family was destined to own the expensive crystal collection. The cabinet and its contents now belonged to Anna. What a treasure she owned. She knew it was appropriate for it to be in her home especially since they lived on the New Castle Air Force base.

When young Charles Jr. was only nine months old his father came home for lunch.

"Where's Charlie?" he asked.

"I guess he's still sleeping. Don't wake him. He was cranky all morning. I can't bear to listen to him crying any more today," said Anna.

"Would you like me to take the rest of the day off so I can watch him?"

"Great, then I can go shopping or out somewhere for a couple of hours."

Charles called his office.

"Judy, this is Charles. I think I'm coming down with a bug of some sorts. I'm not coming back in today. I'll see ya tomorrow."

Anna grabbed her coat to leave before Charles returned the receiver of the phone to its cradle. She kissed him good-bye then ran out of the door. Their small apartment on the base bothered Anna. She was not one to take the restrictions of military life easily. She pouted when Charles would not allow her to break the rules by changing the paint color, or putting holes in the walls to hang pictures in places other than preplanned in the rulebook. She hoped someday to move away from the base to one of the beautiful homes they drove past during their times exploring the city.

Anna stayed on base to do her shopping. She strolled along the sidewalk at the park watching the squirrels and birds. She examined the new blossoms on flowers native to the area. She enjoyed the quiet walk. Most of the families on the base were home having lunch. She bought a book for herself, some new socks for Charles and a birthday card for her sister, Elizabeth, Libby for short. Today she did not buy items at the baby store for Charlie.

Anna felt much better being out of their apartment for an hour or so. She walked back slowly, enjoying the feel of sunshine on her face. When she turned the corner to their building the streets were abuzz with police. An ambulance was parked in her driveway. Her pace quickened. She watched the ambulance crew rush into her building. She ran as fast as she could, aware of the crowd gathering to watch. A frantic Anna appeared in the doorway to her apartment. The paramedics were in the bedroom working on her son while a group of military police surrounded a distraught Charles on the sofa.

"My baby! My baby! What's wrong with my baby?" Anna raced to the bedroom. Two men held her back.

"Please ma'am. Take a seat with your husband. Let them do their job."

They escorted her to the sofa to join Charles.

"Charles, what's wrong? What happened? Tell me he's okay."

She started to get up to run to her son once more, but a police officer restrained her.

Charles cried, "I went in to check on him and he wasn't breathing. I tried to revive him, but..." he paused... "I called for help. I think it was too late."

"No!" she screamed as she buried her face into her husband's shoulder.

Charles sobbed as he watched them remove his son's tiny body from the apartment.

Sergeant Phillips joined the grieving couple. "Mr. and Mrs. Bradshaw, we're going to need to ask you a few questions."

"Can't it wait until later?" asked Charles.

"I'm afraid not, sir. It's better to do this now."

Anna and Charles were questioned in separate rooms. Their stories matched except for the part where Anna said she looked in on the baby before she left to go shopping and Charles told the investigating officers she grabbed her coat and left without checking on him.

Anna excused this by telling them he was on the phone to his office when she checked and he did not notice. Charles agreed it could be possible.

The investigation determined the baby died of sudden infant death syndrome. Both parents were considered free of suspicion.

Anna and Charles' marriage suffered a huge blow as a result of the death of their son; each blamed the other for not checking on him.

Charles wanted to try right away for another son to replace Charlie. Anna refused to go through the pain again. Charles insisted. Anna gave birth to LeAnn. Charles loved his daughter, but his heart desired a son. Two years later Carla arrived followed by in two years by Paula.

Anna insisted Paula would be their last child. When Charles failed his second attempt to make the rank of Major he received his separation date from the Air Force. They lost all of their base privileges as well as his military pension. It was as if his enlisted years were non-existent. His depression affected his job performance.

With Anna's urging they returned to Omaha, Nebraska. They bought a house in the southern part, near the Sarpy County line. Charles worked construction by day and drank by night. The loss of his son hung over him like a black cloud.

When Paula turned four Anna took the girls out for dinner to celebrate. Anna chose the restaurant even though the celebration was for Paula. Paula ran to the door when they returned home. She wanted to show her father the picture she colored on her placemat at the restaurant.

Anna stopped her.

"LeAnn, take care of your sister. I want to check on your father."

LeAnn knew he drank in excess even though Anna tried to hide it from the girls.

Anna walked into the house. She found Charles passed out in his recliner in the living room with the television turned up. She attempted to wake him to help him into bed before the girls saw him.

She shook him gently at first, then with more force. It became obvious she could not wake him. She bent down in front of him, slipping his left arm over her neck, trying to raise him to his feet. His weight was too much for her to handle. He slumped back into the chair.

The door opened, Carla entered.

“Go outside with your sisters!” yelled Anna.

“But I have to go to the bathroom. What’s wrong with Daddy?”

“Nothing, he’s asleep. Hurry up and go to the bathroom.”

Anna waited beside his limp body while Carla went to the bathroom. She studied his face more intently. A sudden chill came over her. She placed her hand on his cool face. Shocked by the feel of his skin she closed her eyes, expecting the worst. She took his arm to feel for a pulse. She could not find one. Aware of her lack of experience checking for a pulse she tried his neck. This time she knew he was gone. She called for an ambulance.

Chapter 3

"Do you suppose mother has always been so calm about death?" asked Paula.

"What do you mean by calm?" asked LeAnn.

"I don't know. I'm going to miss Lawrence. I really liked him, maybe even loved him like he was our real father, you know. He took good care of us and he's the one who sneaked candy to us without Mom knowing about it."

"I remember he was the one who helped us convince Mom to let us keep the kitten we found in the street," said Carla.

When the girls were young they found a white kitten, with a blue collar around his neck, playing in the street. Several cars missed hitting him by only inches. Paula loved animals and could not bear to witness his destruction under the tire of a less cautious car. When she asked her mother if they could take the kitten home Anna refused.

Lawrence ached for Paula and the kitten. He took her aside and told her to catch the kitten and keep it confined while he placed an advertisement in the lost and found section of the newspaper to give the proper owners a chance to reclaim their kitten. After two weeks there were no inquiries. By that time Anna had become accustomed to the kitten in the house, ignoring the fact that he still remained with the family. Paula named the kitten Snowball and he resided with them for over ten years.

"That's what I mean. We can sit here and tell such great stories in honor of Lawrence, but all Mom could do was worry about how much insurance money she'd collect. How can she be so cold?" asked Paula.

"You know, she's been through a lot. She lost her son; she lost her first husband and now her second. Maybe this is just her way of coping. Maybe she refuses to let anyone see the emotional side of her. Remember how she taught us crying in public is a sign of weakness. Maybe this very minute she's sitting home alone crying because Lawrence's gone and we couldn't wait to get away from her," said LeAnn.

Silence fell over the scene. The girls sipped their tea.

LeAnn broke the silence, "I remember when I lost Reed I held my emotions inside. I felt uncomfortable letting others see my weak side thanks to her brainwashing."

"Weak side? How can you call mourning for your husband a sign of weakness? I wondered why I cried more at the graveside for Reed than you did. I remember how everyone thought you married him for his money," said Paula.

"Paula!" scolded Carla.

"Well, it's true. We have LeAnn here struggling to make it as a stockbroker when she meets Reed, tall, dark and handsome, not to mention thirty-five years older and loaded. You heard the gossip yourself. Even Mom thought she was watching out for her financial welfare after watching Mom working hard to make ends meet," said Paula.

LeAnn wiped a tear from her eye.

"No, she's right. The office is still buzzing with gossip. Since Reed and I were married for less than a year before his heart attack, some people say I caused it. You know, in a perverse sexual sort of way."

"How do you cope?" asked Carla. "I had no idea you were going through that."

"I cope the only way I know how. I hold my head high and work like hell to get ahead. I took the money Reed left me, which really wasn't that much after his kids got their share, and I parlayed it into three times the amount using my brains and skills as a broker. Reed taught me well. I plan to retire while I'm still young and then I can look into the eyes of my fellow employees and have the last laugh."

"Good for you," said Carla.

"Here, here," said Paula, raising her teacup in a toast.

"Now here we sit accusing Mom of the same things my co-workers are accusing me of," said LeAnn.

"I feel terrible," said Paula.

"Yeah, me too," said Carla.

"Okay, let's stop by and check on her one last time before we go home. If she's in bad shape, we'll stay and maybe help her in that blasted garden she likes so damned much," said LeAnn.

"Can't," said Paula as she took another sip of her tea.

"Now wait one minute. If LeAnn and I can force ourselves to go over there I'm sure you can too," Carla scolded.

"No, that's not what I meant," said Paula. "It's too wet outside after the rain to work in the garden."

"Maybe we'll have to force ourselves to sit through one of her horrible movies," said LeAnn.

"Yeah, hope you guys have your ear plugs. Can't believe how loud she has that TV turned up," said Paula.

"I think she wants the neighbors to know she's relaxing, watching movies, so they'll be envious," said

Paula. "Who knows what makes her tick. Let's get it over with."

When the girls entered their mother's home they found her throwing out Lawrence's things. He left behind clothes that no longer fit him, hoping Anna's lack of concern for his belongings would not raise suspicion when his suits and other items began to disappear. All of his books and music were gone. The boxes of things he stored in their closet were nothing more than empty boxes he left to make it appear as if nothing had changed.

Anna had brought her large rubber trashcan from her garden shed to finish tossing away the remnants of Lawrence.

"What're you doing back?" she asked.

"We weren't sure if you wanted to be alone today or if there was something we could help you with," said Paula.

"You can help me throw out all this crap. Anyway, what little there is left of it. Did you girls know Lawrence was already clearing his stuff out? Do you think he knew his heart was about to give?" she asked.

Anna had changed out of her proper funeral garb and into a floral housedress that accentuated her plump figure. Although her sewing ability far surpassed most when it came to altering her own clothing, she preferred to remain lazy. The dress she wore hit her at mid-calf, giving her a dowdy look which could have been improved by shortening the length.

“I thought he was perfectly healthy,” said Carla. “He recently had a physical for an insurance policy and he was given a clean bill of health.”

“Well, you know how doctors are these days. Can’t trust em,” said Anna.

Anna’s attitude surprised the girls. With every twitch or pain she rushed into her doctor’s office if not the emergency room of the hospital. With her bad health, obesity and lack of exercise she should have been dead years ago. Somehow she managed to make it in the nick of time, having had several emergency surgeries, which kept her an active and annoying part of the human race. After the numerous times her life was spared, she still chose to degrade the medical field.

“Mom, what’re these?” asked Paula.

She took a stack of unopened envelopes from the trashcan near the desk. They were addressed to Anna.

Anna snatched them from her hands. “My guess is they’re sympathy cards, a damned waste of money. How can a card make you feel any better?”

She tossed them into the larger trashcan with the rest of Lawrence’s things.

“Speaking of feeling better, Mom, how’s your heart these days?” asked Carla.

"Terrible, just terrible. The same as it's been my whole life. I could go at any minute. I hope you girls are aware of that. Maybe you should be spending a little more time around here, you know, to help out. I could be dead for days before any of you would even notice."

When Anna was a child she developed rheumatic fever, causing severe heart damage. The doctors told her parents she would have a shortened life as a result. Her strong constitution, fear of death and multiple drugs kept her going strong all these years.

"How often do you go in for a blood test to regulate your potassium dosage?" asked Carla.

Carla worked in the life insurance division. She found staggering the vast number of deaths which could have been prevented by proper health care. Applicants took physical exams to sign up for the policy and frequently it stopped there with no follow-up exams over the years.

"Whenever I don't feel quite right or a little shaky I have it checked out. It hasn't changed much. The only change has been the cost. The same damned pills cost five times what I paid for them when I first started taking them."

"Mom, when you first started taking them your parents paid for them. When you were married to Daddy the meds were free," LeAnn pointed out.

Anna lived with her parents until she married Charles. Her parents treated her as an invalid because of her heart, never expecting her to work outside the home. They groomed her to become a wife and mother, the only career any woman should need and want. "Education for women is a waste of time and money," her father said.

Anna bristled. She hated to be corrected.

"Well, did you come back to help or sit around planning my funeral?"

With a funeral so fresh in her mind, Anna attempted to play upon the sympathy of her daughters about her own demise. Suddenly her days were numbered.

While the other girls sorted through Lawrence's meager possessions in the bedroom, Carla went into the bathroom to empty his side of the medicine chest containing his razor, shaving cream and deodorant. A large economy bottle of aspirin was his only form of medication.

Carla grimaced as she looked at her mother's side, filled with prescriptions for every ailment. Her weight increased annually as did her need for more meds. She refused to watch her diet or exercise; popping pills became her method of maintaining her health. She had drugs for allergies, drugs to help her sleep, drugs for her heart, drugs for her high blood pressure, drugs to thin her blood and now she was on the verge of becoming a diabetic.

Carla knew the way her mother packed away desserts she could not possibly last long.

Carla removed Lawrence's things, leaving the aspirin bottle in place. She adjusted her mother's drugs, turning the labels outward for easier recognition. She checked the content level.

"Mother!" she scolded. "You're low on both your blood pressure meds and your heart pills. You know how important it is not to let these run out. You should take every dose and not skip any because you forgot to have them refilled."

"Don't blame me, blame Lawrence. He's the one who kept tabs on my prescriptions. I have too much to do already, but now I suppose since he's gone I'm gonna have to add this to my list of chores. Really, I think one of you girls should take charge of my medicines. How would you feel if you came here and found me dead with an empty bottle in the medicine cabinet?"

The girls were perfectly aware of their mother's plans for manipulating them, another excuse to call and have them jump at her request. Many times she decided a sudden illness became so severe she could not possibly drive herself to the doctor's office. She called the girls to beg them to take time away from their jobs to drive her. Frequently, all three girls would arrive at the same time. When they asked Anna why she called all of them, her response was, "I don't think I can trust any of you to get me there on time. I wanted to make sure someone would show up."

After several episodes, the girls wised up and called each other first, deciding to take turns rather than all three appearing at her door simultaneously.

When it came to helping with her drugs, no one volunteered. They looked from one to the other, waiting.

"I'll do it," said Paula. "I'll check her meds and make sure they're always filled."

"That'd be great, sweetie," said LeAnn.

She looked upon Paula as the baby. Once LeAnn married Reed her lifestyle changed. She dressed for business even on her off days. She felt she had a public image to uphold.

She always said, "You must look like money to make money".

She cut her hair short, adding red highlights, and maintained perfectly manicured nails. She spent a fortune on her smile, with braces as an adult and then had her teeth professionally whitened. Her business suits came from the finest dress shops in town and she did not mind letting you in on that fact.

Carla dressed appropriately for her job at the insurance agency. Nice tidy casual office attire filled her closet. Unlike LeAnn, on her down days she sported blue jeans and t-shirts. She wore her black hair shoulder length and curly. She had no problem shopping for sales and even purchased some of her clothes at Wal-Mart. The majority of the work she performed dealt with phone calls, requiring a minimum of actual personal customer contact.

Paula wore her blonde hair longer so she could tie it up or braid it. She lived in blue jeans and t-shirts with tennis shoes or sandals. She was a Kelly girl and requested jobs where the dress code remained less than casual sometimes bordering on sloppy. Several of her jobs required her to upgrade her style. While working in offices where the public entered or when working for the attorneys she liked so well, she had a small assortment of dresses and suits. Frequently, she took a change of clothes along with her so that when she punched the time clock, off came the work clothes and on went the casual attire. She enjoyed working in storage rooms and mailrooms, any place she did not have to interact with the public. Her sisters felt she did not have a real career so, when Anna needed something special, they usually asked Paula to re-arrange her schedule to accommodate.

Once the girls realized Anna experienced no emotional stress over the loss of Lawrence, they made their excuses and left.

As they approached their parked cars, Carla said, “I’m so glad Lawrence set aside money for her. Remember the hardship she went through when Daddy left the Air Force and then when he died without insurance?”

It seemed no matter how hard she worked being a sales clerk by day and waiting tables by night the supply of money remained meager. She taught the girls to be frugal.

Carla paused and looked back at the house. She noticed the curtain close quickly. Anna did not want them to know she watched from her window

"Every Christmas became a gala event. She'd bake all the traditional German breads and pastries. The candies...some of those candies were to die for. I always wondered when she found the time to make the marzipan fruits and vegetables. She made sure Christmas was just as special for us as it was for her when she was a child," said Carla.

Throughout the year Anna skimped on groceries and put together the strangest concoctions. One would quickly think she was the world's worst cook, but her mother had taught her well. During the Christmas season her cooking talents flourished.

LeAnn joined in "I remember the table. Her grandmother's white linen cloth with the hand embroidered runner down the middle and the beautiful china and crystal. I'll never understand why she trusted the three of us with the antique crystal glasses that had been in her family for so many years."

"Something changed in her that year when we sat down to eat and the crystal was missing from the table," said Carla. “I reminded her that she had forgotten to set it on the table, but when I went to the china cabinet to get it, the shelf was empty. She fed us some lame story about being sick of it. I knew then that our Christmas that year and the years before had come from her selling the crystal collection piece by piece.”

“Say, I’m glad you girls brought that up,” said LeAnn. “I found a quaint shop during my last trip to England that sells antique crystal. If you two are interested I think we can replace it for her. It might take a few years but if we all chip in we should be able to rebuild her collection.”

“Sure, sounds great. Count me in,” said Carla. “Do you know the brand and the design?”

“That’s gonna take a little detective work on our part. I’m pretty sure it’s called Newcastle.”

“How expensive is this stuff?” asked Paula.

“Don’t worry Paula, we won’t expect you to kick in as much as we will on each piece with of your part-time employment,” said LeAnn. “Actually, I was hoping to start a crystal widow fund for Mom. We can all put a little in at a time, whenever we can and I’ll invest that money shrewdly, of course.”

LeAnn put on a fake air of superiority mixed with a dab of “rich bitch” attributes. The others laughed at her, knowing she was teasing. All the same, they knew she continued to grow into that personality with each passing year as her abilities as a good broker grew. The wealthier her clients became, the more of a show she put on, desperately wanting to join their league.

"Since we're bringing up the subject of money," said Carla. "Have you and Andy decided on insurance for him?"

"No, what's the rush? I feel funny asking him to look into it so soon after his parents died. Don't you think that's a little tacky?" asked Paula.

"I think tacky is asking you to help with the expense of burying his parents when the two of you aren't even married," said LeAnn.

"He didn't ask, I offered."

"Doesn't matter, the end result was the same. His parents had no insurance so when they had their car accident Andy was stuck with the funeral expense plus other bills," Carla pointed out. "If something happens to him or if he walks, you have no way of recovering your money."

Paula felt the pressure of her two sisters ganging up on her. She glanced up at the sky when she heard a clap of thunder. None of them had noticed the storm brewing overhead while they stood on the sidewalk outside their mother's home. Their own storm brewing on the sidewalk about money made them totally unaware. Her sisters looked up when they heard the crackling sound of lightening.

LeAnn worried her expensive suit would be ruined if she were caught in the rain. She ran for her car, Carla did the same. Paula stood alone on the sidewalk watching them drive away. No one waved. She stood there a while longer as the raindrops began to fall. The springtime rain in Omaha is cold. The drops were large, falling widely spaced on the sidewalk and car. They began to speed up and fell closer together. Paula looked up as the rain poured down on her face. She enjoyed the smell and the feel of rain. She did not care about her hair or her clothes. Finally, she felt her body temperature drop and she started to shiver. She ran her fingers through her wet hair then slipped into her car. She reached into her glove compartment for a stack of paper napkins to wipe her face and hands before driving home to meet Andy for supper.

By the time she arrived at their house her teeth were chattering. She turned the heat on high in the car but her clothes were drenched to her skin, sticking close to her body, drawing the heat from every pore.

She beeped the horn as she pulled into the driveway, a courtesy both she and Andy shared with each other. He ran out the door to meet her carrying an umbrella.

“Gee, I thought I’d be prepared so you wouldn’t have to get wet. What happened?”

“The girls and I were standing in front of Mom’s house talking when the rain hit.”

"I can't imagine LeAnn getting soaked in the rain. She must've been a sight and talk about furious," he chuckled at the thought of it.

"Oh, don't worry. She made it to the shelter of her car before the rain actually burst from the clouds. I'm sure she drove her Lincoln Towncar to her fancy home in Regency where she pulled into her garage, using her garage door opener then stepped out into a dry room and into the house without a hair out of place."

"Ouch, bad day with your sisters?"

"No, not really. Just ended on a bad note."

"Don't tell me the discussion turned to money again and, of course, my lack of it?"

"You guessed it."

Andy slid his tanned arms around Paula. She felt lucky to have him. They shared the simple things in life. He enjoyed evening walks and grilling hot dogs on their Hibachi. He frequently brought her bouquets of flowers. He could not afford long-stemmed roses from a fancy florist but she was just as happy with the choice he made from the local Hy-Vee grocery store on Center Street.

He worked as a sales clerk in the carpet department at Nebraska Furniture Mart. LeAnn hated to shop alone and dragged Paula into the furniture store whenever the mood struck her to add something new to her over-crowded home. LeAnn spent a great deal of time studying decorating magazines for ideas. When she married Reed his home had been professionally decorated but LeAnn needed to add her personal touches to make it feel more like her own.

On one of their trips while LeAnn searched for an area rug for her den Paula and Andy struck up a conversation. He had light blond hair, pale green eyes and a well-toned body. She instantly fell for him. He spent many hours daily dealing with shallow women shoppers. He enjoyed the refreshing change Paula brought into his department.

LeAnn chose the perfect pattern. Andy made the sale. A few days later she had second thoughts. She returned to the department with Paula anxious to go along. She chose an entirely different pattern creating, more paperwork for Andy. He removed the original purchase from her account on the computer then added the second purchase. The delivery truck had already been loaded with the first rug. He needed to stop that delivery.

LeAnn showed her impatience. The transaction took Andy about twenty minutes to be thorough. Paula did not mind. She watched Andy make phone calls to finalize the arrangements. He smiled at her, winking a time or two, as they watched LeAnn strut impatiently, checking her wristwatch.

With the paperwork completed LeAnn signed it and grabbed her handbag to leave.

"One more thing," said Andy.

"Now what?" snarled LeAnn.

"I'll need your phone number," he said.

LeAnn opened her mouth to complain and point out her number was in the computer already when she noticed he was speaking to Paula, who quickly jotted it on the back of his business card.

As the two women walked through the store toward the exit LeAnn said, "Really Paula, you don't even know him. Are you in the habit of giving your phone number out to complete strangers?"

"I liked him. There was something really sweet about him."

"Yeah, Ted Bundy was sweet too, but tell that to all the women he killed."

Paula smiled.

"Now what's so funny?"

"It'd be pretty hard to tell that to all the women he killed. They're dead."

LeAnn bristled in exactly the same way Anna would when she felt she was being corrected.

Later that evening Andy called. Paula met him at Pizza Hut for supper. They talked until it was time for the restaurant to close for the evening. Andy had the next day off so they made plans to have a picnic lunch together. Every evening Andy had free from work he took Paula out to movies or dinner. His grandparents owned a small acreage outside of Omaha. They raised chickens and ducks. They had a couple of old horses out to pasture. When Paula saw the horses she insisted Andy teach her to ride. He spent a great deal of time as a child horseback riding with his grandfather when they still had cattle.

Andy's mother helped Paula pick bushels of fruit from the farm. They took the crop to her house where she taught Paula how to can and freeze. Andy's parents thought the world of Paula.

"Has Andy made any mention of marriage?" his mother asked.

Paula blushed. "I don't think we're ready for that kind of commitment yet."

After they exhausted all the activities at the farm he taught her to bowl. When he learned of her love for animals he made arrangements with an old classmate of his who worked at the Henry Doorly Zoo to give her a private, behind the scenes tour.

At the end of each date they made another and another until they were seeing each other every day. Finally, they decided to move in together. Andy gave up his apartment to move into hers. Shortly after they began living together his parents were killed in an automobile accident during a heavy rainstorm on the highway near Plattsmouth, Nebraska. Their car was totaled.

They moved into Andy's parents' home. He had no siblings so he inherited the home as well as the debts. The house payment was less than the apartment payment plus they had twenty years equity in it at the time so it made the most sense.

The house was located in South Omaha about fifteen minutes or less from Anna's home. The neighborhood was old with huge trees. The house had been well cared for. The basement was unfinished so they made plans to complete it. The upstairs had two small bedrooms and a very small kitchen. The living room was almost never used. Off of the kitchen was a small dining room with a fireplace where they kept the television. It doubled as a family room, keeping the main living room always ready for company. Paula and Andy moved her television into the formal living room and his into their master bedroom.

The exterior of the house had a combination of yellow siding with a reddish stone halfway up the wall in the front of the house. The sloped driveway held both cars side-by-side although only one could fit in the garage.

Andy put a cup of tea on for Paula while she changed from her wet clothes. He called from the kitchen, "What am I not providing you with now?"

Paula joined him as she tied her terrycloth robe around her body.

"Carla's on me about insurance again."

She sipped her tea.

"Maybe she's right," he said. "If my parents wouldn't have borrowed against their policy to send me to school there would've been something left when they died. I wouldn't have had to borrow money from you to bury them."

"I told you I didn't mind. And besides you're paying me back every month. I'm not worried."

"Seriously, though Paula. I don't have a will or anything. If something happens to me I'm not even sure what happens to this house. Your name's not on it. I still owe a few more years to the bank. My guess is they'll throw you out and sell it. I think we should sit down with Carla and work something up."

"Oh, I'm sure that'll thrill her. LeAnn too."

"Okay, let's do it. Hell, maybe I should even think about marrying you," he smiled.

Paula looked at him, trying desperately to read his face. She wondered if this was a proposal requiring an answer or him just kidding around with her.

The next day, he called Carla to set up an appointment to proceed with insurance naming Paula as his only beneficiary.

Then he called LeAnn to ask her to join them. He arranged for both sisters to be at his home for an early barbeque. This time he purchased steaks. When Paula arrived home that evening the girls were there. She knew about Carla coming to sell them insurance but was not quite sure why LeAnn had come.

She joined them in the backyard where LeAnn swatted at flying insects while Carla busied herself spreading the insurance papers across the picnic table.

Andy walked away from the grill to hand Paula a glass of wine and kiss her hello. She gave him a perplexed look. He smiled in return.

"What're you doing here?" Paula asked as she sat next to LeAnn.

"Andy invited me. I suppose he wanted me to witness the fact that he finally came to his senses and decided to protect you with insurance."

"I'm ready," said Carla.

Before Paula arrived home Andy had picked a modest life insurance policy and a health insurance policy. He named Paula as the sole beneficiary for the twenty thousand dollar payoff in the event of his untimely demise as he put it. He also had his friend's brother, an attorney, draw up a simple will leaving his almost nil possessions to Paula. He wanted Carla and LeAnn to witness his signature. Both sisters were notaries.

With the paperwork signed he returned to the grill. Paula witnessed the entire scene, aware that it involved her but somehow feeling left out. Andy, LeAnn and Carla planned and prepared every detail of the paperwork connected to her future with no request for her opinion. She knew she should feel pleased, but she could not help the way she felt.

"Let's eat," said Andy as he returned to the table with the platter containing the steaks. He placed one on each plate. He poured more wine then toasted Paula. "To Paula, may she never need to cash in on this life insurance policy."

The girls laughed and Paula slapped his leg when he returned to his seat next to her.

Paula reached for her napkin. She slid the gold napkin ring off of the paper napkin. For a second she found humor in the fact that Andy had gone through all the trouble to put plastic gold rings on the paper napkins. She quickly noticed the others were ringless. She took a closer look at the ring she so carelessly set next to her plate.

She gasped. Her sisters looked up.

Paula picked up the gold band studying the diamond setting. Realizing the ring was not a fake; she looked into Andy's face for an answer.

"Well, you didn't expect me to sign my life insurance over to a casual acquaintance, did you? You're planning to say yes, aren't you?"

She smiled at him then noticed the shocked look on her sisters' faces.

"Yes, yes, yes," she said. She held his face between her hands to kiss him passionately. The ring dangled from her index finger.

Andy pulled back, took her hands and gently removed the ring, placing it in its correct position on her left hand.

Chapter 4

Paula began making wedding plans immediately. She purchased stacks of bridal magazines. She surfed the Internet for ideas. For the first time in her young life, she cared about the proper dress, the best way to arrange her hair and how to choose flowers. She put in a call to LeAnn.

"How would you like to help me plan my wedding? You have great taste and know all the best shops in Omaha."

"I guess I was unaware that you two were going all out for this. What's your budget?"

"I don't know. What should it be?"

"I guess that depends on how big you want it. Are you planning to invite hundreds of people or have a small discreet ceremony for family?"

"To be honest with you I really haven't thought anything through."

"Have you told Mom yet?"

"No, I hoped if I held off she'd find out from either you or Carla."

"No way I'm gonna break the news to her. Do you know how furious she'd be if she didn't hear it from you first? She's already gonna be livid that we know about it before she does. You'd better tell her and fast."

"Okay, okay. First thing tomorrow I'll stop by and show her my ring. Then will you help me with the wedding plans?"

"Sure. If you live through telling Mom, I'll help you."

"Why do you think she's gonna react so badly?"

"Andy's a nice guy and all, but he's going nowhere. How many times have we had to listen to that stupid saying she has, 'It's just as easy to fall in love with a rich man as it is a poor man'?"

"That's dumb. She can't really mean it. She married Lawrence, didn't she?"

"Yeah, but that was so she could quit working and have him support her. She's already pissed at you for dropping out of college and not pursuing a career."

"I know, but school didn't work out for me."

"Exactly, all the more reason you need a successful man in your life."

"Geez, now you're starting to sound like Mom."

"Wow, thanks. That's quite the insult."

The following day Paula arrived at Anna's house as planned. She came armed with a teacup rose plant with tiny yellow buds ready to open. As she walked up the driveway she saw her mother in the backyard working in her garden. The two story artificial stone house stood in the middle of the lot. In the front a large overgrown maple tree towered over the small lawn. Squirrels had taken up residency in the crevices of the huge trunk, feasting on the seeds shed by the tree each summer.

Anna complained to Lawrence about the location of his house. She felt the old neighborhood on south Thirty-second Street did not suit them. He was proud to be a homeowner and although the neighborhood was antiquated he felt it safe and quiet.

Anna's favorite hobby was gardening. As frugal as she became over the years with food, she chose to grow flowers instead of vegetables. Her garden came to life each summer with daisies, lilies, roses, gladiolus, and foxglove after the beautiful array of tulips, daffodils and crocus died back. Her tastes were drawn to cut flower varieties allowing her to have vases of flowers in the house from early spring until late fall.

Anna looked up when she heard the latch on the gate open. Paula walked toward her. Anna focused on Paula but only for a second then her eyes quickly scanned the neighbor's houses to see if any of them might have noticed her loving daughter bringing her a gift of flowers.

Unfortunately, everyone else was either indoors or away for the morning.

"What's this?" asked Anna.

"I saw these at the store and thought you might like to add them to your collection. I know you already have red and pink, but I didn't think you had the yellow."

"Kinda spindly looking, don't you think? I suppose you got them in time so I can try to save them. Maybe in a couple of years they'll turn into a decent bush."

Paula looked at the plant in her hands. She saw nothing wrong with it. Disappointed and hurt, she handed the plant to her mother. Someday she hoped to be able to accept the rude remarks from her mother as nothing personal, as part of her nasty personality.

"Come on in. Let's have a cup of coffee," suggested Anna.

"I don't drink coffee, remember?"

"I might have some Lipton tea bags in the cabinet somewhere if you want to look for them."

Paula nervously followed her mother into the house, up three stairs from the landing and into the small kitchen. Tea was the last thing on her mind.

Anna poured two cups of coffee. She handed one to Paula who silently looked at the cup.

"Oh yeah, you won't drink this, will you?" said Anna, showing her disappointment in her daughter. "Go ahead and dig for that tea then."

The urge to pace overwhelmed Paula. The tiny kitchen offered no floor space to accommodate that need. She wrung her hands nervously. Maybe she should have brought Andy with her.

"No, that's okay. I really can't stay long."

"So why'd you stop by then? It's not like you to bring flowers when it's not my birthday or Mother's Day."

"I wanted to show you this," said Paula, stretching out her hand for her mother's viewing.

"What's this, a promise ring?" she said insultingly.

"No, it's an engagement ring. Andy and I are engaged."

Paula's voice carried a tone of anger. She loved the ring Andy chose for her. The diamond might have been small but it suited her simple taste. The huge rock LeAnn sported on her finger would not have been to her liking.

"Really, Paula, I think you can do much better. How's he going to support you on his lousy income and what happens when kids come along? What're you gonna do, wait tables like I did? You don't even have the crystal to...." Anna's voice trailed off mid-sentence.

Paula watched Anna's face sadden at the thought of her family crystal having been sold. The topic had not been brought up since the Christmas when the girls discovered it was gone.

More than ever, Paula hoped LeAnn could find the crystal so they could replace it before their mother died. It was the only family legacy Anna was proud of.

"Mom, we'll make do. I'll get a better job and Andy makes a good commission. The house is almost paid for and we have no other debt. We'll be just fine."

"Has he paid you back that money yet? You know if something happens..."

Paula cut her off. "Mom, don't worry about anything happening to Andy. Carla has him all set up with life insurance and Andy had a will drawn up so I won't lose the house. He's really taking care of everything."

"How much?"

"How much what?" asked Paula.

"How much money do you get if he dies?"

"Enough. What difference does that make? He's not gonna die."

"Yeah, well I didn't expect your dad or Lawrence to die either. Which reminds me. I need to get a hold of Carla. Surely she knows by now how much insurance Lawrence had and where all the policies are. I tore this house apart and I can't find any copies."

Anna stood from the kitchen table and went to the telephone on the desk in the dining room. She dialed Carla at work. Anna had a habit of inviting the girls to come visit. At times she nearly threw a temper tantrum to get them to agree to come. After her initial excitement and greeting at their arrival, off she went to her garden to work leaving her guest or guests alone in the house. When they offered to help her she stopped them, telling them they would not know a weed from a rose bush. Insults flowed easily from Anna's mouth. Not once did she think her attitude might be driving the girls away.

"Carla, what's going on with my insurance payment?"

Paula refused to be alone in the house with her if Carla told her about Dorothy or the changes in the beneficiary of his insurance. She walked up to her mother and touched her shoulder. She mouthed, "I have to go now."

Anna waved her away. She had more important things on her mind at the moment then begging Paula to stay. Another reason the girls rarely stopped by was because Anna made them feel guilty for not coming more often and then complained they were leaving too soon. She rarely sat down to visit with them. Not that it mattered, as she did not listen to anything they said. She preferred to talk about herself, politics or her poodle, Muffin. She had a disgusting habit of asking them a question about their lives and part way through their answer; she cut them off to tell them about the consistency of Muffin's stool that morning.

Paula hurried through the living room, onto the sunroom porch then out to her car before Anna could hang up the phone and stop her.

Paula had the day off. As she drove from her mother's home she turned west on "L" Street to Seventy-second. She glanced at her watch. "I wonder if Andy's free to go to lunch?" she said aloud.

She pulled into the back parking lot for Nebraska Furniture Mart. The small lot tucked behind the building always had empty spaces. She avoided using the main doors. This entrance put her closer to the carpet department.

Andy finished with a customer then walked over to her.

"What's up?"

"Are you free to go to lunch?"

"Sure. Where do you want to eat?"

"Let's just run across the parking lot to Burger King."

Paula quietly ate her Whopper and fries.

"What gives?" he asked.

"I stopped by Mom's this morning. I told her the good news," she faked an enthusiastic smile.

"Paula, don't worry about your mother. Nothing anyone says or does is good enough for her. I know she doesn't like me. To tell you the truth, I'm not overly fond of her."

Paula burst into laughter. He had spoken his words so gently. No one liked her mother; at least not once they got to know her. A first impression may cause one to think she was a happy doting parent. She failed to maintain friendships due to her crass attitude.

Andy knew how to make her laugh. Paula had the most contagious, fun laugh causing him to be quite a comic to release her laughter into the room. "Good energy," he always said.

"You know, sometimes I wish we could elope and forget about this whole wedding idea. Can you imagine trying to plan a wedding with my mother's input," she said.

"Is that why LeAnn went to the Caribbean for her wedding without telling any of you until she returned?"

"Probably."

"You know I'll go along with whatever you decide. We can have a big wedding, a small wedding or, my favorite, elope," said Andy.

Paula looked into his eyes and held his hands. He brushed the stray blond hairs from her eyes. "Do you really want to elope? I don't want to force you into a wedding."

"Read my lips. I want what you want, nothing more, nothing less."

He glanced at his watch.

"Gotta go." He jumped up kissed her on the cheek then headed back to work.

Paula watched him bound across the parking lot. He knew she would be watching. He turned and tossed a kiss to her. She smiled as she caught it in the air, knowing full well he could not see into the window, but he knew just the same. He constantly told her they were soul mates and she believed him.

The weeks following proved stressful for Paula. Her mother tried to influence every aspect of the wedding plans. She wanted to invite all of her neighbors, not caring in the least that they did not even know Paula. She even went so far as to invite sales clerks and waitresses when she would drag them into conversation about the upcoming event. Embarrassed, they would jot down their names and addresses so Anna could be sure they received an invitation. If she had it her way, there would be five hundred guests and all the prime rib, seafood and wine they could drink. Money was no object; her daughter was getting married. Of course, she offered no financial assistance, only free advice.

Her criticism reduced Paula to tears each night. Her mother offered ridiculous advice for new plans while LeAnn and Carla tried to tone everything down. If she followed their advice, the wedding would take place in a public park, probably Hitchcock Park off of "Q" Street, with a reception picnic serving hotdogs and potato chips immediately following the ceremony, shaving the cost down to two dollars per guest.

They lectured her repeatedly about expenses. They harped on her lack of career or steady work. "Save for the future" became the slogan for the wedding plans. LeAnn pointed out the money they saved, by not getting extravagant with the plans, could be invested to help provide for their retirement. Paula was being ripped to pieces: her mother wanting this to be the biggest event Omaha has seen in many years, LeAnn wanting her to cut corners for their future and Carla battling for them to increase their life insurance rather than invest their money with LeAnn.

After two months of coming home to find his normally bubbly fiancée sobbing on the bed, Andy finally had his fill.

He scooped Paula up in his arms. He brushed her hair from her eyes and wiped her tears.

"I have something for you," he said.

Through swollen eyes she looked into the envelope he handed her. Inside she found two round trip tickets to Hawaii along with hotel accommodations and a scheduled itinerary. She raised her eyes to his. He smiled at the excitement in her sparkling blue eyes he had longed to see again.

"What's this? Did you win a contest or something?"

"Aren't we the psychic one? I did win a sales contest to Hawaii. I went to the travel agent today to include you and extend the stay for ten days. I also called ahead to make sure we could be married there. That is, if it's okay with you?"

"Married? In Hawaii? What about all the plans here, my mother? I can't do that to everyone."

"Why not? They have no problems making your life a living hell over the wedding plans. Let's do it. We leave in two days if you're willing. We can send them a postcard from the islands. They'll get over it. Don't forget, LeAnn did it."

"I know and my mother never forgave her. She told her God punished for her actions by Reed's death."

"Well, I'm not gonna die. I think we should go."

Paula looked at the photographs on the brochure. She stared off dreaming about the beaches. She looked into Andy's eyes and said, "I love you. Let's do it."

Two days later they stepped off of the plane onto the island paradise where the two shall become one. They would return as man and wife.

With the help of the travel agent, Andy worked with a Hawaiian wedding planner fine-tuning the details. They met with a licensing agent, showing appropriate ID, making it legal for them to be married.

The first night they settled into their hotel. Maybe Andy could not afford the wedding suite, but the smaller suite had all the charm necessary to make the entire experience a romantic one.

After they unpacked Andy took Paula for a walk along the beach. The waves rushed furiously past their feet then fell silently back to the ocean. Birds rushed busily up and down searching for insects disabled by the rush of the water onto the sand. Children played at the water's edge building sand castles to watch them wash back into the sea.

"I could live here forever," sighed Paula.

"You ain't in Nebraska any more, babe."

Andy bent down to pick up a seashell for her.

"Here's my first wedding gift to you."

"I'll treasure it always," she said and he knew she meant it.

The next day their private ceremony took place on the beach. The setting sun blazed in the sky over the ocean. Tiki torches lighted the area where they stood before the local justice of the peace. A handsome Hawaiian gentleman plucked the strings of his harp, serenading the two lovers. The delicate petals of the tropical flowers in Paula's bouquet glowed in the candlelight. Somehow Andy knew Paula would prefer the quiet sunset ceremony to the larger more ornate version offered by the wedding planners. Paula swayed to the music, mimicking the swaying palms in the distance. Once they were pronounced man and wife Andy thanked the crew and whisked her off to their suite where champagne and strawberries awaited them.

Moments after they reached their room a bellboy knocked at their door. While Paula drew a bath in the oversized tub, complete with tropical scented bubbles, Andy tipped the boy who left a large assortment of both hot and cold foods on their table. He lit the candles and called out to Paula.

“I’ll be right there,” she responded. When she entered the candlelit room her eyes caught sight of the enormous feast. She realized, with all the excitement of the day and the ceremony, she had not eaten since breakfast.

They sampled each dish choosing their favorites to indulge in. They toasted to a long life together and sipped champagne. When they felt full and satisfied Paula took Andy by the hand and led him to the bubbly tub. She filled it with hot steamy water that had cooled to the perfect temperature. After their warm bath they slid into bed, making love most of the night.

They slept in the next morning, waking to bird sounds unfamiliar to their Nebraskan ears.

“Well, Mrs. Adams, shall we find breakfast?” he asked.

“I love the sound of that Mr. Adams.”

“What? The sound of breakfast?”

She hit him with a pillow. He rolled her over, tickling her until she could barely breath. He kissed her a long passionate kiss before leaping out of bed to get dressed. Andy, always so full of energy, loved life just for the sake of living it. He found good in everyone and everything. If only Paula's family could see what a wonderful person he truly is, maybe his lack of wealth would not matter.

The remainder of their honeymoon flew by. They spent time alone in their hotel room making love. They also tried to create as many memories as they could. They strolled along the beach every morning after breakfast. Paula loved the feel of the squishing sand between her toes. Andy visited with a tour guide, asking for private places to take his bride. With a map in hand and a picnic lunch they went on an excursion.

"Where are you taking me?"

"It's a surprise. You'll have to trust me."

"Honey, I'll always trust you."

They followed a path through tropical plants. Paula stopped frequently to admire the size of the leaves. Lizards darted playfully across the path ahead of them. She tried to catch them, but they were too fast. Andy laughed at her.

Finally, they reached an area where the vegetation changed to a landscape where the rocks grew larger the further they walked. Now they must climb to advance toward the sound of rushing water. They climbed the last hill and before them witnessed one of nature's most magnificent wonders. A waterfall spilled from atop the rock cliff. Along both sides native plants kept it hidden from the view of tourists passing along the path. Andy set down the basket of food, slipped off his shoes and dove into the water. Paula quickly followed his lead. Together they played under the waterfall. They made a memory never to be forgotten.

As the days progressed they continued to enjoy the tropical vegetation and learned water activities. At first they were both afraid to snorkel, but quickly learned how easy it really was and how beautiful the fish were. They went boating, deep sea fishing, and finally reached a level of bravery and comfort with the water to scuba dive.

Andy took his bride on a tour of the underwater magic, which only the ocean can provide. Once they relaxed underwater with the scuba gear, they held hands and moved slowly through the water, examining every moving animal as well as the plants swaying in the currents.

Paula thanked Andy many times for whisking her away from the pressure of her family interfering with their wedding. She knew he would take care of her for the rest of her life.

The last night of their stay on the beaches of Hawaii they sat on the sand watching the sunset and the stars fill the sky. They curled up together on a blanket savoring every sight, sound and smell of the island.

"Well, by now Mom and the girls have gotten their postcards," said Paula as she watched the ground approaching as they neared Eppley Air Field.

Their unforgettable wedding and honeymoon were now behind them and they must face the wrath of her family. Andy's aunts, uncles, cousins and even grandparents would be very happy for him. They loved Paula. He wished she did not have to suffer at the hands of her disappointed family.

They drove directly to Anna's to get it over with as quickly as possible. Paula led Andy by the hand into her mother's home.

"We're back," she called out as they entered.

Anna stepped out from the kitchen carrying a cup of coffee. It was three o'clock in the afternoon; she was probably on her second or third pot by now.

"So am I supposed to congratulate you for making a fool out of me?" she asked.

"Now, Anna, how did we make a fool out of you?" asked Andy.

"Did I tell you to call me by my first name?" she snapped.

Paula spent most of their relationship keeping Andy away from Anna. She made excuses for his absence at family events and held back inviting him until the last minute, knowing he would not be able to change his work schedule.

"No ma'am."

"I have all my friends and neighbors excited to attend your wonderful wedding and then you two pull this. How could you? After your sister ran off to get married I would've thought you'd learned from her mistakes. You know what happened to her marriage because of it."

"Mom, Reed did not die because they eloped."

"How can you be so sure, Missy?"

She always called her Missy when she scolded her.

"I suppose you're pregnant, too?" she asked.

Shocked, Paula replied, "No I'm not. Look, maybe coming here wasn't such a good idea. I think we should leave."

She took Andy's hand and as they walked to the door she heard her mother say, "Fine with me."

Once in the car Paula burst into tears. Andy reached out to comfort her.

"Drive, just drive. Get me away from her."

That evening LeAnn called to congratulate her for her wise decision.

"You really did the right thing. You kids didn't need to blow your money on a fancy wedding. Did you have fun in Hawaii? How much did that set you back?" she threw in before Paula could answer.

"You'll be happy to know Andy won the trip."

She decided to leave out the part about Andy adding her and extending the time at his cost. It was none of her business.

"When Mom cools down I'd like to have a dinner party here to welcome Andy to the family."

The invitation took Paula by surprise.

Andy went to bed to watch television and wait for Paula. The moment she hung up the phone, Carla called. She, too, congratulated her and agreed with LeAnn about the savings involved.

"As a wedding gift I'd like to give you guys additional insurance on Andy for a year. If you should decide to keep it beyond that you'll have to pick up the payment. That might sound weird, but I think insurance is the best gift for weddings and births of children. Call me strange."

"You're strange," laughed Paula. She felt her sisters were on her side even if her mother was not.

It took Anna two months to stop ranting and raving to LeAnn and Carla about what an ungrateful daughter Paula turned into. She blamed Andy for everything. He took Paula away and talked her into getting married behind Anna's back. She accused him of sabotaging her loving relationship with her daughter.

Carla and LeAnn planned the dinner party around Anna's birthday. They were aware that everything they did as a family must revolve around Anna. There was no way she would attend if she could not be the center of attention.

LeAnn called Carla, "Guess what. I did it!"

"Did what?"

"I was able to locate that crystal Mom had."

"No way!"

"Yep, I found it in a shop in London. The name of the pattern is Newcastle; it's Gregorian crystal made in the late 1700's. It's pricey."

"How much?"

"Five hundred dollars per glass."

"Holy cow! How long do you think it'll take us to complete the set?"

"I'm not sure, but if we get her one for her birthday, Christmas and Mother's Day, it shouldn't take too long."

"Yeah, but that's fifteen hundred dollars a year."

"Not to worry. I told you I'd make it up with investments. The three hundred dollars we started with in the 'Crystal Widow fund' has almost doubled already."

"But that'll only cover the first piece then we'll have to start over and Christmas is only a couple of months away. Paula had trouble coming up with her initial one hundred dollars. I'm not sure she'll have more so soon."

"That's okay, we'll try to cover her for now. You never know, something could come up for her."

"My guess is nothing short of the lottery is going to get her that kind of spare money."

Carla prepared side dishes for the birthday meal. Paula decorated a cake and LeAnn picked up the main course from a caterer.

Andy waited nervously with Paula in the living room while her sisters put the finishing touches on the table. They told Anna they would eat at six sharp. Andy kept checking his watch.

"It's seven o'clock," he whispered to Paula.

"I know, the food is almost ready."

Andy looked at the table as the girls brought in the steaming dishes.

"But we were supposed to eat an hour ago," he said.

"No, we told Mom we would eat an hour ago. She's always late so we never tell her the truth about meal time, or any other event requiring her to be on time."

The door opened and Anna made her appearance with Muffin. The black poodle jumped from chair to chair, then back to the floor, sniffing everywhere.

Anna knew LeAnn did not appreciate dogs at her house, but Anna did not care. She brought Muffin anyway. Strange though, she almost never took her dog to Paula's house, while aware of how much she loved animals.

Along with the poodle she brought a green bean casserole, Anna style. Rather than purchase the crisp onions for the topping, she chose to chunk a white onion and sprinkle it over the top. If she did not have cream of mushroom soup, she would use whatever flavor of cream soup she had in the pantry. Then she would throw in some leftovers for color.

"Don't be surprised if the casserole tastes funny," Paula whispered to Andy.

All three of the girls gagged at the thought of green bean casserole, although they put a spoonful on their plates they managed to get by not eating a bite. Anna, generally too busy talking about herself or complaining about the government and the Republican Party, did not notice who ate what.

Carla passed the casserole around the table first to make Anna feel important. When she handed it to Anna she said, "No thanks, I made it two days ago and I've been eating on it ever since. I'm not having any tonight."

The girls looked disgustedly at the green slimy beans on their plate; now knowing they were swimming with gut-wrenching bacteria.

Anna laid out her pills on the table in front of her as if she were displaying her badge of honor.

"Oh, that reminds me. I picked up your prescriptions today," said Paula.

"Where'd I put them, LeAnn?"

"I saw them on the kitchen counter," said Carla.

Paula stood to get them. "Don't bother, let me get them," said Andy.

He handed the sack to Paula. She poured out the contents. "Here's your blood pressure pills, your digitalis and your sleeping pills. That's all you needed, right?"

"Isn't that enough?" Anna complained. "Almost all of my social security check goes for these drugs. The small pittance Lawrence left me barely gets me by each month."

"Yes, but Mom, be grateful he had a small insurance policy for you," reminded Carla. "Where would you be without it?"

The girls decided long ago to forego telling her about Dorothy. They knew an explosion would ensue if she learned not only were there other more profitable policies but they were in Dorothy's name.

Anna said, "I'd rather have his girlfriend's share. She got more than I did."

The three sisters nearly choked on their food. LeAnn sipped her water, "What girlfriend? Mom, what are you talking about?"

"I figured something was up when Carla kept putting off finding out about his policies so I asked someone else to look it up. That's when I found out this Dorothy person got most of it. I wish the hell I knew who she was; I'd give her a piece of my mind. Of course, I wasn't surprised. I knew he had a thing on the side."

The girls knew even if Anna did not know about Dorothy before, she would say she did. She was too paranoid to allow others to think she was not aware of everything going on in her life.

After Anna blew out her candles, Carla brought in the gift-wrapped box and placed it in front of her. She smiled, like a child, all excited to tear open her birthday present. She looked around the table for additional gifts.

"Is this it?"

"Yes, Mom," said Carla. "We all chipped in to buy it."

She tore open the package, opened the lid and unwrapped the tissue paper. Shock covered her face as she looked at the antique crystal wine glass in her hand.

"Is this....is this a Newcastle piece?"

Paula answered, "Yes, LeAnn found a shop in London that handles them."

The girls could tell they really touched her. They watched as her hands gentling caressed each intricate curve of the magnificent carving. She held it up to the light to watch the sparkle. She turned it over and over, checking it from every angle.

"Thank you girls, you shouldn't have. I mean, I think it's great, but what am I going to do with one glass?"

Andy was shocked to hear Anna complain about such a beautiful expensive gift. His mother would never have said such a thing.

"We plan to add more to the collection over time," explained Carla.

Andy slid his chair back from the table, excusing himself. He went into the bathroom. When he returned his face was pale and his forehead glistened with beaded sweat.

"Andy, are you ill?" asked Paula.

"Maybe a little," he said. "I'll be fine."

Carla looked at him, "Paula, I think you'd better get him home."

They said their good-byes then left.

"It must've been something I ate tonight," said Andy.

"You didn't touch the green bean casserole, did you?"

"Sure I did. It was our first meal with your mom; I didn't want to appear rude."

"Andy, you probably have food poisoning."

"No, I don't think so. I'm sure it's just an upset stomach. I'll be fine once we're home so I can shower and go to bed."

Later that night Paula called Carla from Bergan Mercy Hospital.

"Carla, Andy's in the hospital. Can you come sit with me?"

"What happened?"

"Probably Mom's casserole."

"He didn't actually eat any, did he?"

"Yes, he did."

"I'll be right there."

Chapter 5

"Poor Andy," said Paula. "I can't believe he ate her casserole. He must not have taken me seriously."

"I guarantee he will now," said Carla. "Mom's food should come with a warning label on it."

The girls laughed about her cooking. They told stories of past culinary disasters.

Anna's mother and grandmother were outstanding German cooks. Many friends and neighbors gathered around the dinner table to sample the excellent cuisine prepared. Anna learned from the very best. The ability to be a perfect hostess did not make the journey down the family tree. Anna's self-centered personality prevented it. Fast and frugal became her motto for a meal. If one of the girls or either of her husbands mentioned they preferred one food over another or a preferred choice of doneness, she immediately did the opposite.

Eggs for breakfast were dropped into spattering hot shortening. The edges curled up, turning a crispy brown.

The eggs were taken from the pan scorched with the interior near the yolk still a liquid white. Everyone learned to swallow them down without saying a word. The next one would be even more burned; they were expected to eat them. It was a sin to waste food.

On a cold winter's day the girls may come home from school to a bowl of hot chili. Anna chunked onions in quarters, dropping them into a pan of boiling water with floating bits of ground beef, not all of which had been properly browned. The water contained some sort of prepared seasoning stretched too thin for the amount of chili in the pot. She refused to add tomatoes or tomato sauce to add color and thicken the mixture. The finished product looked like dirty dish water with bits of food floating. No amount of crackers they crumbled into the bowl could help to disguise the flavor or the texture.

Finally, there were the bagged lunches for school. The worst of the worst happened to be a special recipe invented by Anna. She took two slices of bread and rubbed hard margarine onto both slices thus tearing the bread. She topped one slice with two hotdogs split lengthwise and laid open to accept the catsup she slathered over the top. The price of lettuce being more than she wanted to invest, she would top her creation with a slice or two of raw cabbage leaves followed by the second slice of mangled bread. The sandwiches sat unrefrigerated until lunchtime. The embarrassed girls threw them away before any of their friends could see them.

They remembered entire groups of people going home from one of her dinner parties with raging diarrhea.

"What are they doing to Andy? Pumping his stomach?" asked Carla.

"Oh, I hope not. I can't imagine how bad that would be after being sick all evening."

"What happened when you two got home?"

"He tried to ignore it. He took a shower and went to bed. Then he got up and hung out in the bathroom. He kept thinking he had a bad migraine. He was dizzy and nauseous. He said he saw rainbows or some sort of glow around things. He took an Excedrin Migraine, but it didn't seem to help. He started to complain about his heart feeling funny."

"Feeling funny how?"

"I don't know. He said it was hard to explain. Anyway, he must've felt pretty bad to actually let me bring him to the hospital."

The doctor on call interrupted the conversation between the sisters. They noticed him walking toward them. A tall man with blond hair, his eyes swollen from lack of sleep, his voice quiet and soothing. He wore the standard green hospital scrubs.

"Mrs. Adams?" he asked.

"Yes. I'm Mrs. Adams." Paula stood. "Can I go see him now?"

"Are you here with her?" he asked.

"Yes. I'm her sister."

"Mrs. Adams, I'm sorry. We did all we could. If only he had gotten here a little sooner."

He prepared to steady her if she faltered on her feet as many family members do when he has the unfortunate task of informing them of the death of a loved one.

Paula stared disbelieving at the doctor. His words took time to sink in. She looked past him down the hall to where they had taken Andy. She knew she must have misunderstood him. Andy had to be okay.

"Why? What happened to him? He's going to be all right, isn't he? Food poisoning can't work that fast. Can it?"

"Mrs. Adams, did your husband have a history of heart problems?"

Paula looked at the doctor without focusing. Her mind replayed the many conversations she and Andy had about everything important to them. Nowhere in her memory could she bring up a conversation about health issues.

"Andy? No, he's perfectly healthy."

Carla interrupted, "Do you know that for sure? Could he have had a problem he didn't share with you?"

"I suppose so, he always liked to keep bad things to himself. He only liked to talk about up things.

"Oh my God! Is there something wrong with his heart? How bad is it?"

The doctor looked at Paula in confusion. His eyes met Carla's. He realized she had not understood the message he delivered. She remained in a state of denial, very common under the circumstances. He prepared to repeat himself, using different words, when Carla took over.

"Honey, I think what the doctor is trying to tell you is that Andy didn't make it."

Paula looked first at Carla, watching her lips as she spoke. Then her focus turned to the doctor, waiting for him to correct Carla's misconception of the situation.

"I'm sorry," he said.

Paula legs weakened, her stomach churned, she felt suddenly ill. Carla slipped her arm around her to prevent her from collapsing to the floor. The doctor assisted. They guided Paula gently to a chair against the wall. He stood over her ready to assist if she fainted.

When Paula was able to walk Carla went with her to Andy's room. The sight of her husband caused her to lose control. She sobbed so deeply her entire body convulsed. Andy, the love of her life, lay motionless on the table in front of her. How could this be? The color faded from his face, his eyes closed as if asleep but the lack of energy emitting from his body left no doubt of the lack of life within.

Carla said, "Come on Paula, let's get you out of here. You don't need to put yourself through this any longer."

Paula jerked away from Carla's grip. She could not bring herself to leave him there alone. She wanted to believe this was a huge mistake and at any moment he would open his eyes, wondering where he was and what had happened to him.

Carla allowed her to stay with him as long as she felt she needed to. Finally, she leaned over and kissed Andy. She stroked his hair, then turned and walked out of the room.

"You're in no condition to drive. Let me take you home. We'll call LeAnn and Mom from your house. Or would you rather come home with me? You know, that might actually be better."

Paula agreed to go home to Carla's house. She could not bring herself to walk into Andy's house without him there. Paula cried all the way to Carla's. When she entered the house she threw herself on the sofa, buried her face in the pillows and sobbed harder.

She wondered how this could happen to her young, beautiful, healthy Andy. He brought nothing but joy to her life every day. Why would she be punished in such a brutal way? What had she done to deserve this? What had Andy done to have his life cut short in such a harsh way?

"LeAnn, this is Carla. I think you should get over here right away. Andy died tonight. I have Paula with me."

"What? You've got to be kidding. What'd he die from?"

"The doctor said something about a bad heart. We don't have any of the details. I thought it was best to get her out of the hospital as fast as possible."

"I'll be right over."

"Great. Oh, before you come can you call Mom?"

"Do you want me to bring her?"

"I'm not sure. You be the judge when you talk to her."

"Okay, I'll be there soon."

"Hello," said Anna with a harsh voice. She was sure it was a wrong number waking her in the middle of the night.

"Mom, this is LeAnn. Something terrible happened tonight. Andy died."

"How?"

"I'm not sure. Maybe his heart."

"See, I told Paula something would happen to him, the way they ran off and eloped. Just like you and Reed. You two should've known better, especially Paula. You'd think she'd learn from your mistake. So what am I suppose to do? Do you want me to drive over to Paula's or is she at the hospital?"

"You know what, Mom, just go back to sleep. Someone will call you in the morning with more details. I don't think Paula is up to company right now."

LeAnn kicked through the leaves piled high on Carla's walk as she reluctantly approached the door. She looked at her watch, three o'clock in the morning. She looked down the long stretch of sidewalk connecting the houses in the quiet Sarpy County neighborhood, Willow Street and not one willow tree. Tonight the same streets will be abuzz with families going door-to-door trick or treating. Paula loved Halloween, but after this year her favorite holiday will be a painful reminder of the loss of her husband.

She looked up when she heard LeAnn open the door.

"What're you doing out here?"

"Thinking. Do you realize today is Halloween?"

"Yeah, I know. I thought of that. Poor Paula."

LeAnn stepped past Carla. "How is she?"

"Not good. What'd you expect?"

People tend to say the strangest things at a time of loss. There are no correct words and more often than not, the wrong words are expressed. Paula and Andy were not religious people, another complaint Anna had about their union. She felt Andy took her away from her Catholic upbringing, even though she had tossed aside that belief on her own many years before meeting Andy.

LeAnn knew Anna and Paula would butt heads about the type of funeral to have. Anna would not be supportive at all but would worry about how the funeral would look to those who attended. She would gripe about the money and worry about the image and the entire time feel it imposed on her precious time. She repeatedly tried to convince others they were intruding on her busy schedule if they came uninvited. She had nothing to do outside of her garden. When she wanted them to drop everything and keep her company, she complained she was bored with nothing to do. The girls, over the years, could do nothing more but listen to her complaints, roll their eyes then ignore her.

LeAnn went to Paula. She touched her softly on her shoulder. "I'm so sorry, kid. I know how bad this hurts."

Paula looked up at LeAnn, "I had no idea what you went through when Reed died, no idea. I'm so sorry I didn't understand the pain."

"No one does until they've been through it," said LeAnn. "As long as we're on the subject, you need to realize that people are going to say some pretty painful and stupid things. Just ignore them. You grieve as long as you need to, in whatever manner you choose. No one has the right to tell you that it's been long enough or it's time to pick up the pieces of your life and move on. Especially, don't take anything Mom says to heart."

Carla stood next to her sisters feeling helpless in the situation. The two of them shared a bond now that Carla could not possibly understand. She herself had never been married and this was not the time to tell them about Anthony. She wanted to break the news to everyone at the birthday party. She and Anthony had been secretly seeing each other for the past six months. Carla wanted to be sure the relationship showed promise before exposing him to her family.

Carla met Anthony when he made an appointment to meet with her to purchase life insurance. He told her he was on a tight schedule and asked if they could discuss the policy over lunch near his office. She recommended Lola's Deli. The sandwiches were delicious and it was located very near his office building. She told him to tell the owner, Barbara that they would be meeting if he arrived before her and Barbara would make sure they had a quiet table to allow them to work through lunch.

When Carla arrived at the Deli, Barbara looked up at her and motioned to the table where she seated Anthony. Barbara smiled and gave a thumbs up signal to Carla, who laughed it off. Barbara, with her flaming red hair and personality to match, kept the Deli's energy level high and happy.

Carla glanced in the direction Barbara pointed. A dark haired man in an expensive business suit had his back to her. She approached with great curiosity.

"Anthony?" she asked.

He stood as he extended his hand.

"Carla?" he responded.

"Yes. I'm happy to meet you. I hope you didn't have to wait long."

"I just got here myself. Please sit down. I hate to rush you but I only have forty-five minutes. Maybe what we can't finish today we can finish tonight or tomorrow."

"I'll get right down to business then," said Carla.

She secretly hoped they would not finish so she could spend more time with him.

"Have you ordered?" she asked.

"Well, actually I did. I wasn't sure how slow they are here. I'm embarrassed to say I ordered the *Fat Bastard.*"

Carla laughed, "Good, because that's my favorite. I'm sure Barb will be bringing one for me at the same time."

Anthony's brown eyes sparkled as he spoke with her. She admired his flawless skin and perfect smile. As they worked out the details of his request she learned he was single, had no children, his mother was to be his beneficiary, and he was an only child. He owned a high tech computer company that he started from nothing and built into a multi-million dollar business. He recently increased his staff and wanted to add life insurance, as an option for his employees, using Carla's company to handle the details.

Carla took her insurance business very seriously, but Anthony made it difficult for her to stay focused. Her attraction to him was immediate.

A smiling Barbara appeared with two sandwiches.

"Here ya go, two sandwiches with prime roast beef, smoked turkey, smoked honey ham, crispy smoked bacon, pepper-jack cheese, lettuce, tomato, red onion, black olives with smokey chipotle mayo," she blurted out so fast they could not keep up. "Iced tea for the lady and hot coffee for the gentleman. Can I get you anything else?"

Carla knew Barb was teasing her by listing the ingredients and hanging around. Barb gave her a wink then returned to the kitchen.

"You must eat here a lot," said Anthony.

"Actually, quite often."

"Maybe you can join me here again some day for lunch. I think I might be adding this place to my favorite's list for a quick meal."

Carla hoped his invitation would not be forgotten. She would have lunch with him every day; all he had to do was ask.

They finished their lunch and business.

"I'll have the papers for you to sign next week," she said.

"Great, same time next week. We'll meet here for lunch again, maybe I won't be so busy."

He stood, shook her hand then darted out the door. She watched him jog across the parking lot to his car, a Lexus. She could not take her eyes off of him until he drove out of sight and felt her face flush and palms sweat. She met the man of her dreams.

"You go, girl," said Barbara.

"Hey, this was just a business lunch, nothing more."

"Yeah, tell that to the blush on your face. You're hot for him."

"Yeah, right. What do I owe ya?"

"Your gentleman friend picked up the tab."

Carla looked out the window toward where his car had been parked as thoughts of his smile crossed her mind. She closed her eyes and ran the lunch meeting on fast forward to remember every detail.

"See ya next week," said Carla as she left.

They met for lunch the following week. Today he had more time to spend with her. It was Carla who had to cut lunch short to return to work. She lacked the luxury he had of setting his own hours. Disappointed the lunch could not extend into the afternoon he invited her to dinner that evening.

He took her to P.F. Chang. He introduced her to honey crispy shrimp and the marvelous lettuce wraps of which she ate far too many. The numerous years her sisters and she had eaten at Hunan they were unaware of the outstanding menu across town. She made a mental note to tell her sisters about it. They talked through the meal then he ordered a festive banana dessert for them to share. The conversation flowed so easily they did not realize they were the only two left in the restaurant while the staff cleaned around them.

"I guess we'd better let them close up," said Anthony.

Carla looked around the room. During the entire evening she managed to keep her eyes glued to his, not noticing her surroundings.

"Yes, I think you're right. I don't suppose they'll feed us breakfast if we stay any longer."

By the end of the evening she felt he had an attraction to her similar to the one she had for him. At least she hoped she was right.

They arranged their schedules so they could see each other no less than twice a week. Carla knew it was the real thing, but hesitated to tell her family. Now, with Andy's death, she knew this was not the best time to break the news.

Carla pulled her mind back to the crisis at hand. She excused herself from the living room where LeAnn comforted Paula. She walked into the kitchen to prepare tea for the three of them. Her home could not compare to that of LeAnn's but she felt comfortable with it. If you ranked it according to size it was larger than Paula's but smaller than LeAnn's. The neighborhood was newer than Paula's and most of the houses had the same floor plan. In LeAnn's neighborhood each house had it's own individual look, a must for the residents trying to outdo each other. Paula's neighborhood had many tall trees showing the age of the area. Each house, although conservative, had its own personality.

She put a teakettle on the stove to kill time. She could have just as easily heated the water in the microwave. She wanted to avoid being in the same room with Paula. It bothered her to watch the pain her little sister experienced.

Deep in thought over the situation she jumped when the teakettle whistled. She took three mugs from the cabinet. She chose to have mugs and practical dishes rather than the china LeAnn used. The rest of the furnishings in her home were also conservative, nothing flashy or exotic. She put a chamomile teabag in each mug. She watched the water as it poured over the bags with the steam curling above the cup. She poured slowly trying to delay her return to the living room.

"Paula's going to go lie down in your spare room," said LeAnn.

"Sure, fine. That's great. I'll take your tea in there."

LeAnn guided Paula through the hall to the guest room. She turned on the lamp near the bed. Carla placed the tea on a coaster next to the lamp. Paula curled up on the bed while Carla tossed a chenille throw over her.

LeAnn and Carla returned to the small living room to talk.

"She says she wants us to handle all the arrangements," said LeAnn. "She says she doesn't have the strength to do anything. Andy wanted to be cremated."

"Whoa, you know how that'll go over with Mom," said Carla.

"For once, I don't think this is any of her business."

Carla and LeAnn worked out the arrangements to the best of their ability while they waited for the start of the business day to make the appropriate phone calls.

"Andy, don't go!"

Carla and LeAnn jumped up.

"She must be dreaming," said Carla.

They rushed to her side. They found Paula sitting up in bed with her knees drawn to her chest, her eyes searching the room.

"Are you okay?" asked Carla.

"Andy was here. I saw him. He spoke to me."

"I'm sure you were just dreaming," said LeAnn. "You've had a terrible shock to your system."

"No, you don't understand. I was sleeping then I felt someone sit on the bed next to me. I felt a hand brush my hair from my eyes like Andy used to do. I heard his voice. He said, 'I love you baby. I'm okay and I'll be waiting for you.' I opened my eyes and saw him sitting here. He smiled at me. I sat up to touch him. He stood and backed away then I blinked and he was gone. I wasn't dreaming. He was really here."

Paula's sisters were speechless. They were thankful Anna had not been present for her snide words to Paula would surely cut deep.

During the days that followed the girls kept their promise. They handled the arrangements for Paula. Andy's body was cremated as his parents had been. She had his ashes placed next to those of his parents in the cemetery across the street from their home. Anna thought it morbid to live across the street from a cemetery and even more so now that Paula's husband was buried there.

The girls had fought daily to protect Paula from Anna's intrusive ways. She tried desperately to change the arrangements by having a Catholic mass said for Andy. She even asked her parish priest to stop by and talk some sense into Paula. No one should be cremated and if Andy did not have a proper Catholic funeral there was no way he would make it into heaven.

Paula treated the priest with respect and he, her. They shared conversation and a cup of tea. He did not push once he saw her mind had been made up. He offered his condolences and a prayer. Paula allowed him to pray in their home but refused to join him. The temptation to tell him of the visit from Andy crossed her mind, but she soon dropped the notion.

As weeks passed Paula had more Andy sightings. He would appear in their room at night or she would smell his cologne in the house at the end of the day and often in her car when she drove around Omaha. She could tell no one of his visits. She remembered how close-minded her sisters were about the topic and her mother would have her institutionalized if she shared it. Her secret remained private.

One afternoon, while shopping at Barnes and Noble, Paula's search for a good mystery was interrupted by the applause and gasps of a group of people listening to a guest speaker talk about her latest book.

Paula eased her way down the aisle to a spot where she could stand behind and off to the side of the author. A gentleman from the audience raised his hand.

"Yes?" asked the mystery woman.

"Years ago, a few months after my dad died, I thought I saw him when I was in a car accident waiting for the paramedics. I was sure I was going to die. My dad came and sat with me until they arrived. He told me it wasn't my time yet, but he'd be waiting for me when the time comes. Was that really him, or was I just hallucinating?"

"Did you feel as though you were hallucinating?" she asked.

"No, it felt real to me at the time."

"Then it probably was. Human nature, especially in our country, tends to ignore signs from departed loved ones. Ancient civilizations realized the importance of maintaining an open door of communication with the deceased. They needed their knowledge and assistance to grow as a culture. If we were to try to become a little more open-minded and less afraid to share experiences, we would find this occurrence is much more commonplace than previously believed."

A young teenage girl raised her hand.

"Yes?"

"Do you believe in ghosts?"

"I believe in spiritual beings. Some people call them ghosts. Some experts believe a ghost is nothing more than an earthbound spirit. It is often said they do not know they have died so they choose not to go into the light. They are lost."

"So then, what's the difference between a spiritual being and a ghost."

"They are both of the same energy, but a spiritual being who has crossed over has the ability to move back and forth freely across the veil between the two worlds, whereas a trapped soul or ghost has not yet been able to accomplish that feat."

An older woman from the back row raised her hand.

"Don't you think all this talk about communicating with the dead is evil? Isn't it a form of trickery from Satan? Aren't you spreading Satan's word?"

Paula moved from her position behind the woman giving the lecture to an empty seat in the back row.

She saw a tall slender woman wearing a tailored purple suit standing behind the microphone. Her red hair, cropped short but neat, suited her face perfectly. Her green eyes bore a gentle expression. Her face showed sadness brought on by the question she was about to answer. Paula guessed her to be in her early fifties.

"I do not believe the ability to communicate with the dead is evil. There are thousands of accounts of people who have had near death experiences who have seen and talked to deceased family members and then returned to their bodies and are alive and well today with marvelous stories to share. I see nothing evil in it.

"I don't particularly like to attach myself to any one religion. People must believe in something. Whatever works for one person may not work for another. I do not believe I'm spreading Satan's word or anything evil or adverse. I'm simply sharing with you the gift I was born with. I have come a long way trying to understand it and harness it for the good of man. One last question, please."

Many people raised their hands hoping their question would be chosen. She pointed to a handsome young man in his thirties.

"Is it true you work with the police to help solve crimes?"

"Yes, I do. That is one part of my work I find terribly rewarding. I helped find two little girls who had been kidnapped. I've helped with homicide cases. I've had the unfortunate ability to help the police locate hidden bodies. The entire experience is exhausting and painful for me, but if it offers closure to the families I have to feel good about it.

"I would like to take this opportunity to thank all of you for attending my talk. I will take a quick break and then return to the table to sign books. I hope today has been an enlightenment to each and every one of you."

As the crowd began to form a line for an autographed book Paula slipped up to the table to read the name of the author. She read the title, *Is it a Hunch or a Psychic Feeling?* by Jennifer Parker.

She picked up a copy of the book then sat in a chair to thumb through the pages. Her pulse quickened. Could what's been happening to her with the visits from Andy be real? Could this woman validate her experiences? Are others having the same questions? Her mind raced with thoughts while her heart pounded loudly in her chest.

One by one fans spoke with Jennifer as she signed books. Paula planned to stay put until the line diminished. She desperately needed to visit with this woman. She had no one else to turn to. Trying to calm her nerves, she counted the people in the line. Many had left before she began counting, but she still managed to account for forty-seven.

When there were only two people left and Paula was sure no one would step into line behind her and listen to her conversation, she placed herself in the line. She nervously looked around the room to be sure no one she knew might be in the store.

"Who would you like me to address this to?" asked Jennifer.

Paula looked confused. "Huh? What? Oh, sorry. My name is Paula. Just write Paula." She kept her eyes on Jennifer the entire time.

"There you go," said Jennifer as she handed her the book.

Paula stood frozen and speechless.

Jennifer kept the book suspended in air, waiting for Paula to take it from her.

"Is there a problem, Paula?"

"How did you know my name?"

"You just told me, dear. Would you like to have a cup of tea with me? I can tell you have something very important on your mind."

"That would be wonderful," said Paula, breathing again.

Jennifer led the way to a coffee shop located at the back of the store. Paula sat across from her.

"What can I get for you?" asked Jennifer.

"Tea. Any kind of tea would be fine."

Jennifer caught the attention of one of the girls behind the counter. Jennifer, a guest author, received free refreshments and she was watched more closely by the employees to see if she needed anything.

"Two peppermint teas, please."

Jennifer studied Paula for a moment. Being the object of her focus made Paula feel uncomfortable. Sitting with a psychic is like being naked in public. One never knows how much they know about what you are thinking.

"Relax, Paula. Tell me why you are so nervous. What question might you have for me?"

"My husband died and I think he's been visiting me. Is that possible?"

"My dear, it's more than possible, it's probable." She stared past Paula with a fixed gaze. "Your husband's name was Andy, am I correct?"

Paula spun her head around to see who told Jennifer.

"Yes," she replied.

"Andy wants you to know he loves you very much and he treasured every minute he spent with you before he left. He wants you to know he is okay and that you must go on with your life. He also says he's sorry about the problems your mother caused over his funeral."

Paula began to tremble; tears welled up in her eyes. "Is he really here?"

"Yes, Paula. I'm under the impression he's rarely away from you. Did your mother really give you a bad time over his funeral?"

"Oh man, if only you knew."

"Obviously Andy knows."

Their tea arrived, giving Paula something to busy herself with while she sorted out Jennifer's comments.

"What a lucky coincidence that I happened to be here today while you were giving your talk."

"My dear, there is no such thing as a coincidence. Life is planned out for all of us. We have a great deal to do with constructing the plan before we arrive on earth."

"What? I'm not sure I understand what you mean."

"You will once you read my book. Paula, I'm going to give you my home phone number. I must have a mission with you involved. I have yet to learn what it is, but in time it will reveal itself to me. If you feel you can trust me I would like your phone number as well. When the time is right we will meet again. But now I must go. I have a plane to catch. I must return to Denver tonight. Enjoy the book and read it with an open mind."

They exchanged phone numbers and then she stood, extending her hand to Paula. "Until we meet again, Miss Paula."

Paula watched as an escort came for Jennifer to drive her to the airport.

Chapter 6

Jennifer gazed contentedly at her brick home as the cab pulled into her driveway. After many years of traveling around the world learning about herself and other psychics this house beckoned her. She loved her quiet Littleton, Colorado neighborhood. Tall trees and well-manicured lawns lined the empty street. Most residents garaged their cars when they were home from work giving the street a wide-open appearance. Everything looked neat and tidy, as Jennifer liked it. A white birch tree stood guard over the small lawn in front of Jennifer's house. In the past she enjoyed gardening and caring for her lawn, but each year her life grew busier forcing her to join the rest of the neighbors paying for a lawn service.

She unlocked the door and the cab driver set her luggage inside the entryway. She paid him his fare with a nice tip on the side. She appreciated the fact that he kept silent during the trip. During her book tours she speaks to sometimes over one hundred people individually. After each lecture about her life and her books readers and fans stand in line to shake hands and tell her their story. Everyone has at least one ghost story or sighting. With everyone having experienced this wonderful phenomenon she often wondered why it is ridiculed as a possibility and why the people it happens to are ashamed to share their story. They quickly open up when in the presence of a medium such as Jennifer.

She drew back her curtain to watch the cab driver back out of the driveway. Although he remained silent she sensed his stress. His wife's father recently passed. While he drove Jennifer home he stayed unaware of the presence of his father-in-law in the front seat next to him. The driver did not know his own father who had died when he was a baby. He felt as though his father-in law thought of him as his own son. Their close relationship contributed to the pain and sorrow he experienced from his passing.

Ordinarily Jennifer would have mentioned something to bring the two together to share a message from beyond. Today, feeling totally exhausted, Jennifer chose to not tell him, nor to converse with the invisible passenger.

Ming Ming, Jennifer's blue-point Siamese cat surfaced. He stroked her leg while he scolded her for being gone so long. She stooped down to pick him up. Her housekeeper kept his dish filled and cleaned the litter box for what she called the ghost cat. Ming Ming refused to socialize with anyone but Jennifer. Each morning when the housekeeper arrived the dish would be empty, she would fill it then the following morning it would be empty again. She feared the cat might slip out or die while Jennifer was absent and the only way she would know he was gone would be a full dish in the morning.

"Come on sweetie, let's get you a treat."

Jennifer opened a can of cat food for her grumpy pet. She saved the canned food for special treats when she returned home after being gone for a number of days. She felt feeding him canned food any more often would make her already fat cat fatter, not to mention the damage to his teeth.

He meowed incessantly at the whir of the electric can opener. Soon the smell of tuna and salmon reached Jennifer's nostrils.

"I can't believe you like this stuff. It smells nasty," she said as she spooned it into the crystal feeding bowl she saved for the special feedings.

She fixed herself a cup of tea and browsed through the stack of mail on her table. She carried her tea from the kitchen to the living room where she kicked off her shoes and placed her feet on the ottoman in front of her favorite chair. Her home had the feel of a chalet in the Swiss Alps. When the realtor first showed her the house ten years ago, snow covered pine trees lined the backyard.

The scene out the patio window was a winter wonderland. A fireplace at the end of the room added to the warm cozy energy of the house.

For Jennifer, being aware of energy was her life's work. She could only reside in a home where the energy flow made her feel comfortable. She studied Feng Shui before it became trendy, not that she opposed the trend. Quite the contrary, the more people can do to make themselves less stressed in life, the better.

She sipped her tea and tilted her head into the tall back of the tapestry chair. She tried to relax her burning eyes. Ming jumped into her lap, startling her, causing her eyes to open as she sat up quickly, spilling a bit of tea onto her lap and Ming. She stroked his back as she watched the soft cat hair cling to her fingers and grow into clumps of hair between her fingers. Although her hands filled with cat hair every time she petted him his hair seemed to disappear in her meticulous home. She assumed her cleaning lady did a wonderful job keeping it invisible. Of course, the cleaning lady would tell you that an invisible cat has no hair to be seen.

Her eyes caught the blinking light of her answering machine. Someday she planned to use voice mail on her telephone to avoid the reminder to check her messages. Psychic as she was, those flashing messages were still a mystery to her until she pressed the button, unless she put herself into a meditative mood and focused.

"I'll check those in the morning, huh, Ming," she said as he purred under her touch.

She gazed out of the window then back to the machine with the blinking light. Annoyed and curious she chose to listen to the messages rather than slip into a psychic moment, trying to determine who had left them and if any were important. At the psychic school in London she had learned to control her abilities rather than her abilities controlling her.

She stood to walk across the room as Ming jumped from her lap. "Beep….you have five messages."

Jennifer kept to herself most of the time. She had few close friends and liked it that way. She made sure they were aware of her travel plans. Her unlisted phone number rarely collected messages while she was away.

"Wow, five messages."

"Jennifer, Glen. Can you give me a call?"

"Jennifer, Glen again. If you get this message, please contact me right away."

"Jennifer, it's me again, Glen. You must be out of town. If you check your machine please call me on my cell phone, not at the office."

"Hi, if you can't reach me on my cell phone, call me at St. Luke's hospital. I'll be on the third floor, just check in at the nurses' station."

"Guess you're still not back."

"The hospital? I wonder who Glen is seeing in the hospital?"

Jennifer dialed Glen's cell phone.

"Yeah, Jennifer, glad you called."

"Glen, what's going on?"

"I think I need your help with a case."

"Obviously this is more than just a case. You have a personal interest vested in this one."

He started to ask her how she knew then realized who he was speaking to.

"Would it be a terrible imposition for you to come to the hospital tonight?"

"Can it wait until morning? I just arrived home."

"It's really important. I'd come over there, but I don't feel I can leave here tonight."

"Okay, let me change and I'll be right there."

Jennifer rubbed her burning eyes. Bath and bed had been her plans for the evening, with maybe a fire and hot soup to help her relax. Now Glen needed her. Having worked with Detective Karst in the past she knew he would not impose on her unless he felt she could be of great assistance with this case.

She gulped her tea then grabbed an apple from the refrigerator.

"Bye, Ming. I'm off again. Hopefully I'll be home soon."

When she arrived at the hospital entrance she scanned the lobby for the information desk. She pressed the elevator button to the third floor. At the nurses' station she asked to speak to Detective Karst.

"He's down the hall sitting outside of room 312."

As she approached room 312 she saw the figure of a man leaning his chair back against the wall, his legs stretched forward into the hall. Wondering if she should wake him, she crept closer. Immediately he became aware of her presence. He thrust himself forward in his chair, bringing in his legs and standing in one quick motion. So quickly, he spilled the half-cup of cold coffee he had set on the floor beside him.

"Glen, are you okay? You don't look too well. It's not Debbie, is it?"

"No, Debbie's fine. She's at home."

"What's the matter? Are you guarding a prisoner or something?"

Detective Glen Karst from the Denver PD had bags under his soft green eyes. His sandy brown hair clipped close to his head, normally neat and tidy, was in a state of disarray. Jennifer could tell he had been running his fingers through his hair, a habit he had when something bothered him that needed his skills as a detective.

A few years back he was working on a case when his Sergeant introduced him to Jennifer Parker. The parents of the kidnapped child had asked her to help the police on the case. Glen was assigned Jennifer against his wishes. He felt he had enough on his plate without having some damned psychic following him around.

Much to his surprise they worked well together. Jennifer stayed in the background until he needed her. She carefully made comments and suggestions to avoid appearing too confident and bold. She gave him every opportunity to do the investigating on his own. When she offered a tidbit here and there he soon learned to listen to what she had to say. He hated to admit it, but he developed a respect for her ability. Together they solved the case. She taught him much about his own gut instincts and how to react to them. He did not want to say she made a believer out of him, but she did give him much to contemplate. If there was one thing about Karst that made him such a good detective, it was his ability to remain open-minded.

After that first case, she drove to Holyoke, Colorado with him where she helped with another case. He owes his life to her on that one. He went to help an old friend who had many close calls with his life in Denver and chose to live a calmer life in small town of Holyoke. Peace and quiet disappeared when residents of Holyoke began to die causing Dave, the sheriff, to fall back on his skills as a homicide detective dragging Glen and his expertise into the situation. The two men worked day and night to stop the serial killings.

Glen's eyes scanned the hall, first one way then the other.

"Let's go somewhere to talk," he said. "There's a waiting area right over there. I think I can watch the door from there."

Jennifer looked at the door, wondering what or who the mystery was on the other side.

"Where have you been?" asked Glen. He meant to ask out of politeness, but his voice sounded a little gruff. He had been without sleep for days.

"I had a small book tour. I just returned from Omaha, Nebraska this evening."

"I'm sorry. I didn't mean to make it sound like I was grilling you. My shitty attempt at small talk didn't come out right. I'm actually surprised you didn't pick up on me trying to find you like you have in the past," he said.

"Glen, when I'm on tour I try to remain unplugged as much as possible when I'm not in front of a group of people. There is such a thing as the telephone you know. Don't always expect me to tune into you."

"I did use the telephone. You choose to not use a cell phone, remember?" he teased. "You don't even have to be in the twenty-second century, just the twenty-first."

"Oh yes, I'm sorry. That's how you reached me. Forgive me, I'm a wee bit tired this evening."

"Can I get you a cup of coff…" he stopped. "Tea?"

She smiled, "Yes, that would be fine."

He walked to the vending machine. She remembered how desperately she tried to get him off of coffee and on to tea, but that did not fly with this top-notch, extremely masculine detective.

While he waited for the hot water to fill the cup his eyes stayed glued to the door of room 312.

Jennifer followed his gaze.

"Who's in that room?" she asked.

"A couple of friends of mine."

"Can I ask what happened?"

"Someone tried to kill them."

"Oh my. Are they going to be okay?"

"We're not sure. They're still in a coma."

"Both of them?"

"Yep, both of them."

Glen kept his eyes on the door while he spoke.

"What can I do to help you?" she asked.

"I was hoping you could tune in to them or something. See if you can read their minds or find their souls or whatever the hell you call it. I need to catch the son of a bitch who did this."

"Tell me more about what happened. Who exactly are they?"

"Maggi Morgan, the mystery writer. She's a friend of ours and her assistant, Teddi Taylor."

"Where's Debbie?"

Glen rubbed his hands through his hair again.

"She's home."

"What's wrong? Glen, what aren't you telling me?"

"Debbie is, well, overly sensitive right now."

"Define overly sensitive."

Glen sat straight up in his chair as if he were ready to confess to something.

"I met Maggi through Debbie. She's been using me to help with the police protocol in her books. Maggi's neighbor put some fool notion into Debbie's head that Maggi and I were having an affair."

"Were you?"

"Hell no. I care about her, but I've never had romantic feelings for her. I just have trouble convincing Debbie of that."

"Glen, something more than a passing comment from a nosy neighbor had to have happened."

"Maggi got herself in trouble with the New York police department. It's a long story; she was accused of killing people for book publicity. I knew she was innocent. I took time off of work and went to New York with her to help her get it straightened out. I told Debbie I'd be back that night, but we stayed over. We had to meet with a detective in the morning. Shit, to make a long story sound even worse we ended up sharing a hotel room because of lack of vacancies and a screw up with arrangements. Anyway, it looked bad. I'm telling you nothing happened."

"Glen, that's none of my business. Continue."

"Just when I thought we had convinced Debbie that everything was fine the girls, Debbie, Teddi and Maggi tangled with a rapist. The guy ended up dead. Maggi let her guard down..."

Jennifer interrupted, "Why was her guard up?"

"She got these threatening letters and she had some psychos following her asking her to kill their husbands and, well, someone tried to kill these two women. If I hadn't arrived at Maggi's house when I did, instead of the ambulance taking them out unconscious, the coroner would've been called in. They've been in a coma since then. I feel I need to stay here to guard them. Whoever is out there might try to strike again, especially if the girls can identify the assailant."

"Debbie feels you're being here is showing her you care more for Maggi than for her?"

"Yep, that's the gist of it. I can't seem to talk any sense into her. I don't know what makes women so jealous over nothing. She's been going to the cafeteria every day with the neurologist on the case to discuss their progress and I'm not jealous."

"Do they ask you to join them?"

"Yes."

"But you turn them down to stay with Maggi?"

"Yes."

"And you wonder why your wife is jealous. Glen, you have the ability to solve the most intense puzzling crimes, but when it comes to figuring out what makes your wife tick…" she shook her finger at him as if he were a child.

"What? Debbie knows I love her. She knows the life as the wife of a detective is not all romance and fun."

"Why is it I feel you're more married to your career than your wife?"

Glen bristled. "We're supposed to be finding the creep who did this to those two women, not having a marriage counseling session."

"I'm sorry, Glen. I would be disappointed to see anything happen to your marriage. Debbie is such a delightful woman. The two of you make a wonderful couple. I felt her love for you during the time we spent together in Holyoke."

Glen took his eyes from the room where Maggi and Teddi lay to contemplate the events when he came so close to dying himself.

"Can you help me with this case?" he asked.

"I can do my best. That doesn't necessarily mean it'll be what you want or need. I do need to ask you one question that you won't appreciate."

"Go ahead."

"Is there any way Debbie could be involved with the attempt on those two lives?"

Firmly, Glen replied, "Absolutely not."

He knew better than to be offended. He had to follow the same line of questioning when he interrogated family members of his homicide cases. He had to admit it was not a good feeling to be on the receiving end.

A floor nurse stepped into the waiting area, "I'm sorry but visitor's hours are over now. I'll have to ask you to leave."

Glen looked at his watch. He wanted to continue his conversation with Jennifer. He had special permission to stay around the clock if need be, but Jennifer had to leave. He realized he could pull some strings to allow her to stay with him but he could tell how exhausted and probably hungry she was.

She gathered her handbag and teacup from the table next to her.

"Wait," said Glen. "We still need to talk."

"Why don't you call me in the morning."

He glanced at the door again. His trained eyes searched the halls for signs of anyone who did not belong.

"You know, I've been here every spare minute since this happened. I've taken time off of work to watch over them. Every night has been very quiet. I think I can afford to leave with you for an hour or so. Let's find a restaurant. I could use a bite to eat anyway."

Jennifer remembered the bowl of soup she missed out on. She glanced at her watch. If she gave Glen an hour she could still be home before midnight.

"Okay. I'd love to join you for dinner, Detective Karst."

"Great," said Glen. "Just give me a minute."

He went to the nurses' station to tell them he would be away for a little while and to call him on his cell phone if there were any changes.

He guided Jennifer by her elbow down the hall to the elevator.

"You really do look bad, Glen. Maybe you should give up this night watch and go home to your wife."

Jennifer may not have picked up any details of the case involving his two friends, but her psychic ability did bring forth a picture of his crippled marriage. All she could do would be to encourage him to pay more attention to Debbie and hope her premonition of divorce to be an error.

Glen ordered a cheeseburger with all the trimmings. Jennifer ordered a bowl of tomato soup. Glen ordered a beer, Jennifer more tea.

"Now tell me the rest of the story," she asked.

"The doctor in charge the night they came in said there wasn't much they could do. He said they were in bad shape and showed signs of their organs shutting down. He expected them to die quickly."

"But they didn't." said Jennifer.

"When Dr. Collin Fitzgerald, the neurologist on the case arrived, he saw a glimmer of hope with brain activity. The attending physician that evening jumped the gun a little about the organs and kidney failure. But his prediction did come true. They were on life support and weakening rapidly. Dr. Fitzgerald suggested dialysis, but warned that, in their weakened condition, it could be dangerous. Without it they had only one more day before they would poison their own bodies from kidney failure."

The waitress served their food.

Glen took a large bite of his cheeseburger.

"That's probably the first thing you eaten today, isn't it?" asked Jennifer.

"Yep, haven't done anything, no need to eat."

She waited until he managed a few bites before continuing his story.

"They tried the dialysis and it worked, but they remain in a comatose state. The longer they remain this way the greater damage to their brains and less chance of living a normal life if they pull through."

"I'm sorry, Glen, did you say how they were attacked? Were they shot or what?"

"No they were injected with a lethal dose of insulin. Their blood tests showed very high levels."

"Is one of them a diabetic?"

"No. I mean, Maggi's not for sure and I don't think Teddi is. I guess she could be and it never came up in conversation. I really didn't spend a lot of time with her."

"Where did the insulin come from?"

"My guess is our perp is a diabetic or knows one. But with thousands of diabetics around that's not much of a lead."

"What's their prognosis now?"

"No one knows. Dr. Fitzgerald told Debbie all we can do is wait and pray. He said they both had high sugar content in the food they had consumed earlier that evening. Had it not been for that, the insulin would have worked according to plan."

"And who says an occasional binge on junk food is all bad," said Jennifer, trying to lighten the conversation. She worried about the extreme stress Glen exhibited.

"Somehow I can't picture you binging on junk food," he chuckled.

Jennifer appeared to those around her as a very confident and self-controlled woman. She dressed, walked and talked in a proper sort of way. The fact that she wore blue jeans and a blazer this evening surprised Glen.

"Are you telling me you have absolutely no leads?"

"That's right. That's why I called you. I was hoping you could pick up on something, anything that could give me a place to start."

Jennifer looked at her watch one more time. She desperately yearned to crawl into her warm bed and fall into a deep uninterrupted sleep, but she could not ignore Glen's plea.

"Do you have a key to Maggi's house? That is where this occurred, isn't it?"

"Yes. Does that mean you're willing to go over there with me to see what you can sense?"

"I am willing, but not sure how able. I am very tired."

Glen flagged the waitress. She brought his ticket. He laid a twenty-dollar bill on the table and they left.

He drove to Maggi's house. Walking along the sidewalk Jennifer stopped. She turned toward the light in the neighbor's house. "Who lives there?"

"That's Maggi's neighbor, Jean. She's the bitch who caused all the trouble between Debbie and me. When Maggi goes on tour Jean takes care of her dogs. She's caring for them now."

Jennifer looked long and hard in the direction of Jean's house.

"May we walk around the back first?" she asked.

"Sure. Are you feeling something?"

"I am not certain."

Jennifer walked to the back of Maggi's house. The gate to the backyard stopped her. She opened the gate and stepped in. She closed her eyes to help her focus. Glen watched hopefully.

"Sorry, nothing," she stepped back onto the side yard to proceed to the front lawn again.

She stopped, turning toward a cluster of pine trees separating the two properties. She walked through the pines brushing the needles with her hand, crunching pinecones beneath her feet. The scent of pine filled the night air.

"I am not sensing anything. I am uncertain about what I thought I felt."

Once inside Maggi's house Glen led her upstairs to the bedroom where he had found the two women collapsed and motionless on the floor. His mind flashed back to a clear image. He relived the scene where he and Debbie administered CPR in an attempt to revive them. Their fast action, according to the doctors, contributed to them still being alive today. He felt the muscles in his stomach tighten as the perspiration on his forehead began to bead.

Jennifer walked around the room. The CSI team had released the room so she was free to handle any item. She placed her hand on the phone. She drew it back quickly. Glen watched.

"What? What happened?" he asked.

"I felt anger...no, it was fear. No, it was anger followed by fear. Do you think she knew this person?"

"I'm not sure. Did you get that feeling?"

"If she was calling you, I presume because she was angry about something it then turned to fear. I'm guessing the person who made her angry came into the room. Or she was calling you because she was angry about something then felt fear when the intruder approached her."

Jennifer sat on the bed scanning the room with her eyes. She stood and went to the window. She parted the curtains. She could see the side yard below, where she walked through the pine trees, but they were too thick to allow her to see the neighbor's house.

"Is there something now?" Glen asked. He hated watching Jennifer work in silence. He wanted to be kept informed of her every thought.

She walked around the room once again. She went to the door, turned and walked back into the room.

"I'm afraid I'm not getting much, Glen. But I sense four people."

"Four people. Who would the fourth person be?"

"Is it possible there could have been two assailants, not just one?" she asked.

"I'm not sure. I suppose there could've been. I guess I assumed it would've been just one. We figured he had a gun or some other sort of weapon. There was no sign of a struggle in the room so they obviously complied with the orders they were given. Hell, he probably held a gun on them while they watched the insulin being shot up their arms. The bastard."

"I'm feeling four pretty strongly. I'd say you should expand your search for two suspects."

Glen felt his pulse race. For the first time since he discovered his friends lying on the floor, he had a small lead.

"Can you go on? Is there anything else?" he asked.

His cell phone rang.

"This is probably Debbie," he said. He stepped away from Jennifer so he could speak more privately.

"Shit! I'll be right there."

Jennifer studied his face for a second. "Something happened at the hospital didn't it?"

"Yes. Some asshole showed up at their room. A nurse saw him leaning over Maggi. She startled him and he ran out. She called security. Let's get over there."

Jennifer had left her car in the hospital parking lot so she had no choice but to go with Glen. Of course, she would have anyway.

When Glen arrived hospital security stopped him. He flashed his badge. "She's with me." He pointed with his thumb over his shoulder at Jennifer.

Security allowed him to enter the elevator with Jennifer.

When they reached Maggi's room they saw more security and uniformed police officers taking notes. Glen walked up to Bill. He and Glen worked many cases together.

“What happened? Are they okay?”

“Someone has it out for your friend in a big sort of way. The nurses tell me you’ve been here every night. Then tonight you stepped out for a bite to eat and the son of a bitch made his move. My guess is he’s been watching the parking lot for that souped up black truck of yours. Tonight when he saw it was gone he knew you weren’t guarding the door.”

“What? Will you tell me what in the hell happened! Are they okay?”

“Yeah, yeah, no change. The nurse got to him before he had a chance…”

Glen cut him off. “Chance to do what?”

“He came to finish the job.”

He reached into his pocket and pulled out a plastic evidence bag with a syringe filled with a clear fluid.

“When the nurse startled him he took off running. He dropped this in the room on his way out. Our guys found it. We checked with the nurses, no chance it came from here.”

Glen shoved the door open. He went in to check for himself. Both women remained motionless, unaware of the close call they experienced. His skilled eyes scanned the room looking for anything that could have been left behind. Content that nothing remained, he stepped back out into the hall to visit with Jennifer.

"Did you pick up on anything?"

"Yes. The person who attempted to harm Maggi was indeed the same person who originally tried to kill her. He is someone she knows, that much I can tell you."

"Is he someone she knows well or could he be a fan?"

"I'm sorry, Glen, I can't pick up on that. Perhaps if I can hold the syringe."

Glen went to Bill.

"Can I see that syringe again? Jennifer would like to hold it."

Bill had listened to Glen's stories of Jennifer and her abilities in the past but he did not buy into any of it.

"Sure, I guess, if you think she can get anything from it. Be my guest."

Glen took the transparent bag with the tiny syringe inside then handed it to Jennifer.

"Remember, you can't take it from the bag. It's evidence."

"I think I can still pick up energy from it through the plastic."

She walked off to the visitor's lounge to be alone. She sat down on a chair in the corner of the room, cut off from the sounds and movement of the others investigating the case.

She could see a man's hands filling the syringe. She watched as he injected it into himself. Then she watched as he filled it again. She saw the entrance of the hospital. She found herself following this man along the halls to the stairwell. He sat on the stairs for a long time. She had a strong sense of time slipping by before he finished his ascent to the third floor. He slipped into a bathroom and put on a pair of scrubs. The nurses on the third floor wore burgundy scrubs, the same as the pair he slipped on. It became obvious to her that this man spent a great deal of time planning this attack. He knew his way around the hospital and learned each floor wore a different colored set of scrubs.

She watched his shoes as he walked along the hall on the third floor. She felt his presence in this area where she sat. She realized he must have been watching the room from this vantage point. She saw him standing at room 312 then entering quickly. He wasted no time moving toward Maggi. She saw him drop the syringe and run when the nurse stepped into the room.

Unfortunately, she could not see his face. She could not give Glen a physical description. She saw what the killer saw as if she were watching the scenes through his eyes.

Glen joined Jennifer.

"Well?"

"Sorry, Glen. It's the same guy. It's definitely a man. He is a diabetic. He gave himself an injection before he filled the syringe for Maggi. He's a very clever individual. This was a very well planned and executed attempt to finish what he started."

"So nothing about his description?'

"No. I saw everything through his eyes. His image did not appear."

"Thanks for everything, Jennifer. I know you need to get home. I'm gonna stay here again tonight."

Jennifer gave Glen a hug.

He asked a uniformed police officer to walk her to her car.

Chapter 7

Ming rubbed his head on Jennifer's chin. She brushed him away. He purred loudly and rubbed more persistently. She leaned over to look at her alarm clock.

"Ming, it's only six o'clock. Can't we sleep a little longer?"

Having gotten a satisfactory reaction from her he went into full-fledged annoying cat mode. Nothing would stop him now and Jennifer knew it. She threw back her comforter and slipped out of bed. She went to the kitchen to brew her morning cup of tea. While the teakettle heated she brushed her hair and teeth. She went back into her bedroom to make her bed, but found Ming sound asleep on the warmest part of the sheets.

"Why am I not surprised," she said.

The teakettle whistled. As she poured tea she thought of Glen and the previous night. She called him. She knew he would be awake and, if not, he would only be in a state of light sleep.

"Good morning, Jennifer," said a groggy Glen.

"Were you able to get any sleep at all last night?"

"More than most. The department had a uniform here last night in an official capacity so I dozed in the lounge. The rest of the night stayed pretty uneventful."

"What's the plan now?"

"Hell, I wish I knew. I talked to Dr. Fitzgerald last night after you went home. I asked him if we could move them and he said in their condition it's not a good idea."

"Is that your plan then, to move them?"

"As soon as possible."

"Where?"

"I guess another hospital."

"I don't think that's the answer, Glen."

"Why? What other choice do I have?"

"Have you thought about moving them to a different city?"

"No, I hadn't."

"It appears to me this person is desperate to see them dead. I think if they were moved within the city he would go from hospital to hospital until he found them."

"Let him try."

"Glen, I understand you would like to personally take on this man or men. Don't forget, I believe two people are involved. You must remain cool and protect the girls. Let your department handle catching them.

"Did you speak with Debbie last night or this morning?"

"Yes, she's going to breakfast with Dr. Fitzgerald. I asked her to put some pressure on him about moving them."

"Why don't you join them?"

After a slight hesitation on the phone, Glen agreed.

When Debbie arrived with a change of clothes for Glen, his comment surprised her.

"I think I'm going to join you and Collin for breakfast if that's okay with you."

"Sure. Why not? I'm surprised you're going to leave your post though," she said with a touch of sarcasm in her voice.

When she discovered Glen left the hospital last night to go to dinner with Jennifer, she felt hurt. She had desperately tried to get him to leave even for just a short time, to come home or go to lunch with her. Anything to spend some time with him but he refused. Now that he had left, an attempt on the women's lives occurred, exactly as he had feared. She knew if the guard from the department was not on duty at the door he would be staying.

Debbie walked with Glen to the elevator. When the door closed he made an attempt to kiss her but she gave a cool response. He perceived her anger but he lacked the energy needed to put into his marriage. Sleep deprived, stressed, overloaded on caffeine and a lack of food, were taking a dreadful toll on him.

“I’m surprised to see you here,” said Collin.

“I thought we could discuss moving the women again,” said Glen.

“I think you might have good idea, Glen, but they need to be a bit more stable before we can move them.”

“Have you seen any sign of improvement?” asked Glen.

“Tell him, Collin,” said Debbie.

Glen noticed their relationship had taken on more of a friendship than a doctor/ concerned visitor one. He appreciated that Debbie found a friend in Collin. The fact that friend was a man made it even better. He did not feel threatened by him and maybe it would help her to understand one can have friends from both genders without any sexual contact.

“Tell me what?” Glen leaned forward so as not to miss one word.

“I didn’t want to give you false hope. It’s obvious this case means a lot to you. But over the last two days we’ve seen increased brain activity. The dialysis worked, as you know, and the kidneys are beginning to function again. Of course, all of this progress could slip backward and we could still lose them.”

"What does this mean exactly? If they continue to show forward progress is there a possibility of a full recovery?"

"It's too soon to say."

"Look Doc, I'm not gonna hold you to anything. Give it to me straight. I know the worst that can happen. Give me the best scenario."

"The best case scenario is full recovery, but highly unlikely. I'd say if, and that's a big if, if they wake up there will be some degree of damage. Whether it's permanent or not will have to be determined."

"What signs would we be seeing?"

"That's different with each patient. Normally when one has an insulin-induced coma the effects of the insulin wear off and the patient wakes. In this case we're not talking about a slight overdose, we're talking about a dose that should have killed them. The fact they're so young and healthy is on their side. The fact you found them when you did and we were able to administer glucose so quickly is in their favor. But I have to be honest with you. I've never treated a patient with so much insulin in their system before. I'm treading on new ground here. All of the research I've found says their outlook is not good, but the very fact they're still hanging in there is beating the odds."

"Is one in better shape than the other?" asked Glen.

"You know, that's the other odd thing. They seem to be nearly identical with their vitals. Maggi seems a bit stronger than Teddi. Teddi may have had a larger dose or possibly Maggi's system is metabolizing it differently."

Debbie had nothing to add to the conversation. She had difficulty reading Glen's concern. She wanted to trust he was not involved with Maggi, but his actions made that difficult for her to believe.

Glen gulped his coffee. "I think I'll head back upstairs."

"But you haven't eaten your breakfast yet," said Debbie.

Glen grabbed the bacon and toast from his plate. "I'll take this with me. Thanks for the good news, Doc."

Debbie watched him leave. Collin placed his hand over hers.

"You look as though you're ready to cry," he said.

With those words and his gentle touch, Debbie burst into tears.

"I think I'm losing him," she said.

Collin pulled his chair around closer to her. He handed her his handkerchief and offered a shoulder to cry on.

Collin stood six foot two. He had black hair and a dark complexion. His eyes were so brown they looked black. He dedicated himself to his profession during med school. He graduated top of his class and did so with hard work and no social life. Now, as a sought after neurologist, in his forties his practice was well established. He had a huge home in a great neighborhood; he owned two sports cars and a boat. He had every material possession he ever dreamed of but no one to share them with. His work kept him extremely busy.

The female staff seemed to throw themselves at him and he was aware of it. The few women from work he dated left him with a feeling they were hiding their true personalities, trying to be whatever or whoever he wanted them to be. He wanted a real woman, one that could be comfortable being herself. He found himself attracted to Debbie. He used these progress report meals as an opportunity to spend more time with her. Debbie, however, missed the signals he sent.

Two days later Dr. Fitzgerald asked Glen to step into the room when he finished his examinations. Normally, Maggi and Teddi would not share a room, but Glen insisted, for security reasons, they be kept together.

"We've taken them completely off of life support. They're functioning well on their own. There is no trace of insulin in the blood tests. That metabolized long ago. If they're to wake it should be soon. I'm seeing a marked improvement in brain function in both and they're responding to stimuli. I know you would like a better answer, but I can't give you one."

"Can they have visitors?" Glen asked.

"Other than you and Debbie?"

"Yes. I have a friend who would like to see them."

Dr. Fitzgerald frowned. He looked at the women then sighed, "I'm going to trust your judgment on this. If you feel it would help, then okay, but only for a short time. My nurses are a naturally a little edgy about these two after what happened. I'll tell them you're bringing in a guest."

Later that morning Glen escorted Jennifer Parker into the room.

Jennifer reached down and held Maggi's hand then did the same to Teddi. She wanted to see if she could get a reading on one more than the other.

"Glen, could you dim the lights, please?"

She tried to connect with their souls. If they had moved on and the bodies were mere shells waiting to die, she might be able to discern that. She tried repeatedly to make a connection.

"It's no use. I'm not getting anything."

"Damn," said Glen.

"Oh no, Glen. That's a good sign. At lease their souls have not left their bodies. They're still connected. I think they will wake up soon. I know this is difficult for you to understand, but each one of us have guides who help us through our lives. They are energies who communicate to us in a wide assortment of ways. You call yours a gut feeling. So my guides are telling me it will be soon, possibly even today."

Glen wanted to believe her. He knew he should, but her comment about guides and otherworld communication left him feeling very skeptical. He had to draw deep from within to remain open-minded. Finally, he convinced himself if the women wake up today he would give her some credit.

Jennifer gasped loudly.

"What?" asked Glen.

"I sense they are in great danger. I sense the person who tried to get to them the other night is in the building. If word gets out about them possibly waking up...I don't want to consider the possibilities... I think you should make your arrangements now. Be prepared."

When they stepped out of the room Glen paged Dr. Fitzgerald.

Glen met him as he rushed toward him in the hall.

"Is there a problem?" he asked with great concern.

"If they should wake up today, how soon can I move them?"

"If they regain consciousness, since they're not on life support any longer, I suppose you could move them tomorrow. I'd like to monitor them longer, but I understand your urgency in facilitating the move. Would you like me to contact another hospital to get the ball rolling?"

"Yes, but I want a different city."

"I really feel that's a bit extreme, but I'll go along with it. Where did you have in mind? Will you be accompanying them?"

"Of course, I'll be staying wherever they are just like I did here."

"Let me make a few phone calls and I'll get back to you."

Glen called Bill, "Can you do me a big favor?"

"Depends."

"Can you come over to the hospital to sit with Maggi and Teddi?"

"Did they wake up?"

"No, but they're getting closer. The department pulled the uniforms off the case. I need to go home for a few hours."

When Bill met Maggi a few years earlier, he fell for this beautiful dark-haired mystery writer with the sexy body. He pulled out all the stops to impress her with his charm. Maggi, a man-hater, shot him down in a big sort of way. He held a small grudge toward her for embarrassing him in front of Glen and Debbie. Willing to put his feelings aside, he wanted to help his friend, so he agreed.

Glen walked with Bill into their room. Maggi's skin looked pale, her dark hair glistened. The nurses did a good job of keeping her appearance well groomed when there really was not the need. In the bed next to her, Teddi's long red hair fell around her shoulder across her breasts in a braid with a bow on the end. Natural beauties, both of them, no make-up required.

"What's the story on Teddi? Any word from her husband?"

"None, he can't be located."

"Is he a suspect?"

"Of course."

"So what is it you want me to do, boss?"

"Sit outside their door and don't let anyone enter unless you check their ID. I'll take you by the nurse's station and introduce you. Then you can check out what a legit ID looks like. Oh, and keep your grubby hands to yourself. No fondling Maggi. She'd be furious with me if she found out I left you in charge while she's unconscious."

"Man, you're one sick son of a bitch if you think I'd stoop that low."

Glen slapped him on the back then darted down the hall to catch the elevator.

Debbie returned from grocery shopping, surprised to see Glen's pickup in the driveway.

"Finally. It's great to have you home."

She set her groceries on the kitchen counter then curled up in his arms. She kissed him a long passionate kiss. He tried to remember Jennifer's words. He kissed her back. Debbie could tell his mind was elsewhere. She broke free.

"So what are you doing home?"

"I'm packing."

Her heart sank to the bottom of her stomach. Her pulse raced, her breathing sped up. She looked at the suitcases stacked by the bedroom door.

"Glen, are you leaving me? Can't we work this out? I love you."

"I love you too, Deb. But I have to do what I have to do. It has nothing to do with you and me. Your doctor friend is making arrangements to send Maggi and Teddi out of town to another hospital. I need to go with. Jennifer Parker says they're in great danger. This asshole is not going to back off until he kills them or we catch him."

"Where're you going? For how long?"

"I don't have any details yet. I just want to be ready when the time comes. Could be today or could be another week."

"Do you want me to pack and go with you?"

"I suppose you can if you want, but what about your job and the dogs?"

"What about your job, Glen? What're they gonna say?"

"If I lose my job over this, so be it."

His words cut deeply. How could she possibly believe he had no romantic feelings for Maggi? Maybe he was unaware that he had fallen in love with her. Giving up his job to ensure her safety said it all to Debbie.

"Glen, I don't want you to go. Hire a guard for her or do whatever else you can arrange, but if you leave now I don't want you to come back."

Instead of consoling Debbie, Glen felt angry. Sleepless nights, skipped meals, and knowing this jerk had been watching him for an opportunity to strike made this all too personal. No longer did he feel his main objective was to protect Maggi and Teddi. He felt the game was on with the perp and he was not going to lose. He would guard them until they could tell him who did it then he would personally hunt him down. He had no patience for Debbie's jealous attitude right now. He decided to give her a while to cool down then maybe she would understand what he was trying to do. He picked up his suitcases and walked out the door.

His temper cooled as he drove back to the hospital.

"I'll call Debbie when I get to the hospital," he whispered to himself.

His heart ached for her. He knew his dedication to this case was more difficult for her to handle than any of the other cases he worked. She felt threatened and deceived by her friend and her husband.

Glen parked his pickup. He slid outside to take a deep breath. The hospital had become his new home, a home that offered no peace or serenity. He entered the building then ran up the stairs. Jogging on the stairs became his only source of exercise. He prided himself in his ability to remain physically fit and he worked out on a regular basis. He jogged up and down the stairs then went to the cafeteria for a cup of coffee.

He opened the door from the stairwell to the third floor. He walked toward Maggi's room.

He felt his pulse quicken when he saw a group of doctors and nurses rushing around the halls in and out of the room. He hastened his pace. Guilt surfaced for having left again and for taking the time, once he returned, to stop by the cafeteria for a cup of coffee. He set the cup on the floor and ran to the crowd. He searched faces for answers as he approached. Something happened.

His eyes scanned the crowd for Bill. He saw him in the waiting area watching television.

"What the hell happened? Weren't you watching them?"

"Yes. I was sitting outside the door just like you asked me to. A nurse went inside then the next thing I knew the staff rushed into the room. I moved over here to get out of their way. They've been in and out of the room in a hurry."

Glen stared across the hall. He still could not read their faces. He stopped a nurse.

“What’s going on?”

“Oh, Detective Karst, good news. Teddi woke up.”

“Can I see her? What did she say?”

“No, not yet. Wait until the doctor finishes with her. They’re watching Maggi pretty closely to see if she’s showing signs of coming around.”

Not satisfied with the response from the nurse, Glen waited until she left the hall then stopped another nurse.

“Can you tell me what happened? Did Teddi really wake up?”

“She came to for few minutes. She opened her eyes and looked around the room. She raised her hand to her head. She shifted her body in the bed then drifted back off.”

Disappointed, Glen said, “So she’s back in a coma?”

“No, I don’t believe she’s back in a coma just sleeping or fading in and out of consciousness, but not comatose.”

Glen paced the hall. He met Bill again. He slapped him across the back with excitement. If those girls survive they can tell him exactly what happened. He felt the rush of the hunt building.

Too impatient to wait any longer, Glen stopped a third nurse as she stepped out of the room.

"Can you tell Dr. Fitzgerald that Detective Karst would like to speak to him?"

Moments later the doctor stepped into the hall to speak with Glen and Bill.

"Both women show no signs of being in a comatose state. Teddi became conscious and shifted around in her bed. Maggi is moving, but has not yet opened her eyes. I think they're both going to live. Now we just need to evaluate the damage to their brains and nervous systems."

Dr. Fitzgerald looked over his shoulder then whispered to Glen, "I made preparations to move them as soon as they're ready. I contacted a colleague of mine in Omaha, Nebraska to make all the arrangements. I stressed the need for complete discretion and security. It's a ten hour trip by ambulance."

"Omaha, huh?"

Glen had not expected to leave the state, only the city. He thought they might be moved to Fort Collins or Boulder not Omaha, Nebraska. He searched the memory banks of his mind for any connections he may have on the force in Nebraska. He had no idea where he would stay or how long they would be there. Or what he would do for a job if they had to stay for an extended period of time.

He remembered Jennifer Parker had returned from Omaha on the night he asked her to join him at the hospital. He dialed her number.

"Jennifer, this is Glen. Good news, they're out of the coma. Teddi opened her eyes, but didn't stay awake long. Maggi hasn't opened hers yet, but Doc thinks she will soon."

"That's great news, Glen. Do the doctors think there is permanent damage?"

"No one knows yet if there's been brain or nerve damage. The reason I called is they're going to be transported to Omaha. I have no connections there. I know you just got back from there so I wondered if you knew someone there?"

"No, I'm sorry Glen. It was merely another stop on my book tour. I lodged at a hotel. I don't have any friends or family there who could help you out."

"That's okay. Maybe I'll introduce myself to the Omaha PD and see what they might be able to come up with."

"Glen, I'm really happy for you. I hope you can begin your investigation now and put this behind you. I hope your friends return to normal quickly."

"Thanks."

Dr. Fitzgerald walked up to Glen.

"I've made arrangements for an ambulance to leave here at midnight. We'll load them and leave with sirens blaring to not cause suspicion to your man if he's watching the parking lot. I might suggest you ride down in the ambulance and leave your vehicle parked. I can have Debbie come by and move it occasionally."

"Na, that's okay. If he's watching, he'll be watching for me, too. I think he'd pick up on Debbie pretty quick. I'll follow the ambulance in my truck."

"I suggest you go home and pack then. We'll have them ready to leave in about...," he looked at his watch, "six hours."

"I'm all packed and ready to go. I'll wait here at my post until we leave. I'll call Debbie from the road."

Collin was thrilled at the prospect of looking after Debbie while her husband was away. He was anxious to spend time alone with her away from the hospital. Neither Glen nor Debbie were aware of his intentions.

Glen paced the halls. He popped in and out of the room hoping to find one of them awake and ready to talk. The adrenaline surged through his body. The man who did this soon would be his once they gave him a name.

Shortly after midnight the ambulance crew loaded Maggi and Teddi. They closed the doors, knocked on the side and the lights began to flash. The siren blared as the ambulance left the parking lot.

Glen planned to stay behind another forty-five minutes. He paced, repeatedly checking his watch. He tried to watch television to pass the time. He went down the hall for a cup of coffee, but it grew cold. He used the bathroom, then sat back at his post flipping through a magazine without seeing the pages. The time ticked slowly. After forty minutes he left his position at the door, took the elevator to the first floor then went to his truck. His eyes scanned the parking lot searching for anything that might alert his senses. The area remained quiet. He drove slowly out of the parking lot. He headed in the opposite direction the ambulance had driven. He turned back, weaving in and out of side streets, then once he found his way onto the interstate he began making up for lost time.

Somewhere near Grand Island, Nebraska he caught sight of the ambulance. He fell in behind it and followed the rest of the way into Omaha. He met Dr. Regan at the door while the women were being unloaded.

"You must be Detective Karst," she said, extending her hand.

Glen reached his hand out to shake hers. Somehow he had not expected Dr. Fitzgerald's colleague to be a woman. She had dark brown hair, shoulder length, brown eyes and a youthful look. He could tell she had a petite frame but her scrubs hid the shape of her body.

"We've made arrangements to house you for a couple of days in our family quarters until you get situated here. If I can help you locate anything in Omaha or help in any way, please don't hesitate to ask. Now let's get these girls situated. I want to examine them."

Chapter 8

Dr. Natalie Regan did her best to accommodate Glen and his odd situation with the two women. The increased security measures were novel to her. She instructed the nursing staff to assign an exclusive crew of nurses to care for them. The fewer people in and out of the room made it easier to monitor those who needed to be there.

Within hours after their arrival Maggi opened her eyes. She looked around the room. Her nurse immediately buzzed for the physician. Dr. Regan sent the nurse into the hall to find Detective Karst. Although her eyes were open, Maggi did not speak. Confusion surfaced on her face, making her appear totally disoriented. Her blood pressure began to rise. Dr. Megan thought if she recognized Glen, it might help to calm her.

Glen stepped next to the bed. He said, "Maggi, it's Glen. You gave us one hell of a scare. You're gonna be okay now."

She stared at Glen with a blank look then drifted back into a state of unconsciousness just as Teddi had done earlier.

"What do you think, Doc? Do you think she recognized me?"

"There's no way to tell at this point. Her blood pressure did drop back down, but that could be because she drifted out again."

Over the course of the next twenty-four hours both women opened and closed their eyes frequently. Neither of them spoke or responded to those in the room with them. They stirred and moaned as their bodies began to respond to their awakened state. The doctors assumed they were in no pain other than the muscle stiffness from lying in bed without moving. Considering the amount of insulin they had flowing through their bloodstreams, severe headaches could accompany their waking.

Glen and Debbie spoke on the phone each morning and evening. He tried desperately to explain his actions, but Debbie had no patience for his excuses. She simply did not believe him.

Dr. Fitzgerald, realizing how vulnerable Debbie's emotions were, took full advantage of the situation. He sent her flowers. He called her every day and met her for lunches that soon turned into dinners away from the hospital. To reciprocate she fixed a home-cooked meal for him one evening.

Although he enjoyed the quiet private time with Debbie in her home he felt Glen's presence.

"Tell you what. Tomorrow I'll cook," he said.

The next night he asked Debbie to meet him at the hospital to follow him home. He planned every detail. If he could convince her to ride with him and return to the hospital with him when he made rounds, she would be stranded at his home. Tonight he planned to make his move. Not knowing how long Glen would be away he had to make every minute count.

Debbie looked lovely when she met him in his office at the hospital. Her blond hair lay softly on her shoulders while her blue eyes sparkled when his eyes met hers. Their relationship had moved forward from a handshake to a strong embrace for a greeting. He held her closely for a moment longer than etiquette might dictate. He inhaled her perfume. She pressed her head into his chest, enjoying the warmth of his body. She broke the embrace stepping back.

"I hope you're hungry," he said.

"Starved, but you don't have to do this you know. It's getting late. We can go out if you prefer."

"Not a chance. I have it all planned. I have chicken breasts marinating."

"Okay then, I'll follow you."

"I was thinking, since I have to come back here to check on a patient later why don't you ride along with me. I can bring you back to your car when I return."

Debbie hesitated at first. Up until last night, when he came to dinner at her home, they had always met in public places. She had not ridden anywhere with him. In her mind, it made it less of a date if they each drove and met somewhere. Tonight could change the rules. Then she thought, Glen and Maggi have ridden together, they went to New York together. They even shared a motel room. She gave in to his suggestion.

The crisp night air felt cool against her warm cheeks. She fought the feeling of excitement mounting inside of her. She felt like a schoolgirl on a date. She vowed to put Glen out of her mind for the entire evening. Collin proved to be an enchanting host. He grilled the chicken and vegetables while rice pilaf simmered on the stove. He lighted candles around the living room. He played soft seductive music while flames danced in the fireplace. His home was a show place and rightly so, after he paid a small fortune to have it professionally decorated. The wine, the music, the flickering flames set a romantic mood. Debbie drank the wine nervously, falling into his plan. He kept her glass full.

"Everything's doing fine, we'll eat in about ten minutes."

He took Debbie's glass from her as she stood admiring a wildlife painting on his wall. She turned toward him.

"Would you care to dance, madam," he asked in his fake French accent.

Debbie giggled, partly from nerves and partly from the wine on an empty stomach. She bowed to him in acceptance of his offer.

He gently pulled her body next to his. As they danced he tightened his hold on her. She placed her head on his shoulder. He kissed the back of her neck. She showed no response. They danced around the room then he stopped, stepping back to look into her eyes. She returned his gaze. Then he kissed her and she allowed it. He pulled back and looked into her eyes once more. He kissed her again. This time she returned his kiss.

Now he found himself in a bad situation. His lack of patience foiled his perfect plan. Any minute dinner would be ready. How would he manage to sweep her off to make love to her without burning dinner? His disappointment mounted when the buzzer on the stove rang out into the room announcing the completion of the bread in the oven.

The buzzer brought Debbie back to awareness. Collin thought she would insist upon going home.

"I think supper's ready," she said, acting as if the tender moment they shared never happened.

He released his hold on her with plans to serve the dinner, have nice conversation and remain true to his word by taking her back to her car later that evening. He would just have to try again.

She followed him into the kitchen.

“What can I help with?” she asked.

“The table’s set, but you can take the salads from the fridge.”

She opened the refrigerator, which contained many packaged gourmet foods. She wondered if he often entertained ladies in this manner or if he himself had a fondness for special foods.

She assisted him by placing the remaining courses on the table. He pulled out her chair for her and shook her napkin out, placing it in her lap. She could tell he spent a great deal of his time in exclusive settings with wealthy people. He had managed to recreate the atmosphere in his home.

They talked non-stop while they dined. He prepared the meal to perfection.

She stood to clear her place.

“What’re you doing?”

“I’m going to help you clear. The meal was absolutely wonderful. It’s the least I can do.”

“There’s no way you’re going to clear the table. Leave it. I’ll take care of it in the morning.”

He offered her his arm as he guided her to the fireplace in the living room.

As they sat near the fire they talked about their dreams and goals in life. She teased him about his lack of relationships. He laughed at himself with her.

"You know, if I had met you before Glen, you'd be mine. When I'd leave for work in the morning I'd always have you to come home to. My life would be complete."

Debbie looked into his eyes. She remembered how she and Glen met. She stopped herself from finishing her thoughts.

"I don't want to talk about Glen tonight," she said.

He poured more wine. While she watched the flames dance he massaged her feet. She moaned with pleasure. The mood of the room turned passionate. Collin leaned over, her kissing her long and hard. She returned the kiss. He pulled her down onto the floor with him. He made love to her in the glow of the fire. She slept in his arms until morning.

One week after the women had been moved to the hospital in Omaha, Maggi attempted to speak. Her facial expressions and her ability to move her limbs improved each day. Her speech showed no improvement. Teddi struggled more with muscle control than Maggi, but she, too, lacked the ability to speak. Without speech and the ability to control their hands to write, communication remained impossible. Glen could play the blink your eyes and nod your head game with them but, without knowing the right suspects to ask about, their responses were useless.

Glen continued to call Debbie who grew more cold. He also called Jennifer every few days for an update.

"Glen," said Jennifer. "I'm so glad you called today. I just spoke with a wonderful young lady whom I met while in Omaha during my book tour. Her name is Paula Adams. She lost her husband and lives alone not too far from the hospital. I know you've been staying in a motel when you're not with Maggi and Teddi. I explained the entire situation; I did not go into detail about the murder attempt. I told her you were my friend and you were a detective. When I asked her if she knew of any boarding houses or families who rented rooms to college students that might work for you, she graciously offered her home."

"Thanks, Jennifer. That's really great of you, but I'll manage. I wouldn't want to impose."

"I don't think you'd be imposing. Actually, I think you'd be helping her out. Seems there's no men in her family and she needs a few things done around the house. I told her you were a carpenter before you were a detective. I also believe she's terribly lonely."

"I guess I really would like to get out of the high rent district," he laughed. I wouldn't mind helping her out with some projects in exchange for room and board."

"How are the girls today?"

"The progress is damned slow. Some days they look like they might be improving then the next day they seem to slip back. No words other than guttural sounds from either of them. I'm afraid there may be significant brain damage. The doctors tell me I need to be more patient."

"I know the difficulty this presents for you. I know how desperately you want to find the culprits who did this. Do you feel they're safe?"

"At this point, yes."

"Good, that's the most important issue at the moment. Give their bodies time to recuperate. Now let me give you Paula's phone number. It's 555-5521."

"Thanks, I'll give her a call as soon as we hang up."

Glen dialed Paula's number.

"Hello."

"Hi, Paula. This is Glen Karst. Jennifer Parker told me to give you a call."

"Yes, Detective, I'm so glad you called. I would love to help you out if you would like to help me with some work in the house."

"I'd be more than happy to help if you don't think having me under foot would be an inconvenience?"

"No, not at all. I'd love the company."

"I would like to meet you in a public place before I come by your home. A precaution you should always take, young lady, when you're meeting a strange man," he scolded.

"I figured since you were a friend of Jennifer's and a detective I'd be safe."

"Name a restaurant and I'll take you to lunch."

"How about Lola's Deli?"

"Great, where is it?"

"One hundred and fourteenth and Dodge. Do you want directions?"

"Nope, I'll find it. When would you like to meet?"

"How about in an hour," she said.

"See ya there."

Glen left the hospital to check out of his room at the motel and gather his belongings. He put them into the back of his truck then locked the camper top. With his dark tinted windows Paula would not know he had his things with him in case she changed her mind; he did not want her to feel badly. Checking out before lunch would save him a day's rate.

He checked on the girls one last time, told the nurses where he could be reached then drove to Lola's Deli. Paula's instructions were easy to follow. When he parked his truck he realized he neglected to tell Paula what he looked like, she knew nothing of his appearance. He was not sure what she expected. Dressed in jeans and cowboy boots, with a short haircut and facial hair she might not think of him as a cop.

When he walked in, the place was buzzing with chatter. The local business crowd loved the little deli. Most of the tables were filled. The red head behind the counter walked up to him to aid him in finding a seat.

"May I help you? I have a table back along the wall," said Barb.

"Are you Lola?" asked Glen.

Barb laughed, "Long story. My name is Barb, I'm the owner and my nickname is Lola."

Barb checked out the handsome detective with the friendly smile.

"I'm here to meet someone," he said.

"What does she look like?"

"How'd you know it was a she?" he teased.

Barb grew to like him very quickly. "I'm psychic," she laughed.

Glen did not laugh. He studied her face intently then realized she was teasing him. After Jennifer Parker he took that title more seriously.

"Okay Miss Psychic, her name is Paula. Can you find her for me? I have no idea what she looks like."

Three ladies walked in the door behind Glen. He stepped to the side when he saw them coming. "That's her right there with the blond hair," said Barb with her eyes closed and her hand on her forehead, deep in thought.

Glen laughed, "If that's Paula, I promise to eat all my meals here while I'm in Omaha."

"You're on," said Barb.

Two of the ladies walked past them to a table where two gentlemen waited.

Glen looked at Paula.

"Paula?" he asked.

"Yes. Are you Detective Karst?"

Glen shook his head and began to laugh. Barb slipped her hands on his strong shoulders from behind. She whispered in his ear, "You're gonna love the entire menu."

"Hi Barb, do you know Detective Karst?" asked Paula.

Glen whipped around to Barb, who responded, "Just met him."

"I think I've been had." He laughed a hearty laugh.

Barb led them to their table.

The deli had the feel of a quaint Italian restaurant with red and white checkered tablecloths. As they walked through the crowded deli many of the customers spoke fondly to Barb. Glen instantly knew she had many regulars for the lunch crowd. He took that as a good sign; he would enjoy the food.

"So how, exactly, do you know Jennifer Parker," asked Paula.

Glen studied her face. Her skin and hair showed a healthy glow, but her eyes bore a tale of sadness. He tried to imagine the sparkle he guessed had once shone in those eyes.

"Jennifer and I worked on some cases together in Denver."

"Sounds exciting. What's it like working with a psychic? Do you think she's for real?"

"You know, until I met her I'd have said it was all a bunch of phony crap, but she made believer out of me. I'm not saying I agree with everything she says, but..." he stared out of the window, remembering the cases. "The way she could put a story together and make the pieces work without any details from me. Makes ya wonder, ya know?"

Barb stopped by the table, "Are you two going to order or talk through lunch?"

"Oh, I think today I'll try your number nine," said Paula.

"One Philly for the lady and you, sir? Are you going to start with number one and work your way through the menu that way?"

Glen laughed out loud, causing others to glance in his direction.

"I'll have your Al Capone's Favorite," he said.

Paula laughed now, too.

"What? Did I make a bad choice or something?"

"No, it's seems quite appropriate for a detective to order a sandwich named after a mobster."

"I see what you mean. Actually, I like the ingredients."

Paula looked at the menu again and read the list: smoked honey ham, genoa salami, proscuitto, cappacola, provolone cheese, lettuce, tomato, red onion, oregano and oil and vinegar.

"You have to be a detective to figure out what those ingredients are. I'm at a loss."

"Maybe if you and your sisters would take a risk occasionally when you order, you might find something different that you like," teased Barb. "By the way, did you see Carla sitting over there with her guy?"

Paula looked across the room and, to her surprise, she saw Carla gazing intently into Anthony's eyes.

"Excuse me a minute, Detective Karst."

"Please, drop the Detective Karst, call me Glen."

"Okay, Glen. I'll be right back."

Curious about the man who had Carla smitten, Paula, boldly and out of character for her, marched right up to the table and sat down.

"Paula. What're you doing here?" asked Carla.

"Having lunch, and you?"

"Anthony, this is my sister, Paula."

She shook hands with Anthony.

"So how do you two know each other?" Paula asked.

"Carla is my insurance agent," he responded.

"Didn't I see you in here having lunch with my other sister LeAnn?"

"Who? LeAnn? LeAnn is your sister? Then that would make her…"he said.

Carla sat straight up in her chair.

"You dated LeAnn?"

"No, LeAnn handles my investment portfolio. She was the one who suggested I contact your company about insurance. She told me to ask for Carla. I had no idea you were sisters. She neglected to tell me."

"But you told me you'd never eaten in here before," said Carla.

"I hadn't. The first time I came here was with you. When LeAnn called to discuss my account I suggested we do it over lunch. It was my idea to meet her here."

"That's really odd that LeAnn never told him you were sisters," said Paula.

"I guess she sends people my way a lot and vice versa. She probably wanted to keep it on a professional level. She had no idea we'd hit it off so well."

"So I take it you two are an item?" asked Paula.

"Can we talk about this later, Paula," asked Carla, feeling trapped. "Would you like to join us?"

"No thanks, I have my own date waiting over there." Paula pointed to Glen. She did not want Carla to think she was the only one with a secret. She returned to her table.

Now Carla craned her neck for better view of her sister's new man.

"Are you okay?" asked Anthony.

"Sure, I'm fine. Why?"

"You're not eating and you can't seem to take your eyes off of your sister."

"I'm just surprised that she's seeing someone so soon after her husband died. It's so unlike her."

When Paula returned to the table, Glen asked, "Someone you know?"

"That's Carla, one of my sisters."

"How many sisters do you have?"

"Two."

"You do live alone, don't you?"

"Not any more."

"Oh, I'm sorry. I was under the impression you weren't sharing your house with anyone."

"I'm sharing it with you," she smiled.

"Oh," Glen chuckled and wiped his hand on his napkin. "I guess we're roommates then." He reached across the table to shake hands.

Paula checked on Carla first then shook hands with Glen.

Before leaving the deli, Carla stopped by Paula's table.

"Hi, I'm Carla. And you are?"

"This is Glen. He's a detective. We're living together."

Carla was speechless, "Oh," was all she could muster.

"Nice to meet you," followed when she could breath again. She shook hands with Glen then left with Anthony.

"Don't you think you shook up your sister a bit?" asked Glen.

"I planned to. She never told us she was seeing that Anthony guy so I thought I'd play her game. I hope you didn't mind?"

"No. Hell, I like a good game of deceit any day," he chuckled, then continued with his sandwich.

"How soon will you be moving in?"

"How soon can I move in?"

"I don't care. Today?"

"Sounds good to me. What's your address?"

"Why don't you follow me home now so I can show you the guest room?"

"That's fine, but I need to stop by the hospital first. Are you sure I can't meet you at your house?"

"Okay."

She jotted the address and directions on her napkin.

"I'll see you in about an hour," said Glen.

When Paula arrived home she called LeAnn.

"Hey, why didn't you tell me Carla was seeing this Anthony guy?"

"You mean they're dating?"

"They looked beyond dating to me," said Paula.

"Good. I was hoping they'd hit it off. Do you have any idea how much this guy is worth?"

"Now how would I know that if I didn't even know he existed until today?"

"He came into my office and when I saw the growth of his company and that it was relatively new money in the hands of a man who knew nothing about investments, I knew we had to nab him. I figured you wouldn't be interested, being too soon after Andy. I can't date a client so I set it up for him to meet Carla. I had my fingers crossed, but didn't know if she has what it takes to land him."

"So you set them up and neither of them were aware they were being set up?"

"Yeah, brilliant, huh? I saw he wasn't married, had lots of money and only a mother to leave it to. I thought Carla might be interested. Guess she saw what I saw and made her move. Of course, he's pretty easy on the eyes and he's not much of a player, his money's too new. I'm really proud of myself."

"I gotta go, someone's at my door," said Paula.

No sooner had LeAnn hung up the phone then she had another call come in. This time it was Carla.

"LeAnn, Paula's living with some guy!"

"No, way. That's impossible."

"I tell you I met him today. They were having lunch at Lola's. She said they were living together."

"And you believed her?"

"Yes."

"Damn, I wanted to find her someone that could take good care of her. Do you think he has money? What was your impression of him?"

"He's a detective."

"Holy shit! A cop? We don't need a cop in the family."

"That's an odd thing to say."

"I meant, a cop's wages aren't good enough for her. I wanted her to taste the good life. Cruises, touring Europe and glamorous houses, you know."

"I don't think those things matter to Paula."

"They matter to me. I don't want to work my ass off packing away money and knocking myself out with shrewd investments if, when I retire, I have to take care of all of you."

"What in the hell do you mean by that?"

"Well, it's obvious Mom's gonna blow through what little she has. Paula married way beneath her. Andy had nothing to offer. The best thing that could've happened to her was his death. I'm so glad we got all that insurance taken care of before he died."

"What do you mean we?" I'm the one who finally pressured them into it."

"Oh whatever. At least he's gone and she has a small nest egg. Now we have to figure out how to get this cop out of her life."

"What did you mean about taking care of me. I have a decent job and lots of insurance."

"What good is insurance when you're dead? How are you going to live life? What are you going to do, live it like Lawrence? How boring. Not me. I'm gonna work for a couple more years and then I'm outta here."

"Is that why you set me up with Anthony?"

"Hey, congratulations on that one. I'm really proud of you for landing him. Do you think he'll marry you?"

"Gee, I don't know if I can manage the trap without your help," she said, sarcastically.

"Carla, relax. That's what big sister's are for. I plan to do the same for Paula. Maybe you can help. We need to find a doctor or lawyer or someone with old money who can show her the world."

"LeAnn, listen to you. You sound like all you're interested in is money."

"And who isn't? I happen to admit that money is everything. With money you can buy happiness, love and good health. Without it, life sucks. Look at how hateful and nasty Mom is. Don't you think she'd be a different person today if she had money? Don't fool yourself. You do whatever it takes to land Anthony, do you hear me?"

"Yes. I hear you loud and clear." Carla slammed the phone down.

"Ungrateful little bitch," said LeAnn.

With Glen away Collin charmed Debbie at every opportunity. He took her to dinner, the theatre, and the opera. He begged her to accompany him on a Caribbean cruise.

Every time she started to feel guilty about Glen, he found some way to continue to drive the wedge between them. He even found an attorney for her in case she wanted to file for divorce. He offered to pay the fees.

Glen had difficulty reaching Debbie. She often left her cell phone at home, a habit he scolded her for. Her social life with Collin took her away most of the time. Finally, Glen decided to call her at work. She cut him short telling him she had a meeting. Some how she felt if he heard her voice he would know what she had been up to. She was having an affair with Collin. After all the fights they had over Maggi, now she was doing exactly what she accused him of. If she were wrong about he and Maggi, she would be the one who stepped out on their marriage, breaking their vows.

He called her at home and left her a message, "Deb, I found a place to live in Omaha. Jennifer Parker set it up. I'm staying with a young widow friend of hers.

I'm getting free room and board in exchange for some carpentry work on her house. No change with the girls, just very slow progress. Call me." Before he hung up the phone he read the address to her in case she needed it.

Collin stood next to Debbie when she played the message. "Surely you don't believe him. He left you, moved to Omaha and is now conveniently living with some woman and you're supposed to believe there's nothing going on. Come on Debbie, wise up. You really need to leave him once and for all. I love you totally. If you marry me, I promise I'll quit my job and spend every minute with you. We can travel the world. I have enough money for the two of us to live forever."

He held her closely, stroked her hair and kissed her passionately.

"I love you, too," she admitted.

"Great. Let's tidy up details and you're going with me on that cruise."

"Give me a day to think about it. I don't want to give you an answer this very minute."

"Take your time, but not too much. I don't want you to miss that cruise."

Debbie stayed awake the entire night. Sleep was impossible as she weighed the words of Collin against the actions of Glen. She knew their marriage had showed signs of trouble for the past few years. She needed more from a man than Glen had to give. She wanted the companionship he was not capable of providing. The moments they spent together were wonderful, but rare. His work continuously interfered with their personal life. She could not foresee any changes in their future. With no children involved she had to make a decision. Either stay with Glen and be unhappy about the loneliness or leave him and spend every waking moment of every day with Collin. He may not be able to offer more love than Glen but he could give her his time, which Glen could not. She made her decision.

The doorbell rang at Paula's house.

A man in a suit stood on her porch. "I'm looking for Glen Karst," he said.

"Wait here."

Paula ran down the basement stairs into the room that Glen was remodeling.

"There's a man at the door asking for you," she said.

"Howdy, I'm Glen." He reached out his hand.

"Glen Karst?"

"Yes."

He handed Glen an envelope then walked away.

Glen closed the door, opened the envelope and read the papers. "God damn it! I can't believe it."

"What?" asked Paula.

"My wife just had me served with divorce papers."

Chapter 9

After much pressuring from Collin, Debbie finally agreed to accompany him on the cruise. She worried about the dogs. She dreaded putting them in a kennel. She dared not ask any family members to care of them under the present circumstances. The divorce had not yet been revealed to anyone other than Glen and Collin. With extra vacation time accrued at work, requesting time off this season of the year would not be a problem.

The situation with the dogs almost prevented her from going. Madison, her Dachshund and Cheyenne, Glen's German Shepherd, were not accustomed to being without them. Collin, not having any pets, failed to see her concern, but at the same time remained very supportive. If there had been a way to take them with, he would have arranged it.

"Surely you have friends who have pets who wouldn't mind taking care of them for a while."

"Not really. Everyone works and if they're going to be in a strange place, I'd rather it be with someone who could stay home with them."

"What did you and Glen do in the past when you had to leave them?"

"We left them home and had someone look in on them, but we were never gone more than a few days. This trip's different."

"Have you thought about asking Glen to come after them?"

"No way. I'm not telling him about the cruise."

"Exactly how long are you going to wait to tell him about us?"

"He'll find out on his own. Don't forget he's a detective, and a damned good one, so if he wants to know anything about my life he's not going to have a problem discovering that information."

Collin worried his hard work aimed at separating Debbie from Glen might not be permanent. She obviously still maintained a great deal of respect for Glen and probably still loved him. He needed to keep physical distance between them. If enough time passed, with him catering to her every need and showering her with gifts and travel, maybe, just maybe, he could relax about Glen.

This is the first time Collin felt inferior to any man. His high profile job, his good looks, his vast amount of money paled, in his mind, to the hold Glen Karst had over Debbie.

"You know, there is one woman who I could call. She used to be a dog show judge. She's retired now and spends all of her time with her dogs. As a matter of fact, she's taking care of Maggi's two dogs."

"Do you think she'd take your dogs?"

"I guess the only way to find out is to ask.

Debbie called Jean.

"Hi Jean, this is Debbie."

They had not spoken since Maggi and Teddi entered the hospital. Glen tried to convince her that Jean's accusations were lies invented by a lonely old woman.

"Debbie, I haven't heard from you in a while. I talk to Glen occasionally. Are you calling with news about Maggi? I hope she's doing better."

"No, I'm calling about our dogs. I'm going away for a couple of weeks and, with Glen in Omaha, I was wondering if you could take care of the dogs?"

"My dear, you know I'd love to. My Jacks will get along fine with your Shepherd and your little Dachshund. Maggi's two Berners will like having a larger playmate. My little guys are too fast for them so they give up too easily."

"Are you sure having six dogs at once isn't too much for you? I could board them in a kennel."

"Six dogs is nothing. I can remember when I bred for show; at times I'd have over twenty dogs to care for. Bring them on over."

"Great. Is tomorrow okay?"

"Sure, I'll be here."

Debbie finished her last minute packing details, checked her list then left to meet Collin for dinner.

Paula stepped over the lumber and electrical cord stretched across the floor in her basement. She asked Glen to change her one big unfinished room into a laundry room, bathroom, extra bedroom and family room.

Glen, an expert carpenter, loved the distraction from the hospital. Maggi and Teddi were awake and no longer needed his constant guard, especially since security increased their watch around the clock for the two women.

"Here ya go," she said as she handed him a beer.

"Thanks."

He stopped, wiped the sweat from his eyes then took a long drink.

"A couple six packs of these is just what the doctor ordered."

"How're ya doing? Did you call your wife?"

"You know what Paula, I was married to my job before I met Debbie. She's a great person, but she needs more from a marriage than I can give her. She needs a man who can be there for her all the time and be available to take her to dinner and movies and actually stay through the entire movie without being called out. I take my work very seriously, too seriously to combine it with a relationship."

"Do you love her?"

"Hell yes. That's part of the reason I'm letting her go. I've caused her too many sleepless nights worrying and gallons of tears of disappointment when I have to cancel plans to go after the bad guys. I've thought off and on about setting her free, but felt too guilty. If this is what she wants, I won't stand in her way. I just hope she meets the right man soon."

"Do you think she's met someone?"

"Debbie? Na, she wouldn't even notice another guy. Not to sound conceited, but she's completely in love with me. I just wish I could've lived up to her expectations of marriage."

"What will you do now?"

"That's a good question. I just quit my job."

"You didn't."

"Had no choice. They told me to get my ass back if I wanted to keep my position. Those two ladies at the hospital are friends of mine and I'll be damned if a job is going to interfere with me protecting them. I'm going after the son of a bitch who put them there."

"What exactly happened to them?"

Glen gave her a long appraising look, "Can I trust you?"

"Sure."

"I mean don't even tell your sisters."

"Hey, if you can keep my secret about our living arrangement I can keep my mouth shut about your friends."

"Maggi is Maggi Morgan..."

"Oh my God, the mystery writer? I love her books. I think I have every one of them. I saw her on Oprah once. She's gorgeous."

"Yeah, she is."

"Wow, so you're really a friend of hers?"

"Yep, I help her with the police stuff in her books."

Paula set her glass down and sprinted upstairs, returning with one of Maggi's books. She opened the front cover to the acknowledgement page.

"So you're *this* Detective Karst?"

"Yeah, that's me."

"Someone tried to kill her?"

"In her last book the murders she wrote about began to happen in real life. She got herself into a shit load of trouble with the police thinking she was somehow involved in a publicity stunt. Then a stalker stepped into the picture, and a rapist. We don't have the whole story straight yet. The rapist got shot and we thought it was all over until my wife and I found Maggi and Teddi on the floor in Maggi's bedroom barely hanging on. Someone shot them up with insulin and left them there to die. It didn't work and then the sick son of a bitch made another attempt while they were in the hospital in Denver."

"So that's why you brought them here. You're hiding them."

"Exactly."

"Wow, this is just like being in one of her books. I can't believe Detective Karst is putting up walls in my basement. Now I feel terrible. You shouldn't be doing this. You're kind of a celebrity."

Glen chuckled. "My ass, Maggi's a celebrity, I just help out when I can. Besides, I recently lost my title of Detective."

"I think once a detective always a detective. You're on a different assignment now. Sort of like a P.I."

"I guess you could look at it that way." Her comment left a sour taste in his mouth, as blue is blue—P.I.'s don't count.

Debbie pulled slowly into Jean's driveway. She had not returned to the neighborhood since the night they found Maggi and Teddi next door. She felt confused. What if she was wrong about Glen and Maggi, what if divorcing Glen and going away with Collin was the wrong thing to do?

"Follow your heart, girl," she said to herself. She closed her eyes to think of the two men. When she thought of Glen it brought sadness and confusion. When she envisioned Collin she felt warm inside.

She stepped out of the car, stopped and looked over toward Maggi's house. Will she ever be the same? Will their friendship be intact? If she and Glen were not having an affair, how would she ever find forgiveness to accept Debbie again?

Debbie's personality caused her to fret if she felt she hurt someone or they did not like her due to something she said or did. Leaving Glen was a big step in her life. What if, after spending time away with Collin, she discovered she did not want to be with him? Would Glen take her back?

Her thoughts drifted back to Maggi. What will life be like for her if she is permanently handicapped in some way? Would Collin understand if she wanted to be there to help her friend recover and adjust to a new life? Collin would have to be concerned about Debbie and Glen continually crossing paths if she were to remain friends with Maggi. So many thoughts kept creeping into her mind. She knew if she dwelled on them too long they might influence her decision.

She opened the car door releasing Cheyenne, the Shepherd, and picked up Madison, the Dachshund, to put her on the ground. Jean walked out to meet them with her two Jack Russell Terriers and Maggi's two Bernese Mountain Dogs. All six of the dogs went bounding across the huge acreage.

"Do you have time for a cup of coffee?" asked Jean.

"No, I really need to get going."

"Where did you say you and Glen were going?"

Debbie avoided Jean's question. She averted her eyes so they would not meet Jean's. After all, if divorcing Glen was a mistake, Jean would have played a major part in Debbie making the biggest mistake of her life. On the other hand, if Collin became the man of her dreams and she lived happily ever after, she would have Jean to thank for that as well.

"Here's my contact information and here's Glen's."

Jean read the notes.

"What's Glen doing in Omaha?"

"Oh, he didn't tell you?"

"Tell me what?"

"I just assumed since you were taking care of the dogs that you knew."

"Tell me already."

"He had Maggi and Teddi moved."

"Moved? Are they well enough to travel? Does this mean they might live?"

"Gee, I guess Glen hasn't kept you posted at all, has he?"

"Why don't you fill me in, dear."

"The insulin is out of their system. They are out of the comas and off of life support."

"Were they able to tell Glen what happened?"

"No, not yet. Seems there's some problems. They can't talk and they don't have good muscle control. They spend very little time awake. I guess it could be permanent, but we're hoping it's not."

"So they could remain in a vegetative state?"

"I suppose that's a strong possibility."

"How soon will they know?"

"Collin says there's no way of telling."

"Who's Collin?"

Debbie realized she made a careless slip to the wrong person.

"He's the neurologist. He keeps us updated on their condition. We've gotten to know him pretty well. I really better go."

She kissed her dogs good-bye then slid into her car to leave before Jean could ask more questions about Collin.

Glen answered Paula's phone when it rang. Sometimes his cell phone did not work properly in her basement so he gave the hospital her home number.

"Is Paula there?"

"No, she went to the store."

"Who's this?"

"This is Glen, I've been staying…"

LeAnn cut him off. "This is LeAnn. Tell Paula to meet us at Methodist hospital. Tell her our mother's in the cardiac wing. Tell her to hurry."

Rather than call Paula at the store and have her paged he changed his shirt and drove the few blocks to look for her. He parked in Hy-Vee's parking lot then ran inside, searching the aisles for her. His agitated state caught the attention of some of the shoppers, making them nervous. He had seen it so many times, and it always amused him. He found her in the last aisle. He feared she had gone to a different store.

"Glen, what're you..."

"Your sister called. Your mom's in the hospital. She wants you to meet her at there."

"Is she okay?"

"She didn't say. She told me to tell you to hurry. I'll drive. Just leave your groceries."

Paula followed Glen out of the store and into his pickup. Anna was in the same hospital as Maggi and Teddi. Glen could drive there blindfolded. The temptation to use his portable blinking red light when in a hurry had to be avoided when the reasons were personal. Glen followed all the rules, taking his job very seriously.

He found a parking place close to the entrance. He helped Paula out of his pickup then escorted her across the parking lot. Too concerned to look up, she nearly stepped in front of a speeding car. Glen reached out for her and pulled her back, nearly knocking her off of her feet. She fell into his arms as he helped her to regain her balance.

"Oh my God," she said. "Thank you."

"Let's keep you focused on your surroundings, even in a time of crisis. Rule one of being a good cop."

"I'll try. Sure glad you came with me."

Inside the hospital Glen took over. No need to stop at the information desk to ask directions. He knew the hospital only too well, spending many hours walking the halls for exercise while the doctors were with the women or the nurses were bathing them.

He directed her to the cardiac wing. She stopped when she saw her sisters at the end of the hall. Memories of Andy flashed through her mind. She felt ill. The sounds, the smells, the feel of the hospital were too much for her. Her hands began to perspire; she felt light-headed.

"I don't know if I can do this," she said.

Glen slipped his arm around her.

"Hey, I'm here if you need me. You must be pretty close to your mom."

"No, it's Andy. He died here."

Paula never spoke about Andy's recent death to Glen so he politely avoided the subject.

"Do you want me to stay with you?"

"Could you? For just a few minutes. I'll let you know when I think I can handle it."

"Your sisters are here and if you feel you're not ready to face hospitals and the possibility of death, no one has the right to expect you to. Everyone heals in their own time."

"Thanks, Glen. Let's give it a try."

He escorted her to her sisters.

"What happened?" asked Paula.

"Hi Glen," said Carla. She had insurance papers spread across the small magazine table in the lounge area.

"So you must be the mystery man. Glen, is it? My name is LeAnn. I'm the big sister. The one who got all the brains."

Under normal circumstances Carla and Paula would protest, but today their mother pre-occupied their minds.

LeAnn studied Glen from head to toe without hiding her inspection.

He felt as though she undressed him during her visual observation. Now he understood how a woman feels when men check them out openly.

"Will somebody tell me what happened," said Paula.

"Mom had a heart attack," said Carla.

"Is it bad?" asked Paula.

"I think she made it here in time," said LeAnn. "Seems somebody forgot to order her medicine and she skipped a couple doses. She was out working in her damn yard when it hit. She called the ambulance herself."

"I don't think I like the tone of your voice," said Paula. "I keep her meds in order. She had plenty. She's either taking too many or spilled them or something. I've got the prescriptions written on my calendar so I know when each of them runs out. I didn't mess up. You know, it wouldn't hurt you two to check the bottles once in a while when you're visiting her, too."

"I guess we thought you'd handle it. Carla's keeping tabs on all of her insurance policies and I've been handling her investments to be sure she doesn't make bad choices. But if you think you need help with watching her med bottles, then I guess we can do that, too."

"I don't need this," said Paula. "Let's go, Glen."

Shocked by the way Paula was treated by her sisters; he put his arm around her and walked her back to the elevator. While they waited for the doors to open she burst into tears. Glen handed her his handkerchief and offered her his shoulder to cry on. He walked her away from the doors to a bench nearby. They sat on the bench and he held her while she cried.

"I'm so sorry," she said embarrassed. "I think it was more Andy than LeAnn that upset me. I'm used to her going off like that."

"If you ever want to talk about Andy, I'm a good listener."

"Thanks, I'll be okay now. Why don't you check on your friends while we're here? I don't mind waiting."

They took the elevator to Maggi's floor. Paula waited in the visitor's lounge. Security would not allow her past the guard. Glen would have had to pre-register her as a visitor before she would be allowed inside the secured area.

While Paula sat on a chair thumbing through a magazine the feeling Andy was with her overwhelmed her. Sometimes she felt he tried to communicate with her, but she had no idea what he might be saying. She did know that moments like this comforted her.

Glen stepped quietly inside the room. Both girls appeared to be resting comfortably. Having spent day and night with them in Denver part of him felt as if he was slacking off on his duties. Now that they were awake from time to time he wished he could communicate with them, but they were not ready. Seeing them, especially Maggi, in this state added to the depression he felt concerning his divorce. He found himself wondering if it was inevitable. He thought the situation with Maggi and Teddi in the hospital added the final strain to his already doomed marriage. He also wondered, if the girls recovered fairly quickly, if he should return to Denver and try to patch things up with Debbie. He loved her so much, but after giving it some thought, he decided he loved her too much to ask her to try again.

Glen did not spend much time with the girls. He spoke with the nurse who sat in their room. Part of the added security involved a nurse being in the room around the clock, not only to chart any changes and the amount of time they were awake, but to prevent another intrusion like the one in Denver. There was no significant change.

"How are they?" asked Paula.

"They're both sleeping, I think I'll stop by later. It's lunchtime. Let me take you out," he suggested.

"I'll bet I can guess where," she laughed.

"A promise is a promise," he chuckled. "Besides, she fixes a mean damn sandwich. Sure wish she'd open a shop in Denver."

Glen walked Paula through the hospital corridors with ease to the side entrance doors near where they parked. This time when Paula stepped from the curb she looked up to check for oncoming traffic. Glen watched out for her in case her emotions left her less than cautious again.

His truck probably could have found its way from the hospital parking lot to Lola's Deli all by itself, as often as Glen ate there.

"Well, hello Detective Karst. Can't stay away, huh?" said Barb.

"Nope."

Barbara adjusted her apron and primped her hair in the presence of the ever so sexy detective. She turned to Paula.

"Hey, I heard from your sisters that you two are quite the item."

"Long story. I'll tell you someday," said Paula, giving Barb the cue to drop the subject.

"What can I get you?"

"I'll take your squawkin guac'an chicken," said Paula.

"I'll try your number six, the big beefmiester," said Glen.

"Do you really eat all of your meals here?" asked Paula.

"No, but most of them. I grab something for breakfast at the hospital; lunch here and I've been skipping supper. I think I'm sporting a few extra pounds. I haven't been jogging or working out with my martial arts. I'm starting to feel like a slug."

"You've been working up a sweat in my basement."

"I know and it feels really good, too."

Barb overheard the last part of their conversation.

"Hey you two, keep it clean. There are a couple of kids in here," she laughed.

The doctors and nurses finished the work they were doing on Anna. They ran the necessary tests, drew blood, took a urine sample and settled her into her room. Anna hated hospitals. She avoided them at all costs. Her only times being a patient were when she gave birth to the girls and then she hounded the doctors and staff so hard they usually let her go a day or two early. Now they only hold a new mom for twenty-four hours. Had that been the procedure when Anna had the girls she probably would have insisted she be allowed out after only twelve hours. With her ability to make everyone miserable they probably would have agreed.

A nurse, with a look of stress on her face, stepped out of the room.

"Is it okay to see our mother now?" asked LeAnn.

"Of course, she's ready for visitors," replied the nurse wondering why they would want to.

LeAnn and Carla cautiously opened the door and peered in before entering. Secretly they had hoped she slipped off to sleep thus giving them an excuse to leave and come back later.

Anna watched them as they walked in the door.

"Where's Paula?" asked Anna.

"Glen took her home," said Carla.

"Who in the hell's Glen?"

LeAnn rolled her eyes. What was Paula trying to do, kill the old lady? She just had a heart attack and now someone has to break the news to her that Paula's living with some guy she barely knows.

"Calm down, Mom. You don't need to get excited," said LeAnn.

"Don't tell me how to act. Where were you girls when I had my attack? Obviously off doing your own thing. One of these days you're going to find me dead, you just wait and see. So tell me why your sister thought her date was more important than me."

"She just felt bad about your meds," said Carla.

"And she should. Can't she do anything right? I don't ask anything of you girls and when I ask one little favor like watch my medicine, that's too much. You know, one of you should take the time to be with me every day."

"Mom, we work," explained Carla.

"What kind of excuse is that? I worked my whole life and still found time for you girls. What do I get in return? A damned crystal glass for my birthday then I can be ignored the rest of the year."

"We thought you'd like the crystal collection back," explained Carla.

"That's pretty damned selfish if you ask me. Buy me something that you girls will end up with. And how am I supposed to split it up between the three of you without you squabbling over it?"

"Mom, we don't squabble over things," LeAnn pointed out.

"Your sister did good job screwing up my meds. I suppose you forgot to keep my insurance current."

"I knew you'd be paranoid about it so I brought the papers with me," said Carla.

"I'll give you paranoid. Why wouldn't I be with three inept daughters?"

LeAnn threw up her hands and walked out. Carla showed her the insurance papers. Anna flipped through them.

"Why are you the only one down as beneficiary?" asked Anna.

"Because you told me that's the way you wanted it. You didn't trust Andy or Reed. You thought LeAnn would blow it all in the stock market. You asked me to handle your final arrangements and split the remainder between the three of us."

"How do I know you're not going to cash in on my policies and cremate me like Andy to save a few bucks. I can't trust any of you. When I get out of here, I'm going to hire a financial consultant to handle my estate."

"Mom, what estate? You don't have much. Lawrence's house and the little LeAnn has invested for you. That's all you've got. You use all of your social security money in the first two weeks of the month then LeAnn has to cover your expenses from your investments for the remainder. You know, someday, if you're not careful, you're gonna empty that fund completely. Then what're you gonna do?"

"Are you telling me LeAnn's spending my money? I'll bet she's been making bad investments. Can't trust a damn one of you. I'm gonna have an auditor look over my investments then I'll get it away from her before she loses all of it."

"Maybe you should rest now," said Carla. She gathered the papers and left.

LeAnn waited outside the door for Carla.

"Did you hear?"

"Yes, I heard. What a bitch. I can't believe she's our mother. Poor Lawrence, and he had to live with her all those years. The man was a saint. Just when he was about to have some happiness in his life, just when he planned to leave her for a nice woman…bam! He got hit with a heart attack."

"How are her investments going?" asked Carla.

"What? Now you don't trust me either?"

"LeAnn, I didn't say that. If she's gonna hire an auditor I want you to be protected from her wrath."

"Well, I for one hope she doesn't go through with it. If she does, the shit will hit the fan."

"Why? What happened?"

"You know the market, one day you're flying high and the next it takes a dive. I've done a good job building her portfolio, but with this recent terrorist stuff in the news some of the stocks took a dive again. I expect them to make a comeback over the next few months, but on paper it doesn't look the greatest right now."

"Maybe when she gets out of here she'll calm down and forget about it."

"I doubt it. She can't think straight. She's so paranoid the world and everyone in it is out to get her. Remember?"

"I think I'll go back in to try to talk some sense into her," said LeAnn.

"I don't think that's a good idea. Maybe I should go back in and see how she's doing, first. She already blew up at me, no sense in getting her excited again. You wait here."

Carla went back inside the war zone. Anna was watching television.

"What do you want? I thought you were gone, left me like your sisters. Ungrateful, all of you."

"Can I get you anything? How about some juice or tea?"

"I want a Coke. Go get a can of Coke for me."

"But what about your diet? What about your diabetes?"

"I could be dying here and you're refusing me my last wish?"

"I'll go get the Coke. LeAnn wants to say good-bye. Should I send her in?"

"Sure why not. This may be the last time she gets to see me."

Carla stepped into the hall.

"She's dying in there just so you know. The doctors have her totally stabilized, she can go home tomorrow, but she's playing it up as only she can. I'll be right back, I'm getting her a Coke."

"But what about her sugar intake?"

"She doesn't care so why should I?"

LeAnn went in to see her.

"Just so you know, I'm hiring an auditor when I get out of here. Your sister tells me you're spending all of my money. I need that money. I could live another thirty years, you know."

"Carla thought you sounded like you were throwing in the towel already. You sent her after a Coke because you felt you were on your death bed."

Anna bristled as LeAnn stood up to her. Her comeback was interrupted when Carla appeared at the door with the Coke. She handed it off to LeAnn and left.

"Tell me about your sister's new boyfriend," said Anna.

"Which sister?"

"You mean they're both sleeping around and no one's told me about it?"

"Carla is dating a nice business man named Anthony."

"Does he have money?"

"Yes."

"Good, that's all that matters. What about Paula?"

"She and Glen are living together."

"What's this Glen do for a living?"

"He's a cop."

Anna sat straight up in bed with a panicked look. Red in the face she snorted, "A cop ain't gonna support her like she needs. We don't need no damn cop in this family. Get rid of him or there'll be trouble, mark my words."

LeAnn was shocked at her mother's reaction, which came as a surprise to her. She did not think anything out of her mother's mouth could shock her any more. She walked to the window to give her mom a chance to cool down so they could talk.

"Don't turn your back on me," said Anna.

"Look, Mom. You're upset. I think I'm gonna leave now. I'll be back later."

After lunch Glen said, "I can drop you off at home or you can go see your mom if you'd like."

"I think I'll ride over to the hospital with you, but I'm not sure I want to see her. I don't know if I'm emotionally up to it. I'll decide when we get there."

Both Teddi and Maggi were sitting up in bed. The television was on and they were focused on the screen when Glen entered the room.

"Are they watching television?" he asked the nurse.

"The doctor thinks they could be."

Glen walked over to Maggi's bed. He sat on the edge of it. He moved her face toward his.

"Maggi, it's Glen. Do you understand me?"

Maggi closed her eyes, holding them shut then opened them again.

"Maggi, blink your eyes again if you understand me," he said with enthusiasm in his voice.

"That could just be a muscle response," said the nurse as she fluffed her pillows.

Maggi slowly and methodically closed her eyes once again then opened them. She had trouble keeping her focus on Glen.

He reached for her hand. He held it in his. He stroked the back of it with his other hand when she gripped his for a moment.

"Damn it, Maggi, I know you're aware of me. I just know it."

She blinked a second long blink. Her blood pressure monitor showed an increase.

"I believe she's had enough, Detective Karst. Why don't you let her rest?"

Glen let go of her hand, but felt she really did not want him to leave. Torn by the reminder of Jennifer Parker, who tried to teach Glen to listen to his inner voice, and the impatient look on the nurse's face, he left.

Out in the hall Paula was nowhere to be seen. Glen went to the cardiac wing to search for her. He met her in the hall as she walked to the elevator.

"Did you go see her?"

"No, I got all the way to the door and backed out."

"Would you like me to go in with you?"

"No, let's just leave."

Early that evening the alarm went off on the machine connected to Anna. The doctors and nurses rushed into the room to begin working on her. The first nurse to arrive looked through her chart to confirm her do not resuscitate order. That piece of paper meant the difference between life and death for Anna.

"Let's call it," said the doctor.

Chapter 10

"Why are you calling me? I told you not to call until it's over. Are they finally dead?" asked Daniel.

"I called because I hope you have a plan to get us out of this mess you've gotten us into," said Jean.

"What in the hell are you talking about? Don't play games with me. Are they dead or not?"

"No, they're not dead. They're out of the coma."

"What do you mean? Are they talking?"

His voice, breathless as panic set in.

"All I can tell you is they woke up and Glen moved them to a hospital in Omaha."

"Omaha? Why in the hell did he do that? Never mind, I know why."

"If you know, would you mind filling me in?"

"I paid the girls a little visit. That bastard Karst has been at their side nearly night and day. It's tough enough to get to them without him standing guard like some Doberman."

"What'd you do?"

"I'd been watching for his truck to leave. The few times he left and I tried to get to them there was always too much commotion around their room. I knew I had to hit at night when things were quieter. He'd been sleeping at their door. Finally, one night I saw him leave with some woman, so I made my move. I slipped into the hospital, wearing scrubs like the ones the nurses wear. I made it all the way into their room. Just as I was about to inject more insulin into Maggi a floor nurse stepped in. She caught me leaning over Maggi with the syringe. I shoved past her and out the door; she rang for security. I dumped my scrubs in a trashcan, took the stairs to another floor and sat in the family lounge reading a magazine until things cooled down. Then I just walked out."

He laughed. "I even walked right past Glen in the dark parking lot as he came back to the hospital. The stupid son of a bitch had me right under his nose and didn't even know it."

"I'd be mighty careful if I were you. Glen's not going to rest until he finds whoever did this to Maggi and Teddi. I'm making plans to disappear as soon as possible. To make matters worse I have Glen's dog with me."

"Poison the damn thing. It'll serve him right."

Jean was able to assist Daniel with his human killing spree, but there was no way she could kill a dog.

"I'm not going to hurt a dog. I'll have to board them somewhere and get out of here fast."

"Don't be in such a rush. I asked you if they're talking yet and you didn't give me an answer."

"No, Debbie said they're not able to talk and the doctors don't know if they'll come out of it or stay vegetables."

"I guess it's time I pay a little visit to Omaha. Can you tell me which hospital?"

"No."

"What the hell good are you? Find out."

"How?"

"Call Glen with some bogus story about his dog not eating or something."

Jean, too frightened to speak with Glen, called Debbie.

"Hi, Debbie, I hate to bother you, but I lost the information you gave me about Glen. Did you say he was in Omaha?"

"Yes," said Debbie. Then she gave Jean the information again.

Debbie's suspicion began to rise. Jean had Glen's phone number to be able to reach him about Maggi's dogs. She doubted Jean forgot where he was. She had a mind for gossip so details like those didn't slip past her.

"Any word on the girls? What hospital did you say they were in? I'd like to send flowers."

Debbie's instincts emerged warning her not to divulge any further information. Obviously Glen kept Jean in the dark about the move.

"Gosh, Jean. Can't remember. I'm sure Glen will tell you. Why don't you give him a call?"

Jean paced around her kitchen. She went to the pantry for dog food. She filled the six dishes then went into her bedroom to finish packing. She looked up the phone number of a nearby boarding kennel. She called the after hours emergency number.

"Yes, I have a family emergency. I need to fly to see a family member in the hospital. I must leave tonight. Can I bring my dogs by?"

"Under those circumstances, yes. I'll meet you at the kennel."

Jean unloaded the Dachshund and Shepherd. She walked them to an empty kennel inside.

"They can stay together. I think they'd be happier that way."

She followed the attendant to the front desk to fill out paperwork.

"I don't have proof of vaccinations with me, but you can call the clinic in the morning for their medical records."

Jean wrote in the name of Debbie's vet, filled out Debbie's address and home phone number then signed Debbie Karst on the signature line.

It was late and the attendant on call that night wanted to speed up the formalities. She did not bother to ask for Jean's ID or any other information. She wished her well on her travels and a speedy recovery for whoever she was off to see and rushed her out of the door.

Glen, Paula, Carla, Anthony and LeAnn waited in the hall at the hospital to speak with the doctor in charge of Anna's case. LeAnn received the call from the hospital then informed the others of Anna's passing.

"I don't understand. I thought she was fine," said LeAnn.

"She seemed fine to me when she started bitching about her ungrateful daughters," said Carla.

Anthony appeared surprised by the comments the girls made so soon after the death of their mother.

"Maybe, I should have went to visit her one last time," said Paula.

"Why? You're the lucky one. You're last memory isn't of her ranting in her paranoid fashion about how terrible we are. Maybe somewhere in your memory you can find a pleasant thought about her. I know for Carla and me, that'll be impossible."

Neither Glen nor Anthony had actually met Anna. They heard brief passing comments made by Carla and Paula indicating Anna's personality was less than pleasant.

Both men felt helpless as they listened to the girls trying to comfort each other by complaining about Anna and the way she treated them. Something inside of Glen made him wonder about Anna's death. He shook his head. Here are three young women who lost their mother and the detective side of Glen began to look at each of them as a suspect simply because there was a dead body of a very disliked woman.

He walked away from the group. He bought a cup of coffee from the machine down the hall.

"I've been away from my job for too long," he whispered.

"What was that?" asked Anthony.

He had taken Glen's lead to leave the girls to sort out their feelings. Glen knew he had been followed but did not realize that Anthony was close enough to hear.

"Oh, nothing. I haven't been working any cases lately. I'm a homicide detective and my imagination got away from me. You know, dead body and all. I have to process each of them through my mind. It's just the way I think."

"You don't think anything out of the ordinary happened here, do you?"

"Hell, no. We're looking at a lonely old woman with a bad heart that finally got the best of her."

"Maybe the girls will be better off without her when the pain goes away."

“Yeah, maybe. Sometimes these cranky, bitter old folks who make it a point to hurt people as often as they can are better off dead. It allows the family to spend the rest of their lives peacefully. You wouldn’t believe how often they’re murdered to speed up that peace.”

Anthony looked down the hall, “Looks like the doctor’s finally here.”

Glen and Anthony joined the girls.

“No, I can’t believe it. I won’t believe it. You can’t tell me she agreed to that,” said Paula.

“I’m telling you. I have the papers in my car. I never took them out when I came here this afternoon with her file,” said Carla.

“I agree with Paula. I want to see those papers,” said LeAnn.

Carla left to retrieve the papers.

Glen and Anthony were curious what the argument was about, but remained silent spectators.

“So you’re telling us that after you said she was going to be fine earlier today she had another heart attack that killed her?” snarled LeAnn.

“That’s exactly what I’m trying to tell you. She began to feel a little ill this afternoon. We watched her closely. We assumed she was reacting to the treatment we had given her or she had a virus that went undetected. She vomited a couple of times. We gave her a sedative to help her relax and something to stop the vomiting. She became markedly irrational the more ill she became. The vomiting stopped, the sedative made her groggy. She dropped off to sleep. Her blood pressure was slightly elevated, but we attributed that to her sudden wave of illness. Then the monitor showed irregularities with her heart. Her heart began to fibrillate, then stopped completely.

"The orders on her chart were DNR, do not resuscitate. I'm sorry, ladies, but our hands were tied. We weren't allowed to attempt to revive her."

"Mom would never sign those papers," said Paula.

"I agree," said LeAnn. "She was too mean to die and she had such a fear of death. There's no way she'd sign them."

Carla returned with the file.

LeAnn snatched it from her.

Carla snatched it back. She opened it onto the table. She fanned out the paperwork.

"This section is her life insurance policies. Every few years she either added another small one or increased the payoff. These are her property insurance papers. These are her long-term health care papers."

Paperclipped together were her financial papers. Paula picked those up. "Here's her investments with LeAnn and her funeral paperwork. When did she pay for her own funeral?"

"A while back," said Carla.

The last papers were her living will papers.

"Here, is this what you two are looking for?"

Paula thumbed through the papers looking for a signature. LeAnn snatched them away and turned to the last page.

"That's her signature alright."

"I told you," said Carla.

"When did she do this?" asked LeAnn.

"I'm sure it's dated," said Carla.

"Sure is. I can't believe she did it," said LeAnn.

Glen's interest piqued. He studied the three sisters. He wondered why they seemed so uninformed about the final wishes of their mother. Then he excused it away by the fact they seemed to be a dysfunctional family, so this shouldn't surprise him but still....

On the way home Glen quizzed Paula.

"What did your husband Andy die from?"

Paula, with tears welling in her eyes, said, "I really don't like to talk about it, Glen."

"Paula, I understand, but please, just for few minutes."

Glen had always been the kindest gentleman around her. She wondered why he wanted to put her through this.

"He died of a heart attack."

"Was it sudden or had he been having problems?"

"I'm not sure. Andy wasn't the type to want me to worry. He could've had a bad heart and didn't want me to know. At first, I assumed it was freak episode."

"What changed your mind?"

"My family. They pointed out I really didn't know Andy that well and his parents were dead so I had no opportunity to learn much from them about his childhood or any illnesses. He didn't volunteer much about his family. He was close to his parents and it caused him a great deal of pain to discuss them so we didn't."

They pulled up in front of the house. Glen followed Paula inside.

"I think I'm going to bed. I don't mean to be rude. I don't feel like company right now."

Glen wanted to ask her so much more. They should have done a postmortem because Andy was so young. The only way they should have skipped it would be if he had a history of heart disease. But then, in some cases, the obvious can be overlooked.

Glen went to his room. He called Debbie, but no answer. "Just as well," he whispered to himself. "I need to let her make a clean break."

The evening of family and death made him miss her. He fought the urge to think about her. He picked up a book to read until he dozed off. He hurt, deeply.

Daniel called Peter.

"It's about time you answer my calls," said Daniel angrily.

"I figured if I didn't you'd never stop calling. What do you want?"

"I need your help."

"Hell no. Haven't I helped you enough? You killed my wife."

"Relax, weenie, Teddi's not dead."

"What do you mean she's not dead? You told me you killed her. You told me to stay away from the police or you'd kill me next."

"That's right. I couldn't take a chance of them talking to you and you having a wave of guilt and exposing me. I still mean it. You go to the police and you're a dead man, so's your pretty little wife."

"You lied to me. You told me you killed her. I've been watching the papers and nothing. No word about them. What in the hell's going on?"

"Little miscalculating on my part. I should've shot them with a little more insulin. They lived."

"Where's Teddi? I want to see her. I've checked her house and Maggi's, there's been no sign of them."

"Chill, will you. They've been in a coma. Seems they're out now and Karst moved them to Omaha. That's where you come in."

"I'm not helping you any more. If you try to drag me into this again I'll go to the police. I don't care if you kill me. I can't face Teddi if she ever finds out."

"She's not gonna find out and if you go to the police, I'm not kidding. I'll finish her off."

"What do you want from me?"

"I need to find out what hospital they're in and you need to distract their watchdog, Karst, so I can finish the job."

"I'm not going to help you try to kill them again. You never told me you planned to kill them in the first place. I still don't know why you dragged Teddi into this, it's Maggi you were after."

"Look, Karst was about to succeed in keeping Maggi off of death row. I needed her dead and fast. When it looked like she'd walk, I had to stop her. Teddi happened to be in the wrong place at the wrong time."

"I still don't see why I should help you."

"I'll find them eventually, and when I do, I guarantee there'll be three dead bodies for the police. Are you too dense to get that through your skull?"

"I can't just show up after all of this time."

"You'd better make up a hell of a believable story and find them for me. I need you to go to Omaha, check out the hospitals. Explain you're Teddi's husband. That should get you the clout you need to find out if she's a patient. That's all I need from you. Then when I tell you, I want you to show up and call Karst away from the hospital long enough for me to finish what I started. I promise I won't touch Teddi."

"I don't know. I'll need some time. What about Jean? Can't she do it?"

"She's already running scared. I don't think I can trust her."

Peter paced in his apartment. He left Denver but did not return to his home in California. He feared the police would find him and want to question him.

He remembered that night. Teddi and Maggi were waiting at Maggi's house for him to join them for the evening. The story he had been writing for a magazine reached its deadline and he stayed late at the library to finish the final edit. He liked to work in the silence of a library setting. Something about the smell, the look and the quiet brought out his creative side.

When he was about to turn onto the street leading to Maggi's house, police cars screamed past him. Curious, but still fearful of the police after his previous episodes with them, he parked his car and walked through the neighborhood, hiding in the shadows to watch. He made his way close enough to see the paramedics carry two stretchers out to the ambulance. His heart sank to his feet. Those same feet felt the urge to run. He did not want to be accused again.

He ran ducking and diving into the shadows from the huge trees lining the street. He made his way back to his car and drove off. His heart raced as he worried about Teddi. He knew Daniel had been growing impatient, waiting for Maggi to be out of the picture so he could collect on her wealth.

While he tried to hatch a plan for finding out what happened without being implicated, Daniel called him on his cell phone to tell him he killed Teddi and Maggi. He warned Peter to get as far away as possible and to make sure the police never find him for questioning. Peter knew disappearing would make him look guilty, but if Daniel dragged him into it he would still look guilty. With Teddi dead there was no need to go looking for trouble. He drove off and never looked back.

Now he knows Teddi is still alive. His disappearing act is going to be even more difficult to explain but he desperately wants to be with his wife.

"Think, think," he said as he pounded his fists on his forehead. He brushed the prematurely gray hair from his eyes. How was he going to make this work? How could he reappear, save Teddi's life and not implicate himself? There had to be a way. He thought being a journalist should give him the ability to create a magnificent piece of fiction even Karst would believe.

He packed a bag and began his journey from Albuquerque to Omaha. He knew he must travel by car.

With the tightened security, he feared booking a flight and renting a car would leave a trail the police might follow.

Being a traveling journalist from a wealthy family allowed him the privilege of cash in safety deposit boxes at numerous banks. He could grab money and be off on an assignment in a moment's notice. That cash made it easy for him to disappear for a while.

The next morning the girls agreed no autopsy would be performed on their mother. Her death came as no surprise to them given her history of a weak heart and her diet.

Glen overheard the discussion.

"Are you sure you wouldn't like to find out exactly what killed her?" he asked.

"Glen, she wasn't killed, she died. Her cause of death was a heart attack. She'd freak out if she knew we planned to have her cut up. She believes she needs her whole body intact to make it into heaven. I'm sure once we start searching we'll find her plans for us to spend any money she may have had in investments to pay for several masses to pray her into heaven. So no, an autopsy would not be within her beliefs," said Paula.

"I'm surprised you're doing so well today," he said.

"So am I. I actually feel a little guilty. I feel at peace for probably the first time in my life. I really had no idea how much negative stress she put on me. My sisters feel the same way."

"No need to feel guilty. You girls were living a life of abuse even if you didn't see it. Now your abuser has been removed. It's natural you'd feel a sense of peace. I deal with the emotional side of this stuff all the time."

"I suppose you do," said Paula. She watched him as he spoke; trying to imagine him doing his job based on the crime shows she watched on television. Some cops do not look the part, but Glen was very believable as a detective, she thought.

Back in Littleton, Jennifer Parker woke with a start. She opened her eyes to look around her room. Her hand felt the warm bundle curled up next to her. Her senses slowly came back to her. Ming mewed as she stroked him, waking him from his deep sleep.

When Jennifer realized she was safe in her own bed in her own room, she allowed her eyes to close and her mind to drift back to recall what woke her in such a frightening way.

Her thoughts drifted to Glen. She dreamed of him inside of a circle of death. With death surrounding him he had to fight his way out. She saw flashes of Maggi's face then Teddi's. She saw them reaching out for help, but no one would help them. She saw a mysterious figure creep up behind Glen. That scene quickly flashed to Paula replacing Maggi on the bed in the hospital. Faceless figures surrounded Glen as he tried to determine who they were. His instincts failed him. He lost his ability to tell which of the figures were safe and which were dangerous.

The longer she relived her vivid dream the more confused she became. She strained her mind to see the faces, but there were none. People were rising from the grave circling Glen. When he drew his gun it melted in his hand right before his eyes. He tried to defend himself with his martial arts, but with each strike the faceless figures moved before he could connect. The entire dream reflected helplessness.

She opened her eyes again. Climbing out of bed and she went into her kitchen. She stared out of the window, trying to analyze her dream. She had an overwhelming urge to protect Glen. Her teakettle whistled. As she poured her the tea she envisioned a hand picking flowers from a garden. She moved uneasily into the living room and settled in to her favorite chair to think.

"What does it all mean?" she asked. "What does it all mean?"

She allowed her mind to drift into a meditative state once again. She saw a garden-- a beautiful garden or a park perhaps. Yes, it's a park. Then she saw a fence and a trellis with climbing roses. No, it's a yard. It's someone's yard. But where? She struggled to see a street name or something marking the location. Nothing came to her. She drifted in again. A cemetery, she saw a cemetery. There was danger connected there. The feeling grew stronger. She saw a hand put flowers on a grave. The same hand she had seen picking the flowers. The vision blurred enough she could not tell if the hand belonged to a man or a woman. Glen's face appeared for a split second, pale and blue.

She pulled her fingers through her short red hair, gripping it to her head. Her eyes blurred as she attempted to look around the room. She felt ill as the room spun. A headache made its way from the sides of her head to the front and into her eyes. She rubbed her eyes then reached for her the tea to calm her stomach.

When she could not interpret her visions or dreams she was left with an unfinished, uneasy feeling. One that refused to leave until the event occurred and she could put it to rest.

She knew she must contact Glen.

"Morning Jennifer," said Glen.

"Good morning, Glen," she replied.

"What's up?"

"You tell me."

"What?"

"You tell me what's going on in your life right now."

"Nothing, new. I'm still checking the girls. I think Maggi might be showing some response. The nurse thinks I'm nuts, but I think I'm right."

"That's wonderful news, Glen. Are you planning to continue your stay there much longer?"

"As a matter of fact I am. Oh, before I forget. Thanks for hooking me up with Paula. She's a sweetheart. I've been working on her basement, it's the only thing keeping me sane while I wait. There's not much I can do at the hospital and the security there is much tighter than in Denver so I feel I don't have to be there constantly."

"You're welcome. How is Paula?"

"Poor thing, her mother just died. She seems to be dealing with it okay, but her husband's death still has her an emotional wreck. This morning she was so upset I heard her throwing up in the bathroom. I didn't want to embarrass her by letting her know I heard."

"Her mother died, you say?"

"Yes."

"Did you go to the funeral?"

"It's today. I think that's why Paula's so upset. Why the line of questioning? What's going on?"

"Perceptive as always, Detective Karst."

Glen chuckled at the compliment. "Okay, Jennifer, tell me what's on your mind."

"Glen, I had a dream or rather a vision. No, I guess it is best described as a dream. It was not clear enough for a vision."

"Was I in this vision?"

"Yes."

Glen chewed on his upper lip. “So was I dead or alive in this dream?” he asked with caution.

“I couldn’t tell. I mean you were definitely alive, I just don’t know if you stayed alive.”

“Shit, Jennifer. I appreciate you wanting to tell me these things, but not knowing whether I live or die in one of your dreams is a bit unnerving.”

“I know Glen, and I apologize, but I couldn’t let it rest.”

“Okay, let’s work through it. What did you see?”

Jennifer went on to explain the details as best she could.

“Don’t you think being at a hospital all the time could explain me being surrounded by death? Don’t forget Paula’s mother’s death.”

“I would like to agree with you, but you have a more active role in this dream than that. People are not who they seem and you could very well be in danger. You had difficulty judging the intensity of the danger you were in, and who put you in that danger.”

“Now, Jennifer. If there’s one thing I’m comfortable with, it’s judging human nature. I’m sure if someone meant to hurt me, I’d be well aware of it. Hey, I know what it is!”

“What?”

“Yesterday I wanted to go for a walk to get some fresh air and give Paula some time alone. I’ve had my fill of sitting at the hospital. Across the street's a cemetery. I walked through there for over an hour yesterday reading tombstones and enjoying the weather."

"Across the street? Glen, where exactly is this cemetery?"

"Its across the street from where I'm staying with Paula."

"Would you mind if I came to Omaha for few days. I need to be there to try to set this straight in my mind."

"Sure, come on down. I can sleep on the sofa and you can have Paula's guest room. I think she'd be thrilled to talk to you. Maybe you can say something that can help her with the loss of her husband. I manage to upset her whenever I bring him up. Beside, I have a few unanswered questions you can help me with."

"I'll pack this morning and be there by tonight. Can you give me directions to the hospital? I'll meet you there."

Chapter 11

Jennifer waited until she felt the rush hour traffic in Denver was behind her. In Denver almost any hour feels like rush hour. She remembered when she first moved there the traffic seemed more tolerable in the middle of the day. Now each day of driving, she puts her life in jeopardy when her mind wanders. Times like this she appreciates the psychic school she attended teaching her to shut off her gift.

Before she attended the school, everywhere she went she saw dead spirits around the living. They knew she had the ability to communicate with them and she felt obligated to do so on a regular basis. If she ignored them she felt as if she was being rude. During one of her classes, her instructor pointed out to her that it was actually the spirits who were being rude. They pushed their way into her life without an invitation, hoping she would get a message across to a loved one left behind.

As a teenager she nearly lost her job as a waitress because she would tell her customers of the deceased family members or friends who accompanied them at their dinner. Some customers became so upset with her they would walk out without paying. Her manager, aware of her abilities, asked her to refrain from making a connection between the two worlds on his time.

Jennifer wanted to be as helpful as possible since that was part of who she was. She learned to use the conversations with the dead and the interaction with them as part of her amusement when she met new people. She remembered waiting on a table where two customers were unaware of the five dead people who joined them. Now with her ability to shut off whenever she wanted to, it made life easier, especially while driving.

Once out of the city limits of Denver, Jennifer relaxed and prepared herself for the long journey to Omaha. She began to feel danger all around her. She looked in her rear view mirror. She scanned the road ahead of her, half expecting to see an accident up ahead. She remained confused but on guard just the same.

She knew from her past work with the police once she approached a crime scene the intensity of the danger increased, but for her today there seemed to be a constant flow both ahead and behind her. What Jennifer did not know was that danger traveled with Peter and Daniel, who were also driving to Omaha that same day. With the many miles she had yet to travel, she tried relaxation methods to hold back the stress of the unknown. Even a psychic cannot always discover what every feeling and vision means on demand.

The funeral service for Anna was a private family service. At least, that is what they told the priest who assisted with the arrangements. How could they tell him Anna had no friends? No one really cared if she lived or died. She managed to drive away everyone who she befriended after a short while. The girls were the only constant in her life. If she had it her way, she would have insisted the girls invite every hairdresser, sales clerk and waitress who ever served her, convincing herself they would want to be there.

The priest insisted that many of the parishioners would feel left out if they could not attend her service. They felt it their duty to be present at the funeral of members of the church. Anna rarely missed a Sunday, but even then never managed to make friends with anyone. She called them all hypocrites.

After Anna was laid to rest, LeAnn offered her home for the church members and family to gather. She hired a caterer so she would not have to prepare or serve. Many of the guests brought food along with them to add to the buffet table.

Paula excused herself from the group after eating. Her stomach felt queasy. She thought lying down might help. She slipped into one of the guest bedrooms to rest. The room felt chilly to her. She was unsure whether it was her nerves or the actual temperature of the room. Rather than disturb the perfectly made bed with a dozen pillows adorning the tapestry bedspread, she went to the closet in search of a spare blanket or throw.

She opened the closet door. LeAnn had it filled with her clothes. The large walk-in closet in her own room failed to meet the capacity she required to house her wardrobe. Paula parted the clothes looking at the business suits and glamorous evening gowns that LeAnn had no opportunity to wear. She slid her hands over the fine quality fabric. Even her rough hands from working outdoors could tell the difference between the feel of LeAnn's clothes and her own t-shirts and cotton blouses.

She stepped back to look at herself in the mirror. Today she actually wore a dress. She felt it appropriate to purchase a new conservative black dress for her mother's funeral. Somehow she felt her mother would be watching to see what she would be wearing and would find some way to chastise her for wearing the wrong outfit.

She removed one of LeAnn's dresses from the closet. She held it up to herself. She fluffed her blond hair back then gathered it on top of her head. She turned and twirled, imagining what it would be like to be in the dress. She returned it then took another. After a half dozen new looks she shook her head and thought no way would she be happy dressed up.

She continued to look for the extra blanket. To her left stood a tall built-in shelving unit. She could not help but notice the markings on the boxes. The shipping label read London. She flipped open one of the boxes whose top was not completely sealed.

When she looked inside the contents shocked her. There, in a divided box, were eleven more Newcastle crystal glasses to match the one they had given their mother for her birthday.

Paula lifted a glass from its tight fit within the box. She held it to the light in the room to examine it. There was no doubt. This was the remainder of the set that LeAnn had planned for them to purchase over the next few years. What was it doing here? Why didn't she tell them about it?

She carefully replaced the glass. Her curiosity got the best of her. She wanted to know what was in the other boxes. Suddenly, there was a tap on the bedroom door. She shut off the closet light, closed the door and jumped onto the bed.

"Yes?" she said.

"Paula, are you okay?"

She heard Glen's voice.

"I'm fine."

Instead of Glen leaving her, he opened the door a crack to check for himself. When he saw her lying on the bed, he entered.

"What happened?"

"Nothing, really. My stomach's upset so I thought I should lie down for awhile."

He walked over to her on the bed and felt her forehead. "You don't have a fever. Probably just stress."

"Yeah, I guess."

She wondered if she could trust Glen. She knew from watching him work around her house that he always carried a pocketknife. The perfect tool she needed at the moment to snoop in LeAnn's closet. She looked up at him then past him to the open door.

"Close the door, will you?" she said.

Glen looked puzzled.

"Do you want me to leave or stay?"

"Stay."

Glen closed the door then stood next to it wondering what she wanted.

"Do you have your pocketknife with you?"

"Sure. Why?"

"Can I borrow it?"

"Absolutely."

He reached into his pocket to remove the knife. He opened one of the blades and wiped it, out of habit, on his slacks before handing it to her.

She slid off the side of the bed then peeked out of the door. She walked to the closet, opened the door and turned on the light.

Glen watched.

"Let me know if you hear someone, okay?"

"Wait a minute. What are you up to? I'm a cop remember. I don't want to go along with any burglary plan you're hatching."

She smiled at him. "You're not a cop anymore and I promise I'm not going to take anything. I'm just snooping."

Glen opened the door to look out. Paula jumped, thinking someone had entered the room. She fumbled with the knife.

"Here. Let me do that before you cut yourself. You want these boxes opened?"

"Yeah, slit the tops and let me see what's inside."

"How do you plan to pull this off without being caught? Once you cut these open it'll be obvious someone got into them."

Paula frowned, he was right.

"I have an idea," he said. "I'll be right back."

He left the house, searched his tool chest in the back of his pickup then returned unobserved.

He reached his hand into his pocket and pulled out a roll of clear packing tape. He carried quite the assortment of tools and other paraphernalia with him for both his construction and detective work. You never know what you will need at a crime scene.

He pulled the first box off of the shelf. He turned it upside down on the bed then cut open the bottom tape. He slid the contents out.

“Why upside down?” she asked. “Did they teach you that in detective school?”

“Hell no. I learned this at Christmas time as a kid. I had to know what was in the packages so I devised several ways to get into them and reseal them without my parents knowing about it.”

“You devil,” she laughed.

He handed her an exquisitely carved serving bowl that matched the set of glasses. She examined it carefully then handed it back to Glen to return to the box and work his magic to disguise the fact he had opened it.

“Do you want them all opened?” he asked.

“No, I think we’re pushing our luck here. Someone’s bound to come in looking for me. Thanks for your help.”

“Would you care to explain to me why we did what we just did?”

“I’ll tell you later. I promise.”

Glen checked his watch. “I think I’m going to swing by the hospital to check on the girls. I’ll come back by to pick you up later. You get some rest.”

"I feel fine. I think snooping took my mind off of my stomach. I want to leave now. It's too depressing hanging around here."

Paula took Glen by the arm and marched up to LeAnn and Carla who were talking in the kitchen.

"I think we're leaving now," she said.

"Paula, we still have guests," said Carla.

"Oh, you mean the guests alone in the other room while you two are hiding in the kitchen?"

She slipped out the back door with Glen.

"We have to do something about those two," said LeAnn.

"What do you mean?"

"We can't let her continue with him. Heaven forbid they get married or something insane like that."

"I really don't think they're headed in that direction, especially so soon after Andy died."

"He's a pretty good looking guy. What do you suppose he sees in Paula?" asked LeAnn.

"I can't believe you said that," said Carla, shocked.

"Oh, she's cute, but she doesn't have any money."

"I have a news flash for you, LeAnn. Not all relationships are based on money. You make it sound like you really did marry Reed for his money."

"So what if I did. That's why you're sinking your hooks into Anthony and don't try to tell me you're not."

"It just so happens Anthony is a wonderful guy. He treats me well and we're happy together."

"And he's loaded. Admit it, Carla. I know you've waited all these years without getting married until you could find Mr. Money."

Carla turned when she felt someone enter the room. Anthony stood in the doorway.

"Are you two okay in here?" he asked.

Carla worried he heard everything they said.

"Have you been standing there long?"

"No, I just opened the door? Why? Were you talking about me?" he teased.

"Always," said Carla as she slipped her arm into his. She turned to LeAnn. "I think we'll be leaving now."

Anthony walked with Carla to his car.

"Was there a problem back there? Did I interrupt something?"

"No. Sometimes it's hard to deal with LeAnn's obsession with money. Her entire world revolves around it."

"I'm sorry. I hope you don't think I'm obsessed with money."

"Oh, heavens no. You don't flaunt what you have. LeAnn flaunts what she doesn't have. She wants everyone to think she's independently wealthy. She keeps telling us she's going to retire in two years."

"Maybe she will," said Anthony.

"I don't see how. When Reed died he gave most of his money to his sons. She got the house and a decent amount of cash investments in her portfolio, but certainly not enough to live on for the rest of her life."

"I wouldn't underestimate your sister. She's done a hell of a good job with my investments. On paper she's already made me a tidy sum in a short amount of time. I'd be willing to believe she has what it takes to build a huge nest egg out of nothing."

LeAnn feigned a migraine to encourage the remainder of the guests to leave. The guests meant nothing to LeAnn. Her thoughts drifted back to Anna and her lack of friends. She thought about how she had lived in a fantasy world she created where she thought every waitress and sales clerk, even her hairdresser, were her best friends. They were being nice to her, treating her as they would any of their customers. They did pick up on the point that when they gave her a little extra attention she spent more money. Anna thought differently, inviting them to family functions and dinner parties they never attended. Anna refused to accept the fact she was nothing more than a customer to them. She could almost hear her mother scolding her for not inviting them.

LeAnn hurried the catering staff along, urging them to clean faster so she could get rid of them.

As LeAnn gathered plates she saw a briefcase standing in one corner of her massive living room. She set the dishes down, looking around the room as she went for the briefcase. She picked it up by the handle then went off to her bedroom.

She closed the door and laid the briefcase on her bed. It had a small lock on it but fortunately for her, it was unlocked. She popped it open to reveal a stack of papers. Upon closer examination she realized they were her mother's insurance papers. The briefcase belonged to Carla.

LeAnn leaned across her bed to the nightstand. In the top drawer she found one of her many calculators. She pulled the papers out onto her bed. She flipped through them one by one totaling the lump sum death benefit payments. She put the property, long-term health care and car insurance policies aside. Then changed her mind and quickly totaled the premiums for her own curiosity.

"Damn it, Carla," she said. "I can't believe you had her so heavily insured on garbage where she'd never show a return."

LeAnn knew if she underinsured everything and carried only liability on her car then the extra money could be invested in a mixed portfolio that she could cash in on if she had an occasion where insurance was truly needed. No wonder Carla had no real money of her own. She obsessed over insurance.

LeAnn totaled the life insurance policies. “My God, you’ve got to be kidding. She’s been paying in to this all these years and all she has to show for it is a measly half a million and a worthless house. Damn. I could’ve done so much more if she would’ve given me a chance.”

She continued to look through the policies to see how soon they would collect their money so she could invest as quickly as possible. Maybe she could get Paula to let her invest her entire share. LeAnn stopped when she saw Carla’s name appear at the base of the last page of the first policy as the sole beneficiary. She flipped back through the policy. There must be some mistake, she thought.

She set it aside and picked up the next policy. Carla, once again, was the only beneficiary. She doubled checked her mother’s signature. How could this be? Anna had many small insurance policies. The largest was two hundred and fifty thousand taken out less than a year ago. Each policy added over the many years she was married to Lawrence had Carla as the beneficiary. Surely if Lawrence would have been handling her policies, he would have his name or, at least, all three of her daughters on the policies.

LeAnn stressed all night about how to get her share and convince her sisters to entrust their shares to her for investing.

At the hospital Maggi and Teddi were much more alert. They were sitting up feeding themselves when Glen walked in. Maggi smiled at him. He went to her side and kissed her on the forehead.

"Shit Maggi, you're back."

When Maggi tried to talk her speech came out unclear.

Glen turned to the nurse. "Why didn't someone call me about the change?"

"We tried but you didn't answer your cell phone."

Glen reached into his pocket to check his phone. He had turned it off during the funeral service and neglected to turn it back on the remainder of the day.

No sooner had he turned it back on then it rang.

"Glen, Jennifer Parker. I'm in the parking lot of the hospital. Where are you?"

"I'm in Maggi's room. I'll come out to find you. Which side of the building are you on?"

He rushed out of the door, elated with the changes. He had forgotten Paula sitting in the hall.

"Jennifer Parker's here. I'm gonna run down to the parking lot and bring her up. I'll be right back."

When Glen made his way to the parking lot he found Jennifer walking in his direction toward the door he exited.

"How'd you know which door…never mind. I don't know why I ask those questions."

Jennifer smiled.

He gave her a hug. She sensed danger around him, making her feel uncomfortable.

"Come on upstairs. Paula's waiting in the lounge."

"Maggi is better, yes?"

"Yes, she's sitting up eating and trying to speak."

"What do you mean trying to speak?"

"I'm not sure. I need to talk to one of the doctors. She seems to lack the muscle coordination for speech or something like that. My guess is, it's not gonna last."

Glen guided Jennifer to where Paula was seated. She stood up to greet Jennifer.

"I think you two ladies remember each other," said Glen. His eyes scanned the halls looking for an available nurse so he could ask to speak to the doctor.

"Congratulations, my dear. You look wonderful," said Jennifer.

That caught Glen's attention.

"Congratulations on what?" asked Paula.

"Why on the new baby," said Jennifer.

Glen looked at Paula with excitement.

Paula had a blank look on her face, "What baby?"

"My dear. Are you not aware you are with child?"

Glen looked from one woman to the other. He wanted to express his excitement to Paula, but was uncertain as to whether or not the news was happy news.

Paula placed her hand on her stomach. She slid down onto her chair. Her thoughts raced through the calendar she drew up in her mind. She counted the weeks since Andy died. She knew she had skipped a couple of periods, but assumed that was stress-related.

"I'm sure you must be mistaken," she said.

"If there's one thing I can be sure, of it's a pregnancy. Those are so easy to detect. The new life growing inside of you has a soul who follows you around, waiting until the birth of the baby to slip into the newborn's body. It's during this time the soul gets to know the mother and the family and friends who will surround the baby. No room for error on this one."

"You mean to tell me I have a soul hanging around all the time?"

"I suppose I should clarify that. It does not stay with you twenty-four hours a day, but pops in and out at will. Spending time on earth as well as the spiritual world until the moment of birth and the baby breathes its first breath. When a medium such as myself is near a pregnant woman, the baby's soul sort of pops in to make its presence known. I've told many, many women they are pregnant before they have any idea. Rest assured you're not the first."

Glen looked at Paula.

"Does this news make you happy?" he asked.

"I think so. It'll take a minute to get used to the idea. But yes, I think I'm going to love having Andy's baby."

Her eyes welled with tears. "I wish he would be here to see it."

"Oh goodness, Paula. He was there when the baby was conceived, he'll be at the birth and he'll watch and guide his child throughout his life on earth. Don't worry. Andy will love and care for the child from his vantage point. You and the child will be aware of his presence, but not in a physical way."

Daniel called Peter. "Where are you?"

"I'm on the road. I should be in Omaha tomorrow. Where are you?"

"I'm at the Friendship Inn near the Sapp Bros. Exit south of Omaha. Get a room here when you arrive. We need to make a plan."

Before Peter arrived, Daniel unpacked his things then drove into the city to find another motel room. He chose a small one in south Omaha on L Street, the Satellite Inn. He checked himself in then called a florist to order flowers.

When the delivery boy arrived, he watched him from the window of his room overlooking the parking lot. He waited until he heard the knock on the door.

"Yes, who's there?" he asked.

"Delivery for Glen Karst," said the delivery boy.

Daniel unlocked the door. The young man stepped inside the room.

"Glen Karst?"

"Yes, just put them on the table. I'll get my wallet."

When the boy turned his back to him, Daniel raised the tire iron high over his head and came down hard on the boy's skull. He fell to the floor. Daniel wasted no time stripping the boy of his uniform. Fortunately for him they were nearly the same size. Daniel had a slight frame for a man his age.

He gathered the clothes into a plastic laundry bag, courtesy of the motel, grabbed the flowers and left. He had paid cash at the front desk when he registered. He got into his Ford Escort, the same car Jean warned him to dispose of, and drove back to his first motel room.

Once inside he removed his new uniform from the bag and hung it in his closet. Phase one of his plan was in place.

The next morning Peter arrived and checked into the motel then called Daniel.

"I'm here."

"Okay, get your ass to work. We can't waste any time. Find them."

"I'm still not quite sure how to go about that."

"Start out with the phone, asshole. Call all of the hospitals, explain who you are and ask for a progress report."

"Just like that you think they're going to give me information?"

"I doubt if they'll give you an update, but I'm sure you'll be able to weed out a few hospitals if you sweet talk the broad on the other end of the phone. Give them a real sob story, someone'll break."

Peter thought of a line he could use. He took the phone book from the drawer and began his search.

"Hello, my name is Peter Taylor. I'm a journalist. I've been out of the country on assignment. I got word my wife is in a hospital in Omaha. I arrived this morning, but after tearing my luggage apart I can't seem to find the name of the hospital or my contact information. Can you tell me if she's a patient there? Her name is Teddi Taylor."

He waited while the person searched her computer database.

"I'm sorry, I have no information on that patient."

"So you can't tell me whether or not she's ever been a patient there?"

"Well, I'm not seeing her name anywhere on the computer, not even in the restricted information section."

He repeated his line call after call. Most of the hospitals responded the same way. There were a handful who refused to give him any information, at all citing the HIPPA laws.

Now he knew which hospitals to eliminate. There were four possibilities. He changed his method.

He called back to one of the eliminated hospitals to avoid causing suspicion.

"Hello, I'm writing a novel with a hospital scene. Can you tell me what floor in a hospital you would have a patient that was, say... a criminal with a police guard. Oh, and this patient has just come out of a coma. Would his room be isolated from the others because of security reasons?"

"We would keep a patient like that on the second floor for general patient care."

"Would that be the case with all hospitals?"

"Not all, but most. Each is a little different in how they handle things."

Next he called the hospitals on his possible's list. When the operator requested the room number, he asked to be connected to the nurses' station for general patient care.

"Nurses' station. How can I help you?"

"I need to speak with Detective Karst. Is he still on duty?"

"Who?"

"Detective Karst, he's guarding a couple of patients. I'm his sergeant and I need to speak to him."

"Just a minute, please."

He waited nervously, wondering if he would hear Glen's voice on the phone.

"I'm sorry, but no one here is aware of your Detective Karst. Could you have the wrong floor or the wrong hospital?"

"You know what? I think I did dial up the wrong hospital. I'm so sorry. Thank you."

He hung up the phone and took a deep breath. He wrung his hands. He went into the bathroom to throw cold water onto his face.

He picked up the phone and repeated the process. The third hospital he called brought success.

"Hang on, I don't think he's here right now. I'll go check."

"No, I'm afraid he hasn't come in yet today. Would you like to leave a message?"

The nurse heard nothing but a dial tone when Peter hung up.

He thought of Teddi. His wife lay in a hospital bed no more than twenty minutes away. After all of this time he knew where she was and she was alive.

Daniel called.

"Any luck?"

"No, not yet. These things take time. I'm gaining on it though. I'll call you when I find them."

"Damn it Peter, don't make me do this myself. I'm ready to hit the hospital tonight. Don't disappoint me."

"Or what? What happens if I can't deliver their location to you by tonight?"

"Don't get smart. You'd better watch your back and don't screw with me. Do you understand?"

Peter hung up the phone. He grabbed his jacket and headed out the door. He pulled his hood up over his head in an attempt to stop Daniel from recognizing him as he went to his car.

He drove away from the motel then drove down Eighty-fourth Street pulling into Wal-Mart's parking lot. He took out a map of Omaha he picked up at a service station along the way. He found the location for Methodist hospital. He continued north on Eighty-fourth Street until he had to detour on Center. Confused, he weaved his way through the residential area until he came out on Dodge Street. He continued west on Dodge until he reached the hospital.

His heart raced. Inside the tall building Teddi awaited whatever fate Daniel had in store for her. He refused to let that happen. He had to protect her. He needed a plan.

If both women were still alive and he went to the police to expose Daniel, what could really happen to him? After all, he did no harm Maggi and Teddi himself, nor did he even know about Daniel's plan to kill them. All he did was keep Daniel informed as to the whereabouts of the women so Daniel and Jean to could pull off their scheme.

On the other hand, if Daniel tried to pull him into the plan and connect him to the other murders, how could he possibly defend himself? What good would he be to Teddi if he spent the rest of his life in prison or worse, received the death penalty for multiple homicides?

He continued to sit in his car as the minutes turned to hours. Time was slipping quickly and he still had no plan.

Inside the hospital, Maggi and Teddi both continued to improve in leaps and bounds. The recovery that seemed to take forever happened more quickly each hour of the day.

Speech for Teddi was coming more easily than for Maggi. Glen wondered if Maggi was too embarrassed to try because of the way she sounded trying to speak.

He asked Teddi if she knew where she was and she nodded. "Do you know how you got here? Or why?"

She struggled to get the sounds out, but managed a good "no".

He asked the same questions to Maggi, who responded with a shake of her head.

"Do you remember who I am?" asked Glen, wanting to be sure they were truly understanding his questions.

"Gggllllennnn," said Maggi.

"That's right. Okay let's move forward."

Maggi nodded.

"The night I found you I had a call on my phone from you. I tried to return it, but you didn't answer. Debbie and I went to your house and we found you in your bedroom unconscious. Do you remember any of this?"

She shook her head no.

"What about you, Teddi. Does any of this sound familiar?"

She also shook her head no.

"I'll go on. Someone broke into your house and injected the two of you with insulin. It nearly killed you. You were in a coma for a long time. I want to find the son of a bitch who did this, but I need your help."

Maggi shrugged her shoulders.

The doctor stepped into the room to examine them. Glen moved out into the hall. When the doctor joined him, he asked, "What's going on with them? Are they gonna get any better?"

"To be honest I'm surprised they're coming along as well as they are. Their muscle control is coming back quickly. I suspect their speech will return in just a day or so, it's their memories I'm worried about."

"Don't tell me they have amnesia," said Glen.

"No, no it's nothing like that. Their bodies have been through a lot. Their brains suffered from the lack of glucose that may or may not have caused some permanent damage. People experiencing insulin-induced comas frequently have difficulty with the speech and memory portion of their brains. These two were in comas longer than most I've seen. I've had patients under for a shorter duration who have not recovered to the point these ladies have. I've also had patients experience a full recovery. I don't have any recovery data from patients with their history."

"They're healthy and beating all the odds so far. That's a good sign, isn't it? Especially since you really can't compare them to anyone," asked Glen.

"That's true, they have a lot going for them. You got to them relatively soon, they had eaten shortly before the insulin, and they were able to get glucose into their systems quickly. I will always wonder why they went into such deep comas and for so long."

"I think I'm going to let them rest now. I'll be back tonight," said Glen.

He walked to the elevator with the doctor. Paula and Jennifer stayed a polite distance behind them.

"Why don't you follow my pickup over to Paula's," said Glen.

"I'll ride with Jennifer. Don't worry about us following you," said Paula.

Glen walked to his pickup. Peter saw Glen as he walked in his direction. For a split second, he thought Glen was walking directly toward him. He slid down in his seat, turned his back to him and pretended to talk on his phone.

He watched in his rear view mirror as Glen pulled away. Teddi would no longer be guarded.

Chapter 12

Peter watched as Glen pulled away. He made his way into the hospital. He asked at the information desk which floor contained the med/surg unit or general patient care. She gave him instructions to take the elevator to the second floor.

When he got off the elevator he looked both ways down the hall. How would he ever find their room? Were they even in the same room? he wondered. He turned to his left and started to walk. He peered in the open doors and made note of the closed doors. He passed nurses who seemed oblivious to his presence. He politely spoke to patients walking the halls in their hospital gowns, pushing an IV stand ahead of them.

There were many visitors walking the halls with their family members who were patients creating a quiet buzz. Peter continued to go unnoticed. He turned down one hall after the other. Nothing indicated where he might find them. He walked for over half an hour and other than being in the correct hospital and probably the correct floor, he had no hope of discovering which room to find Teddi in.

All the halls looked the same to him. There were slight color changes to help the patients find their way back to their rooms. He started to walk down yet another hall when a nurse walked up to him.

"Can I help you?" she asked.

"I've been sitting so long. I thought I'd take a little walk."

"Most of the floor is fine to walk on but no one's allowed down this hall," she said.

He glanced down the hall trying to count rooms.

"Is that hall quarantined or something? Is there something dangerous or contagious I need to worry about breathing in?"

"No, nothing like that. It's just a restricted area."

"Oh, is that where you house the celebrities when they come here?"

"I suppose you could say that."

"Thanks, for the warning. I'll keep walking."

Peter continued to make laps always returning to where he could watch the nurses' station and the restricted hallway without drawing too much attention. He had been in hospitals before and knew, sooner or later, the nurses would be busy. He waited for that moment when no one would be watching the hall. He planned his move.

If he could make it to the end of the hall and dart into a room then he could weave his way back and forth checking each room. His pulse quickened as he waited for the opportunity.

A momentary absence of nurses allowed him to dart down the hall. He opened a door and slipped in. The room was empty. He opened the door and peeked out. Some nurses had returned but no one was looking in his direction. He ran to the next room. It, too, was empty. The next two rooms were also empty.

When standing in the fourth room he heard a television in the adjacent room. He knew then someone would be there. Whether it was Teddi or Maggi he had no idea. He also knew if he went into the wrong room he stood a good chance of getting caught. Was the gamble worth it to him? If he were to be arrested or even picked up by security for questioning, chances were good Glen would be called in. Immediately, Glen would take over and he would have to explain the entire thus story exposing Daniel and Jean.

Once he decided the risk was worth it, he slipped out the door and into the next room. Teddi looked at Peter.

"Peter," she said in a voice unfamiliar to him.

Maggi was sleeping in the next bed. He raised his finger to his lips to stop Teddi from talking.

Peter glanced around the room, planning an escape if someone came in. The only thing he could do would be to bolt out the door and run like hell or try to hide in the bathroom and hope the staff had no reason to go in.

He opened the bathroom door to prepare it for his rushed entry. Then he went to Teddi. Her eyes gleamed with excitement. He held her in his arms. She melted into his chest. He tried to pull away to kiss her but she held tightly to his shoulders, refusing to release him.

When she felt she had absorbed enough of his energy, his scent and his warmth she released her hold on him. He kissed her tenderly caressing, her long red hair. He breathed her in as he held her.

"Teddi, forgive me. I thought you were dead. I couldn't find you until today. Oh Teddi, I've missed you so."

He smothered her with kisses.

"I love you," said Teddi.

"I love you, too. There's so much I have to tell you. I need to get you out of here. You're still in danger."

"How?" she asked.

Aware she was still far from normal when struggled with her speech, he was concerned about her ability to leave the room.

"Can you walk?"

"Not very well." She pointed to a walker against the wall. The nurses had been getting them both up on their feet to move around the room.

Peter, too nervous to stay any longer, said, "I'll be back for you in a little while. We'll have to move quickly. I need to get you out of here without being seen. We may get caught and I might end up in jail. But damn it, Teddi, saving you is worth it."

He kissed her one last time then peered out the door, hoping to find a clear path down the hall. Unfortunately, the only way out was the way he came in, past the nurses' station.

He noticed the nurse who had stopped him earlier. He watched her intently, waiting for her to leave. She walked away from him and entered another room. He made his break.

Before he got to the end of the hall a nurse stopped him.

"What're you doing here? You shouldn't be here, this is a restricted area."

"I'm sorry, I got lost. I'm trying to find my sister's room. I went for a walk and got disoriented. You know what though, that hall looks familiar. I recognize the painting. I think I've got my bearings."

He walked away without the nurse calling security. A second nurse joined the first and they ran down the hall to check on Maggi and Teddi.

"Are you okay?" one nurse asked Teddi.

"Yes."

"Did you have a visitor just now?"

"No."

Maggi stirred.

"What's wrong?" she asked.

"Nothing you should worry about," said the nurse. She helped Maggi sit up and fluffed her pillows. "I can't believe how well you two are doing. Who would've guessed, walking and talking. Amazing."

"I'm not doing either too well," said Maggi.

"I think your detective friend will be surprised once again with your progress."

Their bodies were coming to life. Their speech was slow but very easy to understand. Their ability to walk resembled that of someone who had been weakened by a bad episode of a nasty flu virus. They were too shaky on their feet to walk unassisted but in the next day or so they should be more than capable of short walks alone. The memory issue still remained a problem. The doctors were relatively sure the damage would not be permanent to their brain. The worst-case scenario would be damage to their pancreas, requiring one or both of them to take insulin for the rest of her life. How ironic the very drug that nearly took their lives might be the drug needed to sustain it.

The nurses left the room.

"Maggi, Peter was here."

"What?"

"Peter came to see me."

"You were probably dreaming."

"No, he held me and kissed me. I know he was here for real."

"No one is allowed in except Glen."

"Maybe Glen fixed it so Peter could visit. He says we're still in danger and he wants to get me out of here."

"Teddi, for all we know Peter could be the one who put us here."

Teddi glared at Maggi.

"He loves me. He'd never do that."

She rolled over, turning her back to Maggi.

When Peter returned to his motel room, Daniel waited outside his door.

"Been sight-seeing?"

"I went out for something to eat. I don't have to account to you for my every move."

Daniel, although smaller in frame than Peter, threw him against the side of the building. Peter, about to shove him back, felt the gun in his ribs.

"I'd better be able to trust you or you're a dead man. Tell me what you know."

Peter gave him the names of three possible hospitals, leaving out Methodist hospital from the list.

"How do you think you're going to get to them? I'm sure they're guarded around the clock."

"I have a plan. Don't worry about me. You'd better be available when I need you to distract Karst. I've decided it would be better if I made my move in broad daylight. Tomorrow. Now narrow down those three hospitals to one."

"How?"

"I don't care how you do it but if you want to live to see beyond tomorrow you'll figure out a way."

"Can't very well distract Glen if I'm dead, now can I?"

That comment infuriated Daniel. He slammed his fist into Peter's stomach causing him to double over in pain. Daniel walked away as Peter struggled to insert his key into the door. He stumbled into the room locking the door behind him. He sank onto the floor up against the door and remained there until he could breathe without pain.

Carla called Paula.

"Hey sis, how're you feeling?"

"Good, what's up?"

"I was planning an insurance party and wondered if I could use your house?"

"What's an insurance party?" laughed Paula.

"Remember how nice it was when we all met at your house and Andy bought his insurance and presented his will? It was such a nice time with the barbeque. Anyway, I want it to be on neutral ground."

"What do you mean neutral ground?"

"I don't want it to be here or at LeAnn's. We had words again."

"Over money?"

"Yep."

"What does one do at an insurance party?"

"I need to go over Mom's papers with you two and I also want to check to be sure you guys are current on your policies."

"I guess you can use my house. I do have company, though. A friend of Glen's is staying with us."

"Great. I'll sell him insurance, too."

"He's a she."

"Glen's got another woman staying there with you? Are you nuts?"

"It's a long story. When would you like to have this little get together?"

"Is this evening too soon?"

"Tonight! That doesn't give me any time to prepare."

"Not to worry. I'll pick up some KFC and all the trimmings. You just supply the house and the dishes.

Besides, LeAnn won't expect anything fancy if it's at your place."

"Oh thanks, that sounds really nice."

"You know what I mean. You're not into trying to impress everybody like she is."

"Speaking of LeAnn. I saw something at her house when I went to lay down."

"What?"

"Well, maybe I shouldn't say anything until I talk to her about it."

"Now, you have to tell me. You shouldn't have said anything unless you wanted me to know."

"I went to her closet in the guest room with the tapestry bedspread. Anyway, I was cold and went there for a blanket and saw a bunch of boxes on shelves in there. They had London shipping labels on them so I looked inside."

"I'm not surprised, you know the way LeAnn loves to shop. What'd you find?"

"I found Mom's crystal."

"What do you mean, Mom's crystal? She sold it."

"I know but it was the rest of the set to go with the glass we gave her for her birthday. LeAnn has the entire set including serving bowls and I'm not sure what else. I didn't open all the boxes."

"I can't believe she took some of her money out of her precious portfolio to buy crystal. What about the crystal widow fund she started?"

"That's what I was wondering," said Paula. "Why did she start the fund in the first place if she had the crystal all along? And why didn't she just give Mom the whole set all at a once? And why didn't she tell us about it?"

"That is odd. Maybe we should ask her about it tonight."

"No! Please don't. She'd be furious if she knew I snooped. Let's wait until the crystal comes up again and see what she has to say about it. Promise you won't say anything."

"I promise. On one condition."

"What?"

"That you call LeAnn and invite her over tonight like it's your idea. She might still be mad at me."

"Okay, what time?"

"Seven."

Paula immediately called LeAnn.

"LeAnn, I've asked Carla to come by tonight and explain Mom's insurance to us and make sure my stuff is current. Can you come over?"

"I'm glad you called. I sure would like an explanation from her about Mom's insurance."

"What are you so mad about?"

"She left her briefcase here. I found Mom's papers."

"You snooped?" asked Paula, feeling a sense of relief.

"Yes, I looked inside to find out who owned the briefcase so I could return it. When I saw Mom's papers I thought I'd do the math and see the best way to invest our money."

"Invest our money? Who said I want to invest it? I might have other plans."

"What other plans could you have? You and Glen aren't making any plans, are you?"

Paula was beginning to feel guilty about the charade she and Glen were pulling on her sisters. She decided to come clean when she tells them about the baby. Maybe tonight would be a good time, she thought.

"I'll explain tonight. What has you so mad about the papers?"

"You know what, we'll discuss that tonight, too. See you then."

LeAnn hung up the phone without saying good-bye. It made her angry that Paula would not tell her what she wanted to know when she wanted to know it. No way would she divulge her private information to Paula. Two can play at that game.

"She's getting more like Mom every day," said Paula, as she hung up her phone.

Glen and Jennifer were in the basement. Proud of his handiwork, Glen gave her a tour of his finished work and an explanation of the work to come. Paula joined them.

"I guess we're having a family party here tonight," she said.

"Oh heavens, I don't want to impose. Perhaps I'll go to the bookstore to browse or see a movie. I really don't want to be a bother," said Jennifer.

"Yeah, me either. I'll spend the evening with Jennifer. That is, if you don't mind my company," said Glen.

"I would be delighted to spend time with you," she replied.

Paula's face wrinkled into a frown.

"What?" asked Glen. "Is there something wrong?"

"I was sort of hoping you'd be here so we could explain our relationship, or lack of it, to my sisters. I think it's time they know the truth."

Jennifer looked from Paula to Glen.

"I know there's no romance here, so explain to me what you two are talking about."

Glen walked over to the new wall he had installed. He rubbed his hands over his perfect seams. He turned to Jennifer.

"Debbie filed for divorce."

Jennifer said nothing.

"You knew, didn't you?" asked Glen.

"Yes, I saw it coming. I had hoped it was one time my psychic feelings were wrong. That does happen you know."

"Why didn't you tell me?"

"It's not my place to tell someone their future when I have a premonition. What if it was wrong? Besides, I believe I warned you to take better care of your marriage, didn't I?"

"I don't need a lecture."

"What do you plan to do about it?"

"I'm letting her go. I think she needs to find someone else."

Jennifer changed the subject. "So what's going on with you two?"

"It's my fault," said Paula. "My sisters are always trying to match me up with someone. They think I can't find a man on my own."

"That's not true. You found Andy, didn't you?"

"That's part of the problem. They only want me to have a man with a huge expense account."

"Money superceding love?"

"Yes. My mother brainwashed them into thinking it's just as easy to fall in love with a rich man as a poor man."

"Oh dear, not that old cliché," said Jennifer.

"In my family it's not a cliché, it's a motto. I knew after Andy died they'd be pushing me to find some wealthy guy and settle down. I actually think they were both relieved when he died," she cried.

Jennifer put her arms around her.

"I'm sure that's not true," she said.

Glen found himself deep in thought.

"They were about to make my world miserable. I ran into Carla, that's one of my sisters, at a restaurant with a guy. It was obvious they were close and she never told any of us about him. I wasn't up to her rubbing my face in it or trying to have him find someone to fix me up with so I dragged Glen into it."

When he heard his name he rejoined the conversation.

"You didn't exactly drag me into it. I was happy to oblige."

Jennifer shook her head.

"What did you two do exactly?"

"Paula told her sister we were living together and neglected to inform her of the type of arrangement we have. They think I'm her new guy."

"Oh my. I see. They must be quite upset."

"Oh hell, thanks a lot, Jennifer," laughed Glen.

"No. That's not what I meant. I meant they must be quite upset they didn't get to hand pick her new beau. Sounds like they intended to control the situation."

"Paula, you tell us what you want us to do and we'll do it."

"I'd appreciate it if both of you could hang around tonight for support. Carla's already upset with me for allowing you to move another woman into my house. Before this gets blown out of proportion any worse than it is, we need to come clean."

"Are you going to share the wonderful news about the baby tonight as well," asked Jennifer.

"I'm not sure how wonderful they'll think it is, but yes, tonight's the night."

Peter shopped the remainder of the afternoon avoiding Daniel. He returned to the hospital to wait. He ran his plan over and over in his mind. He convinced himself if getting caught meant saving Teddi, it was worth it.

He parked as close to an exit as possible. Then he carried his shopping bags inside. He went to the floor where Teddi waited. He set his bags behind one of the chairs in the visitor's lounge. Then he took the elevator back down to the gift shop. He picked out a large balloon and two flower arrangements. As he approached the cash register he picked up a little pink bear. Teddy bear for my Teddi, he thought.

He went to the same floor but this time chose a different visitor's lounge to drop off the gifts. He went back to the vantage point he used earlier in the day to watch the hall. This time his nerves were less tense. He had convinced himself it was okay if he got caught.

He waited and he waited. It occurred to him Maggi might not be asleep this time. She could ring her buzzer and this whole crazy plan he hatched could end before it started. But he had to give it a try.

Finally, some of the nurses went on break. It must have been time for the shift to change. The scene showed nurses explaining patient charts and events of the day as they changed shifts. One nurse went down the hall to the girls' room.

Peter could not believe his eyes. There in a wheelchair sat Maggi. She was being wheeled across the hall to soak in the tub, leaving Teddi alone.

Peter looked up at the ceiling. "Thank you, God. You must know this is the right thing to do."

He made his move down the hall and into Teddi's room.

"Peter," she said. "I knew I didn't dream you up."

"Shhh," he said. "I have to be fast. I brought you a change of clothes, a blond wig, make-up and a cane. Is there any way you can make it down the hall with the cane?"

"I don't know. I've only done it with the walker."

"Teddi, baby. You have to do this. There's not much time. You have to go as fast as your little feet can carry you. If you get stopped tell them you're lost. When you get to the end of the hall turn toward your left. There'll be a visitor's lounge tucked around the corner. You'll see the vending machines. Get there as quickly as possible. I'll be waiting."

He helped her out of bed and into the clothes he bought for her. He helped her tuck her hair into the wig. He ran out the door when the coast was clear. She applied the make-up.

Peter paced in the lounge area. He stood at the vending machine as if he were trying hard to make a choice. He eyed the wheelchair he had stolen from the entrance and tucked into the corner. The flowers and other gifts were in place.

Teddi opened her door a crack to watch the hall. There seemed to be another rush of staff. She knew Maggi would return before there was an opening for her. Her legs began to tremble from standing so long, waiting. The hall was empty. The two nurses at the station were both working on the computer together. They had their backs to her.

It's now or never, she thought. She gathered all the strength she could muster and hobbled down the hall. She struggled with the cane and nearly fell to the floor. She tried to run but it was more of skip or a hop. She lost her balance a number of times as she forced her legs to carry her.

At the end of the hall she made her turn to the left. One nurse looked up at her, but turned back to the computer. Her disguise and the cane set off no alarms.

At the vending area she found Peter waiting with the wheelchair. She knew her legs could not hold her up much longer. He helped her into the chair. He tied the balloon to the back of the chair and filled her arms with the flowers and teddy bear.

"Keep the flowers in front of your face if we pass anyone."

He calmly walked to the elevator. He pressed the button. It seemed like an eternity before the doors opened. He worried someone would discover her missing before they had an opportunity to get out of the building. He knew if the empty bed was discovered they would lock down the hospital, trapping them inside.

Once on the ground floor his confidence mounted. He pushed Teddi out the door.

"I'm gonna have to leave you here for a minute while I get the car. Don't talk to anyone if you can avoid it. I'll hurry."

Peter bumped into a man as he ran through the parking lot to get to his car. He started the engine and backed out quickly, nearly hitting the car behind him.

"Calm down, old man," he said. "You've almost done it."

He waited at the edge of the parked cars while others drove by. He frantically wanted to cut into the line but thought he would call attention to his car. Someone might remember seeing him.

He pulled up in front of Teddi. He set the flowers on the ground and loaded her into the car. He closed the door, jumped in on the other side and drove away.

He constantly looked over his shoulder, expecting a stream of police cars behind him. Nothing happened. All was calm. No one saw him; no one followed him. He did it.

Maggi finished her bath and the nurse returned her to her room.

"Looks like your roommate made it to the bathroom without help. She must really be getting better."

She walked to the door and tapped on it.

"Teddi, are you okay?"

There was no response.

She tried again. Then opened the door to the empty bathroom. She set off the alarm button in their room and raced down the hall to the nurses' station to inform them of the missing Teddi.

Security locked down the hospital. A frantic search began. They hoped she had gone for a walk and would show up quickly. The nurses felt terrible, but knew they must call Glen. Soon the hospital would be swarming with police.

Glen's cell phone rang.

"Holy shit! I'll be right there." He ran to his room grabbed his gun and started out the door.

"Glen, what happened?" asked Paula.

"Teddi's missing."

Chapter 13

Jennifer Parker barely managed to get Glen's attention as he peeled out of Paula's driveway. He slammed on the brakes and rolled down the window.

"I'm going with you."

She climbed into his pickup, barely closing the door before he hit the accelerator with a hard stomp. Jennifer grabbed for her seatbelt as they rounded the corner. Her body fell toward Glen.

"Sorry," he said.

She righted herself and tightened the seatbelt.

"That's fine. You do what you must do. I'll manage."

Weaving in and out of the narrow streets he finally made it to Sixtieth Street where he increased his speed. In record time he was at the hospital parking lot.

"I'll jump out here. You park. I'll get clearance for you to come inside. Give them your name and tell them you're with me," he yelled as he ran from the pickup to the door.

Jennifer had never driven a pickup before. She slid down from her side, walked around the back of the pickup and climbed into the driver's seat. She studied the instruments, which looked familiar enough, until she realized that it had a manual transmission. First gear seemed like the logical choice, so she stepped on the heavy clutch and found first, not familiar with the torque in a Cummins Diesel. She let out the clutch as slowly as she could and stepped on the throttle. The tires squealed as she lurched forward. Instinctively, she let off the throttle and the same torque that had pinned her to the back of the seat, threw her forward into a very intimate introduction to the steering wheel. Thinking to herself, maybe I'll start out in second gear...clutch, brakes, and second gear, did the trick.

She slowly guided the vehicle, much larger than any other she had driven, into the widest parking spot she could find. She assumed Glen would prefer she park it safely rather than try to ease into a tighter spot closer to the entrance.

She let out a deep sigh of relief then climbed out, locking the door behind her. She stepped back to inspect her parking job. Feeling content with herself she focused on the case inside.

She had no difficulty making her way through security. Glen did an excellent job with the clearance. She found Glen with Maggi.

"I told you, I didn't see anyone," she said.

"You're absolutely sure?" asked Glen.

"Look, my past memories are a little shaky but I can remember everything that happens now just fine," she responded angrily.

Jennifer walked over to Teddi's side of the room. She picked up her hospital gown, then the bag on the floor next. She sat on the bed.

Glen requested the staff on duty meet with him in the lounge individually for questioning.

"Excuse me," said the detective in charge.

"Yes," said Glen.

"Who are you and how are you involved in this investigation?"

"I'm sorry, I thought you knew who I was. My name is Glen Karst. I worked this case in Denver. I arranged for them to be moved here for security reasons and I came along to guard them."

Glen flashed his badge. Detective Larson jotted down his badge number.

"You won't care if I call this in?"

"No, go right ahead. I will tell you though I quit my job to follow through with this case."

"You do know you're out of your jurisdiction?"

"Of course, but these are personal friends of mine and some bastard tried to off them twice. I'm offering added security. I want to be there when the son of a bitch gets caught."

Larson handed the sheet of paper to one of the officers standing nearby to check Glen out.

Karst and Larson discussed the details of the case, starting when he found the girls in Maggi's bedroom.

"Excuse me, sir," said the assisting officer.

Larson stepped off to the side to talk with him.

"Glen, seems there's a problem."

"What kind of a problem?"

"Maybe we should talk about this down at the station. I'm sure my men can handle the situation here."

"I'm not leaving here again. Every time I do something seems to happen."

"I'm afraid you have no choice."

"What the hell. You're kidding, right?"

"No. You can come along quietly as a police courtesy or I can cuff you."

"Cuff me? You don't have enough cops in your department to cuff me. What in the hell's going on?"

Jennifer followed the two men down the hall and to the elevator.

"Glen, what's happening?"

"Jennifer, follow us in my pickup. There's got to be some misunderstanding."

Once downtown the two men walked into Larson's office. He opened the file that had been placed on his desk prior to their arrival.

"Where were you yesterday afternoon, say around two o'clock?"

"I was at the home I've been staying at since I arrived in Omaha."

"Can you give me the address of that location?"

He jotted down both the address and the phone number Glen recited.

"Are you going to tell me why you're wasting my time here when I should be at the hospital checking the scene?"

"Do you have anyone who can vouch for your whereabouts yesterday?"

"Yes, Jennifer Parker, the lady sitting in the hall. I was with her all day yesterday. Also there's Paula, the lady who owns the house where I'm staying. We were all together yesterday."

"Okay, we'll check that out. Can Paula be reached at this number?"

"It's the house number. If she's there she'll answer. I'm starting to lose my patience here. Tell me what the charges are or let me go."

"Officer Karst, you're a suspect on a homicide."

"What! That's insane. Who?"

"Are you familiar with a motel named the Satellite Inn?"

"No."

An officer slipped in the door to speak with Larson. Glen stood up and paced. He knew this had to be a screw up that was wasting far too much of his time.

Larson returned to the table. Glen sat down, leaning forward to hear what he had to say. Hoping to clear things up in a hurry and he could be on his way.

"Officer Karst, your alibis check out. If you could just be patient for a few minutes longer the clerk from the motel will be here. If he clears you then you're free to leave with my apologies."

"I know procedure, and that's fine. But bad things happen at the hospital because I'm here; I'll rip your damn lungs out."

"Just a few more minutes. Please."

He left the room. Glen stood up and kicked his chair. His anger was difficult to control.

Larson returned. "I showed your snapshot to the clerk. He didn't recognize you. I do apologize for the inconvenience. We'd be happy to allow you to work this investigation with us."

"Not so fast. What the hell is going on?"

"A delivery was made to the Satellite Inn on L Street. Glen Karst was registered for a room, the clerk's description does not match yours and he confirmed that when he came down here. Yesterday afternoon a Glen Karst ordered flowers from Kush Florist. When the delivery boy entered the room, someone hit him over the head, cracking his skull open. His clothes and the flowers were removed from the room. The maid found the body this morning."

"Shit. Can't you see the connection? Someone's using my name and impersonating me. That's the bastard who now knows where the women are and he's got Teddi. Maggi's next. We've got to get to her. I need to move her out of there."

"I'm sorry about all of this, Detective Karst. You're free to leave and you can have all the help you need from us, just say the word. I'll assign a team to work with you. We need a briefing ASAP."

"Thanks," said Glen, still angry about the situation. He was furious they would not take him at his word, but deep down, he knew he would not have, either.

Jennifer stood to follow Glen out the door. He spotted his pickup in the parking lot. The large shiny black pickup stood out among the smaller cars and vans.

"There's part of the problem," he said.

"What?" asked Jennifer.

"My pickup is too high profile. The bastard can always tell when I'm at the hospital and when I'm gone."

He and Jennifer climbed in and drove back to Paula's house.

“I thought you wanted to go to the hospital.”

“I do. I want you to bring your car, and park on the opposite side of the building from where I park. I’ll pull in where I normally do and stay at the hospital for an hour or so. Then I’ll leave. I want you to exit out the other side and meet me at Lola’s Deli. I’ll give you directions.”

“Okay,” said Jennifer, happy to work on this case with him.

“I’ll grab a hat and coat from Paula’s to put in your car. I’ll leave my pickup, go inside the deli and I want you to bring in the hat and coat. I’ll slip them on and leave with you.”

“I see. Then you would like me to return you to the hospital so your stalker will think you’re no longer there.”

“Exactly. I frequently eat at Lola’s. If he’s been following me, he’ll know that’s part of my routine and he’ll think he’ll have time to make his move.”

When Glen and Jennifer met again in Maggi’s room she continued the work she began.

“Glen, I’m a little confused here.”

“Why?”

“I have no sense of Teddi being in danger. Whoever took her knows her and she’s very happy at the moment.”

Maggi listened in.

“Are you absolutely sure?”

“Yes.”

"Now you have me confused. Who took Teddi and why? Is he the one who killed the kid at the motel?"

"I don't believe so. I feel no malice in this individual."

"Peter," said Maggi.

Both Glen and Jennifer looked at Maggi.

"What?"

"Peter. Teddi told me Peter came to visit her earlier while I was asleep. I didn't believe her. I told her she must be dreaming. She said he wanted to protect her. He said she was in danger and he wanted to get her out of here."

"Why didn't you tell me this before?" scolded Glen.

"I didn't think she knew what she was talking about."

"Maggi, you know better than that. Where are those keen detective skills you're always wowing me with?"

No sooner had the words left his mouth than he realized her mind was far from the sharp Maggi Morgan mystery writer. Her keen senses were damaged by the drug and coma.

"Geez, I'm sorry, Maggi. I didn't mean..."

"No, Glen. That's okay. I'm disappointed in me, too."

He walked over to her bed and sat next to her holding her.

“Get this guy, Glen. I have to admit knowing Peter could slip past security has me pretty scared.”

She cried.

“Jennifer, you’ve been telling me it’s two men. Could Peter be one of them?”

“Who is Peter?” she asked.

“Peter is Teddi’s husband. He suspiciously disappeared the night this happened. Somehow he traced them here and made his move.”

“Hmmm... I’m really not getting that sense. I still feel there are two people, but I don’t feel like this Peter is one of them.”

Glen looked at his watch.

“It’s time,” he said.

“Time for what?” asked Maggi.

“I have to leave now for a little while, but I’ll be back. Don’t worry, there’s uniforms right outside your door. I’ve left orders that one of them must accompany every doctor and nurse into the room with you. No one can be alone with you until we catch whoever is responsible.”

Out in the hall Glen took the officers aside.

“Has Larson informed you of my work on this case?” asked Glen.

“Yeah, Detective Karst. He told us to do whatever you asked of us.”

"Groovy. Right now I'm leaving here with Jennifer Parker."

He touched Jennifer's arm.

"When I return I'll be wearing different clothes. When I give you the high sign I want you to leave your posts and go to the cafeteria for coffee. When you hear the security call, haul your asses back here as fast as you can."

"I don't understand, sir. You want us to leave our posts and return when the security call comes across the speakers? What makes you think the alarm will go off?" asked one of the officers.

"I'm beginning to figure this creep out. He's watching me. He's using me. He thinks he's playing a game. No way is he even gonna come close to scoring any points in this match. I'm gonna see him destroyed."

"What're you planning to do?"

"Like I said. I'll come back and slip into Maggi's room. I'm going to place myself behind her bathroom door and wait. He's been watching my pickup and when it's gone he makes his move. I'm guessing he's gonna hit while he thinks I'm away this afternoon. I'll be returning with Jennifer, leaving my pickup parked at a restaurant on Dodge Street.

"It's imperative he sees no one on duty. He may case the area a bit before making his move. Give me about fifteen minutes in the bathroom before you two take off. And be prepared."

Next, Glen went to the nurses' station. "I need to see the roster of the nurses who'll be on this afternoon and on evening shift," he said.

He ran his finger down the list. There were only two nurses assigned to Maggi's room.

"I want you girls to be a little careless today. I don't want more than one nurse at the station at a time and whoever is here, I want her back to that hall at all times. Is that understood?"

The head nurse appeared nervous.

"Detective Karst, are you expecting the murderer to return to this floor today?"

"Let's say I'm hoping he will."

"Am I or any of my nurses in danger?"

"I wish I could guarantee you weren't but I can't. Keep yourselves alert without looking alert. One nurse at a time at the station should minimize the amount of danger. This isn't the first time you've done this, right?"

She began to tremble as she straightened papers on her desk.

Glen slipped his hand over hers.

"I'm gonna do my best to protect all of you. You'll just have to trust me and work with me. If you see someone who doesn't belong, ignore him."

"Are you sure it's a man? Can you give us a description?"

"It could be a man or a woman. It could also be two people instead of one. You know what? If you see someone heading down that hall, get your butt out of here. Go into a patient's room and wait. No exceptions."

" I don't want to be a hostage, Detective Karst, I'm a mother. I have three little kids at home."

Her eyes filled with tears that she struggled to hold back.

Glen slipped his strong arms around her. She cried on his shoulder. His gentle ways calmed her.

"Look, if you do as I say and get out of the way quickly, everything will go smoothly. Now get your nurses together and explain the situation to them and nothing leaves this area. I don't want the entire hospital talking. Got it?"

"Yes, sir," she said, trying to hide her fear.

"Let's go."

Jennifer and Glen left the hospital through different doors. Glen drove his pickup to Lola's Deli. He drove around the block first then stopped. He got out to check his tires with his tire gauge in case he was being followed. He wanted Jennifer to have time to go into the Deli unobserved.

From his vantage point he saw Jennifer enter the door. He parked in front of the Deli next to her car, blocking the view with his large pickup. He went inside.

"Back for more?" teased Barb.

"Not today," he responded. His face remained void of his usual smile and lacked the gleam in his eye.

"What's wrong? Is Paula okay?"

"Yes, she's fine. I'm working today so I can't stay."

He walked to the bathroom and saw the sack sitting on the floor where Jennifer left it.

Jennifer ordered a sandwich to go. Glen was pleased she thought ahead in case she had been seen going inside. Carrying a sack out made it look more realistic.

He came out of the bathroom wearing the coat and hat. He walked slowly and methodically with his head down and his arm holding a cell phone to keep the exposed side of his face covered.

Together he and Jennifer entered her car and pulled carefully but quickly out of the parking lot. He instructed her to take the back roads to the hospital rather than the one he normally took. All the extra precautions probably were unnecessary but Detective Karst was a pro and a stickler for details.

"Drop me off up here then go home."

"No. I plan to stay with you."

"It could be dangerous. I don't want you involved. You've been great. Now please go home and wait for my call."

He slipped out of the car and into the hospital. He took the stairs rather than the elevators. He ran up the stairs two by two. Burning off a little energy helped him calm down. The distance was such that his breathing barely increased.

Once on the second floor he made his way quickly down the halls to the room housing Maggi. When the nurse at the station saw him she knew the killer had arrived. She kept her back to him the entire time. Then he spoke to her.

"It's me, Glen."

She turned to him. He winked and she turned back around trying to slow her racing heart.

His eyes scanned the entire viewing area. There was no one in the halls, not even nurses. He made his way to the door. The officers watched his approach. He flashed his badge quickly revealing his plan was about to begin. One made his way to the head of the hall to look for any visitors strolling. Glen slipped inside.

Maggi gasped when she saw him.

He stood up straight and lowered his collar as he removed his hat.

"You scared the hell out of me," she said.

"Sorry, I didn't mean to. I'm gonna get situated in your bathroom. Don't be afraid to scream if you need to."

"I hope I won't need to."

Maggi tried to watch television as the time ticked away. Glen could not find a comfortable position in the cold bathroom.

They waited.

Daniel made numerous phone calls to Peter with no results.

"Bastard," he mumbled.

He left his room and went to the office of the motel where they stayed.

He checked to make sure the desk clerk was not the same one who checked him in.

"Can I help you?" asked the clerk.

"Seems I've locked myself out of my room. I'm Peter Taylor, room 247."

"Not a problem."

The clerk handed him a new keycard.

Daniel let himself into Peter's room. His things were gone.

"That stupid fool. He'll live to regret the day he screwed with me."

Daniel kicked the trashcan out of anger spilling the contents across the room.

He opened every drawer and checked the bathroom to see if Peter left anything behind that could lead him to Maggi's whereabouts.

He kicked through the water bottles and pizza box that spilled out onto the floor. Crumpled napkins and candy wrappers were all he could find. He spread the trash once again with his foot and he noticed a crumpled piece of motel stationery.

Finding Peter's list of hospitals in the area set his heart pounding. He set his gun on the table next to the lamp. He flattened the paper, smoothing out the wrinkles.

The meticulous Peter scratched through each name as he eliminated them one by one. In the middle of the list he circled Methodist Hospital.

"Idiots shouldn't leave clues hanging around. How stupid."

He opened the drawer of the desk and removed the telephone book. He checked the address for the hospital. He flipped the pages until he found a map of the city. He located the hospital on the map. He checked his watch.

"I think it's time you got your flowers, ladies."

He raced back to his room and changed his clothes. He straightened the florist delivery uniform as he looked in the mirror. Pleased that a hat went with the uniform he pulled it down over his eyes. He picked up his vase of flowers and adjusted the card hanging from a pink ribbon.

He drove to the hospital without much difficulty. Once inside he asked for Maggi Morgan's room.

"I'm sorry, but you can't deliver those directly to the patient. Just leave them here and we'll have an aide take care of them."

"I'd really like to ma'am but it would be my job. This is a special case. These need to be hand delivered as ordered by"... he stopped to read his invoice, "by Detective Glen Karst."

The receptionist looked confused.

"Wait here. Let me call ahead and clear it."

"Hey, I have a flower arrangement for Maggi Morgan and the delivery person says his orders are to deliver it directly to her room according to a Detective Karst."

Ordinarily, they would have refused to allow the delivery but under the circumstances today she made an exception.

"Sure, that would be alright."

"Ask her if Detective Karst will be there to sign for them?" he asked.

"Okay. He wants to know if Detective Karst will be there to sign for them."

She paused. Should she tell Karst or should she assume any unusual visitor today could be the killer? She took Glen's advice to ignore everyone strange today.

"No, he's not available today. I can sign if he needs me to."

"She said he's not there right now, but she'll sign for them."

"Thanks. Now if you can give me directions to the room."

She checked her computer and gave him instructions of which floor to go to and which halls to go down. She even wrote it on a piece of paper for him.

"Thank you. You've been so kind. I owe my job to you."

He scanned the halls then following her directions. This is almost too easy, he thought. He froze in his tracks. Too easy...maybe it's a setup. He shrugged that thought off.

When he arrived near the nurses' station he saw the guards outside of Maggi's door.

"Fine" he muttered. "I got this far and now those jackasses are gonna screw up my plan."

The two officers approached the station. At first he thought he may have been spotted or they may have been alerted to his coming by the head nurse.

"We're going down to the cafeteria for some coffee. We'll be back in about thirty minutes."

"Okay."

Daniel could hardly believe his ears. They were leaving together for thirty minutes. That would be more than enough time to take care of Teddi and Maggi and get out of the hospital.

The nurse saw him through the corner of her eye. She so desperately wanted to alert the police officers as she watched them walk toward the elevator. She tried to remain calm and remember her instructions from Detective Karst. She left her post and went into a patient's room, leaving the coast completely clear for Daniel.

He quickened his pace down the hall to where the two empty chairs sat on either side of the door. He eased the door open. His eyes caught a glimpse of the empty bed. Then he saw Maggi. Her eyes were closed but the television was on.

He quietly placed the flowers on the table near her bed. Her eyes opened.

"Daniel? What are you doing here? Don't tell me you've decided to bring me flowers after all these years?"

Surprised by her response, he asked, "So Mags, how long has it been since we've seen each other?"

"Years."

Now he knew she had no memory of the night he tried to kill her, just like Peter told him.

"Why is it that when two people get a divorce they can't seem to remain friends? At least stay on the Christmas card list."

Maggi stared at Daniel. Something did not feel quite right.

"Maggi, what's wrong?"

"I'm not sure?"

She bolted straight up in bed, scooting herself as far away from him as possible.

"Oh my God, it was you! You tried to kill me!"

"Very good, your memory's coming back."

He pulled a revolver from his pocket. He held it to her head.

"Now lay still while I finish the job."

He fumbled for his syringe filled with insulin to inject her one last time. This time he planned a larger dose. He was not taking any chances.

"When I finish with you, I'll have to find your little friend, Teddi."

Glen waited until he felt the time was right to get a clear shot without harming Maggi.

She prepared herself for Glen's entrance. She slid down flattening herself on the bed.

"Very good. I'd hate for you to fall out of bed. Now give me your arm," said Daniel, still holding the gun to her head.

Glen burst from the bathroom. Before he could yell anything, Daniel shot at him, the bullet penetrating his left arm.

Glen returned fire, dropping Daniel with one shot. His limp body fell on top of Maggi.

Maggi screamed.

The nurse, not comfortable with the delivery person, alerted the two officers in the cafeteria. They waited at the end of the hall for the deliveryman to leave the room. They rushed in when they heard the gunshots and Maggi's scream. Guns raised they made a quick sweep of the room.

Glen helped Maggi out from under Daniel's body. His arm oozed a steady flow of blood from his wound. The officers called it in while the nurses attended to Glen's arm.

"It's over Glen. I can't believe it's over," said Maggi, shaking.

Glen did not think this was a good time to tell Maggi Daniel might have an accomplice still at large.

Chapter 14

Maggi insisted upon being released from the hospital. Glen moved her into Paula's house. She and Jennifer shared the guest room while Glen stayed on a roll- away bed in the new bedroom he started in the basement. The walls were up but no painting or trim work was completed.

When LeAnn discovered Paula now had three houseguests, she voiced her opinion.

"I sure hope they're paying you rent," she ranted on the phone.

"They offered, but I declined. I like having the company. I can't believe Maggi Morgan is actually staying in my house, not to mention a famous psychic medium."

"Sounds like a bunch of crazies if you ask me. What kind of cop would put your life in danger by moving a woman in whose being stalked? You might have a killer outside your door this very minute."

"Well, if I do, I'm sure Glen can handle it like he handled the other one."

"I thought you said his arm's in a sling."

"It is. He shot and killed that guy at the hospital after he was shot in the arm. I think he's more than capable."

"I guess love's blind."

"What do you mean by that?"

"The guy's taking financial advantage of you and you're letting him. Can't very well be working in your basement now, can he?"

"For your information he has all the walls up and the electricity wired. He's waiting on me to pick the paint colors and I'm sure I'm capable of painting walls while he's recovering."

Paula really wanted to hang up on her sister. She tired of LeAnn's criticism of everything she did or did not do.

"You cancelled our little insurance party when Glen took off to save the world. When are you planning to reschedule that?"

"How about this Saturday night? He should be feeling better by then."

"Why do we need him to handle our family business?"

"There's something we'd like to talk to you and Carla about."

"What?"

"I tell you on Saturday."

Angry again because she could not control Paula she hung up.

LeAnn called Carla.

"Guess we're due at Paula's on Saturday night. She says she and Glen have something important to tell us. I suppose she's engaged."

"Or worse, maybe their married."

"Speaking of marriage. What's the status with you and Anthony?"

"I'm moving in with him."

"You're what?"

"I thought you, of all people, would be excited. He asked me to move in with him in his big beautiful house. I can rent mine out. I'll have extra money to help pay off my house more quickly."

"Why don't you let me invest that money for you instead."

"LeAnn, drop it. I'm a big girl. Let me handle my finances the way I want to."

"Fine. See ya Saturday."

LeAnn managed to make both sisters angry with her in one afternoon. She thought about their attitudes. She felt they did not appreciate her skills.

"Ungrateful," she said.

She gasped as she heard her mother's voice come from her mouth. "Surely I'm nothing like her. I won't let that happen to me. It's the girls. They bring out the worst in me," she said, as she stood before the hall mirror primping.

Paula thoroughly enjoyed her three houseguests. Glen spent a great deal of time resting. The pain remained intense but he refrained from taking his pain medication. He preferred to remain alert. The medication made him groggy.

Paula quizzed Maggi about her books.

"How do you come up with your amazing plots?"

"I get some from the newspapers and some from Glen. The rest just pop into my head."

"Will you be writing a book about what happened to you?"

"You mean a biography?"

"Sure."

"No, I don't think so. I think I'd prefer to stay in the mystery genre."

Paula then asked Jennifer, "When you write your books how do you know what to write? I started reading the one I bought at your book signing. It's very deep. Some parts I had to read a couple of times to be sure I got it."

"I channel my writing, dear."

"What the hell is channeling?" asked Maggi.

"I open myself up to a higher self. The words flow from somewhere within. I type whatever comes into my mind."

"How do you know your not just plagiarizing someone else?" asked Maggi.

"Sometimes I think I am. I don't take credit for what I write. I tell my readers the words are given to me from a higher source."

"On that note," said Maggi. "I think I'll get another cup of coffee."

"I'll get it," said Paula. "You stay put. Jennifer, tea?"

"Yes, please," she responded.

Glen appeared in the kitchen from the basement.

"I was just pouring coffee and tea. Can I get you something?" asked Paula.

"Bourbon. I need a tall one."

"I don't think you're supposed to drink with your medication," said Paula.

"Hell, bourbon is my medication. Those damn pills make me too sleepy."

"Sleep is probably good for healing."

"Yeah well, the bourbon is good for my mental state at this point."

"Sorry, but I don't have any bourbon."

"Yes, you do. Look in the cabinet over the refrigerator."

Paula opened the cabinet to find Glen's bottle.

"Where'd that come from?"

"Don't leave home without it," he laughed.

Paula returned carrying a tray. Glen felt badly that he could not carry it for her.

She passed around the drinks. Glen raised his glass.

"To one hell of a strange group."

They laughed and toasted each other.

Carla and Anthony were the first to arrive Saturday night. LeAnn made a late entrance.

"Boy, you're getting more like Mom every day," said Paula. "We had to wait dinner on you."

LeAnn bristled. "There's a difference between being socially late and Mom."

"Really? I don't see the difference," said Carla.

Anthony squeezed her knee with his hand to stop the argument before it started.

LeAnn filled her plate then joined the rest of them in the living room. Carla called LeAnn when she realized her briefcase was missing. She promised to bring it to the meeting tonight but she did not carry it in with her.

"Where's my briefcase?" she asked.

"It's in the car. I forgot to bring it in. Anthony, be a doll and go and get it for me, please."

She tossed him her keys. He returned with the briefcase.

Carla spread the contents on the floor. She also opened a folder she had brought along with her.

Jennifer said, "If you'll excuse me, this is family business. I think I'll retire to my room."

"No, please wait," insisted Paula.

All eyes fell upon her.

"Glen and I have something to tell you."

He stood up and went to Paula's side. He could sense how nervous she was. He decided to take the heat for her.

He slipped his good arm around her.

"This lovely lady and I have a confession to make. It's about our living arrangement. You see, we're not engaged as some of you seem to think."

"I should hope not. You're married," said Maggi.

Glen realized, with all that happened recently, the topic of Debbie had not come up.

"Not exactly, Maggi. Debbie filed for divorce."

"What?" gasped Maggi.

"He's married!" blurted out Carla.

"No, now wait a minute. Let me explain this. I needed a good cover," he lied. "So I asked Paula to go along with me being her boyfriend while I stayed here. I can guarantee you, ladies, nothing happened. I've been staying in the guest room the entire time. Paula here was gracious enough to go along with my story."

Paula looked at Glen with a shocked expression on her face. What a sweet man to protect her in the way he did. He took all the blame onto himself.

"Thank you, Glen," she said, as she tipped her head to touch his cheek.

"Yeah right and pigs fly. I smell a rat. What's really going on?" asked LeAnn.

Maggi looked confused.

"I think you two concocted this story to cover up your illicit romance since Maggi showed up in the house with the two of you," said LeAnn.

"If there's one thing I can tell you about Glen Karst, he's honest," said Maggi.

Glen and Paula looked at each other and exchanged grins, knowing he just lied to protect her throwing thus the honesty issue out the window.

"Maybe if you tell them the rest of your news, dear," suggested Jennifer.

She had a dual purpose in changing the subject. She wanted to give them something to be happy about and she wanted to be able to exit the room. She questioned the happy part when she sensed the presence of their mother in the room with them. Somehow, when she appeared a few minutes before Glen began to speak, a negative energy filled the room.

Paula looked at Jennifer and Glen with pleading eyes. She so wished they could handle this for her as well but neither offered assistance.

Jennifer watched as Paula struggled to find the words. Suddenly, she saw Andy appear next to Paula. He put his arm around her shoulders. Paula rubbed her crossed arms. She sensed something but was unaware it was Andy's presence.

The fear of her family faded and a feeling of elation came over her.

"Well?" said Carla.

"I'm going to have a baby," she blurted out excitedly.

"A what?" said LeAnn.

"No way. You've got to be kidding," said Carla.

Even Maggi looked surprised. She knew Paula was a widow but had not yet been filled in on the details of his passing or how long it had been. She glanced at Glen.

He took a drink from his glass of bourbon that he carried around the house with him during his recovery. He raised his eyebrows teasingly to Maggi, knowing full well she would get the entire story any moment now.

"No, I'm not kidding. I'm three months along."

Carla counted on her fingers. "That means it's Andy's baby."

"Of course it's Andy's baby. Who did you think...." She paused and looked at Glen, then burst into laughter.

"No, it's not Glen's."

He smiled at Maggi, who glared at him for teasing her. He winked.

LeAnn caught that wink. She wondered if the story they told was true.

"Why didn't you tell us sooner?" asked LeAnn.

"I just found out."

"Have you been to the doctor yet?" asked Carla "Does your health insurance cover maternity?"

She shuffled through the papers in the folder she brought.

"No, I haven't been to the doctor yet. I have an appointment next week. And I don't really care if my insurance covers maternity."

Now it was Carla's turn to gasp. How could she be so careless to get pregnant without checking into her policy?

"You said you just recently found out?" asked LeAnn.

"I had no idea until Jennifer arrived. She's the one who told me."

Jennifer cringed. This is not the type of crowd who should know of her abilities. A room full of skeptics is a difficult audience to deal with, especially angry skeptics.

"Why would a stranger know you were pregnant?" asked LeAnn.

Paula left the room and returned with Jennifer's book. She handed it to LeAnn, who looked at it then handed it to Carla and Anthony. He read the back cover aloud.

Jennifer summoned her guides to help her through this unsettling event.

"Oh Paula, you don't believe in this kind of garbage, do you? No offense Jennifer, I applaud anyone who can come up with an idea that makes them money," said LeAnn.

"Can't you be sued for telling people bad things or things that aren't true? What kind of insurance do you have to have to cover you?" asked Carla.

Paula stood in the middle of the room totally disappointed. She finally told her family the good news of her upcoming child and they were more interested in the financial value of being a psychic and the insurance to protect those claims.

Glen's heart went out to Paula and Jennifer. He felt the overwhelming urge to protect them from the vicious comments of the two sisters.

"Hey. Isn't anyone going to congratulate Paula on the new baby?" he asked.

He raised his glass in a toast, "To Paula and the luckiest baby in the world to have her for his mother."

"His? Do you already know it's a boy?" asked Carla. "Did she tell you that, too?"

Paula looked at Jennifer to confirm Glen's comment. She nodded her affirmation. Glen then realized he guessed the sex of the unborn baby. He, too, looked to Jennifer for confirmation. She smiled at him thinking how intuitive he is and how badly he fights accepting his gift.

She remembered the beginning of his training with her. How, when he applied her meditative techniques, he saw the train tracks that helped put an end to one of his cases. She recalled the occasions when he saw and spoke to the dead, but tried to excuse it away as most do. He made great progress but still had a long way to go. Today, relaxed and not thinking about it, his gift surfaced.

LeAnn and Carla, feeling badly, went to Paula to hug and congratulate her. Glen slipped into the kitchen to refill his glass. Anthony followed.

"I hope that little boy has a better chance in this family than the rest of the men in their lives," said Anthony. He poured another cup of coffee.

"What do you mean?" asked Glen.

"How much history do you know about this family?" he asked.

"Nothing really," said Glen. "I knew Andy died and then of course their mother. I guess I didn't know if their mother was divorced or what happened to their father. The subject never came up. When I tried to talk to Paula about Andy she shut me off."

"The men in this family are cursed. Really has me wondering if I want to continue my relationship with Carla."

Glen leaned up against the cabinet to steady himself.

"How's the arm?" asked Anthony, noticing Glen's discomfort.

"Hurts like hell."

"Aren't your drugs working?"

"Not taking them," Glen answered. He sipped his bourbon.

"Why the hell not? I'd never miss a dose. Jesus, man, you were shot. It's not like running a splinter up your arm."

"I can't take any chances of being doped up. I need to stay alert. I'm not sure Maggi's one hundred percent safe yet. Jennifer thinks there could have been two people involved."

"At the expense of such pain?"

"This helps dull it," he said as he raised his glass.

"Yeah well, how much of that can you down and still stay alert?"

"A lot. I'm really good at it. Now tell me more about the cursed men of the family."

Glen's detective senses were awakened.

Anthony looked over his shoulder to see if anyone could hear them.

Glen walked past him into the living room.

"Hey, I'm taking Anthony downstairs to show him my handiwork. Call us if you need us for anything."

Anthony followed Glen to the basement.

"You don't mind if I lay down for a minute while you talk. The throbbing is getting uncomfortable, lying flat helps."

Glen cleared his neatly folded clothes off of the chair in the unfinished bedroom. He plopped down on the bed, slipping his arm out from the sling to relieve the pressure on his neck.

"How far back do you want me to start?"

"As far back as you know."

"Anna was married to a man named Charles. They had a little boy before the girls were born. The little boy died in his crib while Anna was out. She blamed Charles for not watching him."

"Was it crib death?"

"I guess. Anyway, then they had the girls. Anna didn't want any more kids. Charles was disappointed because he still wanted a boy. He was in the military and got canned for his drinking and depression. I guess he planned to be a lifer but couldn't pass some test and they sacked him. That's when they moved to Omaha."

"Where were they living?"

"Somewhere in California. I guess one day after they were here they came home and found him dead in his chair in front of the television."

"What was the cause of death?"

"Hmmm...I think Carla said a heart attack. Then she married this guy named Lawrence. He worked at the insurance company with Carla. He was her boss. Anyway, Anna was a real bitch to live with. I'm sure Paula told you that much."

"Oh yeah. I got an earful around the time she died."

"Seems Lawrence was making plans to walk out on Anna. He met someone else at the insurance company. Just when he was about to make his move, he keeled over from a heart attack."

"That's what Anna died from," Glen pointed out.

"Yeah, so what's your point?"

"No point. Don't you think that's quite the coincidence?"

"Oh and there's more. LeAnn's old man, Reed, died from a heart attack, too. But he was quite a bit older so that one was not much of a surprise."

Glen mulled the deaths over in his mind.

"Do you know what Andy died from?" asked Glen.

"That's the sad one. He was pretty young and appeared to be in tiptop shape according to Carla. He died of a heart attack, too."

"No shit?" said Glen, as he swung his legs around off the bed and sat up.

He eased his arm back into the sling.

"Let me get this straight, we have a baby boy, two husbands for Anna, one husband for LeAnn and one husband for Paula and they all died of a heart attack. Except for the baby, but who really knows what causes crib death, especially that long ago."

Paula went down to check on the men.

"That's what I mean. Any man they come in contact with dies. That's why I'm not sure about keeping up this relationship with Carla. I'd worry less about Paula's baby if he were a girl. Some dark cloud hangs over the men in their life," said Anthony.

Paula froze outside the bedroom door. She overheard what Anthony said. She covered her belly with her hand as if to protect her baby. She backed up to the base of the stairs and called out, "Are you guys gonna stay down there all night?"

"We'll be right up," yelled Glen.

"Look, this is between you and me. I don't want Carla to know how I feel. Makes me look a little paranoid. I'm sure it's nothing but a coincidence, but it does make a guy wonder, ya know?"

"Hell yes, it makes ya wonder. I'll figure it out."

"How would you do that?"

"Hide and watch. Something doesn't feel right."

"Now you sound like that psychic upstairs," laughed Anthony.

Jennifer's words haunted Glen. "Follow your gut feelings, you can't go wrong."

"Ah, yeah. We'd better go up now before they all come down here," said Glen.

When Glen and Anthony returned to the living room, Glen's eyes scanned the room out of habit.

"Where's Maggi?" he asked.

"She went in to lie down," said Jennifer.

"Come join us," said Carla. "Jennifer's going to do a reading for us."

"We've got our very own *John Edward* show happening," said LeAnn.

Jennifer began, "This evening I became aware of two energies with us. One is your mother, Anna and the other is Andy."

Carla looked around the room, "Isn't that just like Mother. She's still wanting in on everything, even from the grave."

"Anna is much stronger than Andy, so let's do him first. He wants you to know he's with you and the baby, Paula. He's going to be there every step of the way. He says he knows you're suffering but he feels you're strong enough to move on."

LeAnn clapped, "Very good. I could've told her that one. Tell us something you shouldn't know."

"I see a ring, a gold ring. I see a table. It's a barbeque. There's a napkin with a gold ring on it."

Paula wiped away her tears. "That's my engagement ring. He put it on a napkin to surprise me. That's the day he asked me to marry him."

"You told her that," said Carla.

"No, I didn't. No one knew that except the three of us, unless you told Mom.

"Everyone can find out engagement stories, tell us something else," said LeAnn.

"He wants to know if you like the rug you bought?"

LeAnn stopped butting in.

"He said you returned the first one and were…how should I say it more nicely than he?"

"Just say it," said Paula.

"I'm seeing a dog urinating, so generally that means he's saying you were pissed off. Oh, I hate using those words."

Everyone in the room laughed. "Even if he's not here, Jennifer has you pegged," laughed Carla.

"He's gone," said Jennifer.

"Do you want to hear from your mother?" asked Jennifer. "She's anxious to come through."

The girls looked at each other, not one of them answered.

Finally, Paula said, "Sure, what's Mom got to say."

"Before I tell you what she has to say you have to know something about her. Your mother has not crossed over."

"What does that mean?" asked Carla.

"When people die, I'm sure you've heard the stories, they go into the light. When people die, friends and family who have left before them greet them. Even pets can come to help them cross over. Leaving the human body to return to spirit form is a difficult transition, especially for those souls who have not yet reached higher levels. They have a more difficult time remembering their spiritual form."

"Oh brother," said LeAnn.

Even Anthony rolled his eyes.

"I'm giving you more information than you need at this point. If you would like to learn more about it, you can read it in my books. For some reason your mother has chosen to stay behind, an earthbound spirit or ghost, as some put it."

Carla and Paula looked around the room feeling uncomfortable.

"I need a drink. Glen, can I have some of your bourbon?' asked LeAnn.

"Sure, help yourself."

"Me too," said Carla, jumping up to help in the kitchen.

"Might as well bring one for me, too," said Anthony.

When they returned with their drinks Jennifer continued.

"Your mother says she wasn't ready to go. She said there were things she wanted to attend to before she left and hopes you girls will continue with those."

"What's that mean?" asked Paula.

"I don't know. I'm only the messenger," said Jennifer.

Anna stayed on a while longer discussing family holidays and made comments about personal conversations to help the girls believe she was truly present.

Jennifer was relieved when Anna left. She excused herself and joined Maggi in the bedroom.

"I'm hungry," said Paula.

"I can't believe it, but so am I," said Carla. "I think we ate all the chicken."

"How about a pizza?" asked Paula.

"Not one of those frozen things," said LeAnn.

"No, I was hoping we could get the men to go out after one," said Paula.

"Not a problem. We'll go pick up a couple if Anthony here is willing to drive." Glen raised his wounded arm.

The men left to get pizza.

"Carla has an announcement to make, too," said LeAnn.

"What?" asked Paula.

"Anthony and I are going to live together."

Paula's face gave away her confusion.

"What?" asked Carla.

"Nothing. I'm really happy for you."

"No, you're not. What're you hiding from me? You're such a bad liar."

"Now whose acting like Mom?" said LeAnn. "You'd better tell her or she's gonna badger you all night."

"It's nothing really," said Paula.

Carla crossed her arms and puffed out her chest in much the same way she did when they were kids and she made it obvious she was going to stand her ground.

"Okay, okay. But it's probably nothing more than guy talk," said Paula. "When I went downstairs to get the guys I overheard Anthony talking about the men in our family being cursed and it makes him nervous. He mentioned to Glen, probably just kidding around, that he was thinking about breaking up with you because of it."

"I knew you couldn't keep him. You'd better do something. You can't let that money slip away," said LeAnn in a loud voice.

"Shh," said Paula, pointing to the guest room.

"What a terrible thing to say," said Carla.

"I know, the bastard," said LeAnn.

"I was talking about you," said Carla. "He's not going to leave me. Rest assured that's not going to happen."

When the men returned no one said a word about the conversation Paula overheard. They laughed, told stories and ate pizza. Anthony picked up a couple of bottles of wine. Paula stayed with her iced tea while the others got a little tipsy.

"It's getting late and this wine's getting the best of me," said Anthony. "Why don't I take you home?"

Carla, who had turned on the charm that evening, agreed. LeAnn decided she should go also. Glen and Paula walked them to the door. He tried to help Paula straighten up the mess from the party with his one good arm.

"You look like you're in pain. Why don't you go to bed? I can handle this," she said.

He refused. He stayed with her until everything was cleared away.

At breakfast the next morning, Maggi and Jennifer made their announcement.

"Glen, I'm going back to Denver with Jennifer. I miss my dogs and want to go get them," said Maggi.

"Hell no, you're not going back."

"Yes I am," she said defiantly.

"Then I'm going, too."

"You're not in any shape to drive. The doctors said you need to take it easy for at least another week. Besides, you're not supposed to drive on your meds."

"He's not taking them," Paula butted in.

"Why am I not surprised?" said Maggi.

"Doctors don't know shit. I'm coming, too."

"Glen, please calm down. Maggi will be fine with me. I promise. I'm not taking her back to her house. She'll be staying with me. I'll contact your friend in the department. What was his name? Oh yes, Bill. I'll have him pick up her dogs and keep a watch on my house. It's only for a week and no one will be aware she's back in Denver."

Glen felt the women were ganging up on him and his arm did hurt like hell.

"Okay, one week and then I'll be there. You are not, under any circumstances, to call anyone else or leave Jennifer's house. Is that clear?"

"Yes sir," she saluted.

Paula and Glen walked them to Jennifer's car and said their good-byes.

"I'm sure she'll be fine," said Paula. "Relax."

"I'm not gonna relax until the police find Peter and Teddi and I get the whole story."

"Oops! That's my phone ringing," said Paula, as she sprinted back into the house.

Glen picked up the newspaper and casually walked in while reading the headlines.

"I can't believe it!" she cried as she hung up the phone.

"What?"

"Carla found Anthony dead in his house this morning."

Chapter 15

Glen's mind raced with possible scenarios as he rode with Paula to meet with her sisters at LeAnn's house. He worried about the stress in her life affecting her pregnancy. Glen, not having kids of his own, felt a connection somehow to this widowed woman with child. His protective instincts emerged. He found himself torn between returning to Denver to protect Maggi and staying behind to help Paula.

Inside they found LeAnn and Carla sitting in front of the fireplace drinking wine. Carla's mascara streamed down her face with the tears. LeAnn, at a loss for words, looked relieved when Glen and Paula entered the room.

"What happened?" asked Paula, as she went to Carla.

"I'm not sure. He was fine when he took me home last night. This morning I called him, like I always do, before work. There was no answer. I assumed he was in the shower so I waited and called back. I wondered if he was mad at me or something I said so I drove over to his house. I pounded on the door and kept calling him on my cell phone. I looked in the garage and his car was parked inside.

"I looked in all of the windows and saw he was still in bed. I pounded on his window but he didn't move. I went into his backyard where he hangs the spare key and let myself in."

She burst into tears again.

"When I went to the bed he looked terrible. His color was bad and he didn't seem to be breathing. I called 911 and tried CPR, but it was no use. When the ambulance arrived they said he was gone."

"Did the coroner's investigator show up?" asked Glen.

"Yes."

"They're gonna do an autopsy, aren't they?"

"I'm not sure. I guess that would be up to his mother, wouldn't it?"

"In most cases it would be," he said.

"Who else could make that kind of a decision?" asked LeAnn.

"If the investigating officer suspected foul play, he could request an autopsy or if there was no reasonable medical explanation that a doctor would sign off on. Did you meet the detective on the case?"

"I don't remember who I met," said Carla.

Glen walked around the room. He wondered how far to push these girls today. He had a million questions. He could not help but notice the differences between Paula's home and LeAnn's. Her obsession with money and fine things, under any other circumstances, would have made her a prime suspect. After all, she had a connection to nearly all of the deaths Anthony had told him about the previous night.

How odd, he thought, hours ago he had told Glen he might end the relationship and now his life had been ended instead. He thought back to their conversation. They were alone in the basement when he told Glen. His mind raced to the layout of Paula's house. How could their voices have been overheard? He visualized the duct system in the basement before he covered it with sheetrock. He ruled out their voices being heard that way.

Then he remembered Paula's voice from the basement stairs, calling them to return to the dinner party. He looked at Paula with her soft crystal blue eyes and her creamy blond hair. She oozed the look of the girl next door; her look of innocence would stop most people from thinking a negative thought about her. Glen knew from experience sometimes the most innocent looking and acting could also be the most dangerous.

He studied LeAnn. Her love of money should not have had anything to do with Anthony. She had nothing to gain by his death. As his thoughts continued, he could not come up with a reason why Paula would want to see Anthony dead. The only one with an excuse would be Carla, if she felt she would soon be jilted. She had no way of knowing the gist of their conversation. Women do keep their secrets. He remembered a group of women who were involved in a mess of husband murders in a previous case. Secrets were the glue of their relationship.

"Excuse me for being such a bad hostess," said LeAnn. "Can I get you two something to drink?"

"I'll have coffee, if you have some made," said Glen.

"I know Paula, tea for you," she said.

"Yes, can I help you with it?"

"Sure."

Paula heated a cup of water in the microwave. LeAnn poured Glen a cup of coffee.

As Paula reached for a box of tea, LeAnn stopped her. "Wait, I have a new blend for you that I picked up at the health food store. Supposed to be organic and have extra vitamins or something in it, good for the baby." She handed her a decorated tin filled with a loose leaf tea. When she opened it a minty aroma escaped from the tin.

"The lady at the store said it might take a little getting used to. The flavor is a little bitter, but hey, nothing good for you tastes good, right?"

Paula scooped some into a tea ball to swirl around in her cup. LeAnn was right, it had a horrid taste. She sipped it slowly.

"Would it be alright if I left you for a while. I'd like to go to the police station and see what they've come up with," said Glen.

"Sure, go ahead," said Paula.

"I'm glad he left," said Carla. "Sometimes he makes me feel uncomfortable."

"Why?" asked Paula.

"I don't know, it's like he looks at everyone, like he's sizing them up as a suspect or something. He gives me the creeps. How much longer is he gonna be staying with you?"

"The doctor says he may be able to travel next week. My guess is, he's gonna want to go back to Denver to watch over Maggi," said Paula.

"So what is it with those two, anyway?" asked LeAnn. "Are they lovers or what?"

"They're good friends. He works with her on her books," said Paula.

"Yeah, that's a new one," said LeAnn.

Now Paula wished she had gone with Glen. Seems LeAnn was about to put her claws out and she was not in the mood to defend herself or anyone else.

"You know, it's too bad you two didn't rush into this marriage. You could've had him as heavily insured as his money would allow," said LeAnn.

There was no response from Carla. Paula shot LeAnn a disgruntled look.

"What?" asked LeAnn. "I just meant the guy was loaded, too bad she couldn't cash in on some of it."

Carla began to tremble, the flames from the fireplace failed to keep her warm.

"I'll get her a blanket," said Paula.

She went to the closet in the guest bedroom. Once again, those boxes caught her eye. LeAnn followed her. She saw her looking at the boxes.

"Doing a little snooping, are we?" she asked.

"Now that you mention it, I do have a question for you. Why do you have all that crystal? You wanted us to take up a collection to buy it for Mom. You already have the whole set. Why didn't we just give it to her complete and pay you back?"

"Silly, silly girl. If we would've given her the entire set at once, then not only would we all be out for the price of the crystal, but we'd have to come up with money for other gifts throughout the year. It was a wise financial choice," said LeAnn.

Carla wondered what took them so long. She set down her glass of wine to search for them.

"What's a good financial choice?" she asked.

"I have the complete set of Mom's crystal in here and Paula thought we should've given it to her all at once. I merely explained doing that would cost us more gifts throughout the year."

"Just as well. She wasn't too thrilled with the glass she got, anyway," said Carla.

"I'm a little surprised you spent your own money on the entire set," said Paula.

She had time to contemplate the crystal since her mother's funeral when she first discovered it. To spend money in such a way was too out of character for LeAnn. She could come up with no conceivable reason why.

Carla climbed up on the bed while Paula draped a lavender chenille throw over her shoulders to ward off the chill.

Carla studied LeAnn's face.

"You did spend your own money on it, didn't you?"

"In a roundabout way, yes."

"How roundabout?" asked Carla.

"Look at it this way. If Mom had not sold the crystal, what would happen to it after she died?" asked LeAnn.

"I suppose it would belong to you, the first born daughter in the family," said Paula.

"Exactly. The crystal is my birthright. It's been handed down to the oldest daughter for generations. When I was a little girl I used to spend hours admiring it in the china cabinet, knowing someday it would be mine. I looked at it as though it were mine. It broke my heart when she sold it. She had no right to sell my crystal."

Her voice grew louder and her face transformed into a look neither of the girls were familiar with.

“LeAnn it wasn’t your crystal. It was Mom’s,” said Carla.

“No, you’re wrong it was meant to be mine. I’m the oldest. You wouldn’t understand, it was never going to be yours. Why should you care if she sold it? You had all your Christmas gifts and yummy food at the expense of my crystal. I feel justified with what I did.”

Paula stunned, said, “LeAnn, we all had the gifts and the food Mom bought with the money from selling it. You sure didn’t mind those gifts back then. Cut Carla some slack here, don’t forget what happened today.”

“No, no. I want to know what she means by feeling justified,” said Carla.

“I bought the crystal with Mom’s investment money,” she blurted out.

“You didn’t,” said Carla.

“It was my right.”

“The hell it was.”

Paula paced in the room. She felt guilty for having started this discussion, not knowing it would turn into such a huge battle. She looked at LeAnn with her perfect hair and makeup; she looked at Carla who had black lines running down her face. At this moment it was difficult to believe they were sisters. She stood in an elegantly decorated room with tapestry drapes and bedspread.

Expensive sculptures adorned the room. No wonder she felt uncomfortable lying down in the room the last time she was here. This room looked as if it should be on the page of a decorator's magazine and it would be a crime to touch anything. With all of this wealth surrounding her, why did LeAnn have to care so much about that damned crystal?

"Does Mom know you used her money to buy the crystal?" asked Carla.

"Duh, of course not. I invested her money carefully. I had hoped she would've lived long enough that we could've all chipped in."

"That damned crystal widow fund. You had no intentions of doing something nice for Mom. All you wanted was for us to repay you for that crystal, for your own greedy reasons."

"You both owe me. That was my crystal. Get out! Get out of my house."

Paula drove Carla's car to her house. She wished Glen would be there. She really did not want to continue this argument against LeAnn and with Glen present the subject would be dropped.

As she thought of Glen, she remembered his arm. He should not be driving. She hoped he would be okay.

When Glen entered the police station, he realized he should have called ahead. Detective Larson could be out on a case. He recalled the few hours he himself actually spent at his desk compared to the hours out on investigation. His armed throbbed. He took the pain pills from his jacket pocket. He opened the bottle pouring a couple out onto his hand. With his index finger he rolled the two yellow pills around his palm. He put them back into the bottle and closed the lid. His strong desire to stay alert overpowered the pain.

He introduced himself at the front desk and asked to speak with Detective Larson. Luck was in his favor. Larson had not yet gone out for the day.

"Glen," he said as he answered the tap on his door. "How's that arm?"

"I'll live."

"What can I do for you?"

"I'm not sure. I may have a case for you to investigate."

"Here in Omaha? How'd you get yourself involved in another case so fast? Or are we still dealing with your writer friend?"

"No, and I may be way off base here but something doesn't smell right to me. I thought I'd discuss it with you and see what you think."

"Shoot," said Larson. "Er a, sorry. What's your story?"

"This morning I found out about a guy I know being found dead in his house."

"You know this guy?" he asked, flipping the file around to Glen.

"Yeah. I had pizza with him last night. He was perfectly fine when he left. Do you know the cause of death?"

"I'm waiting to hear back from the coroner's office, still researching family history and his medical records. You know the drill."

"What's bothering you about this? You suspect something, don't you? The guy lived in a pretty nice neighborhood. Did he make his money with drugs?"

"Nah, computers," said Glen. "Last night he was talking to me about breaking up with his girl and today he's dead. I can't say I'm completely comfortable with that scenario. He had a theory about the men in his girl's family being cursed."

"Wait a minute." Larson dialed his phone. He spoke with the coroner.

"They're leaning toward a run of the mill heart attack," said Larson.

Glen ran his fingers through his hair. "I had really hoped you weren't gonna say that."

"Why? Does that blow your theory of a scorned lover?"

"No. It actually makes me more worried. Did his mother give clearance for an autopsy?"

"I'm not sure. You really think I need to dig into this a little deeper, don't you?"

"Yes, I'd appreciate it."

"You know, Glen. I have a lot of respect for you and the work you did on that attempted homicide involving your friend. But to go over his mother's head and order an autopsy, you're gonna have to give me a little more to go on."

"I don't have all the facts and this could be hearsay but it sounds too coincidental to me. This case goes back a long time and crosses out of your jurisdiction."

"I've got the time. I like a good story. Let's have it."

"There's these three women. I'm staying with one of them, her sister is the girlfriend in question for our deceased."

"And the third one?"

"The third one also lost her husband. Anyway, there's these three women and their mother. The mother and their father lived in California. They lost their infant son. Screwed the dad up in a big sort of way and he got dropped from the Air Force. They moved to Omaha and then the dad's found dead. No autopsy, booze and tranquilizers. She remarries this new guy. He plans to leave her and suddenly he shows up dead, a heart attack."

"I'm not sure where you're going with this, Glen. Heart attacks are pretty common."

"I know. That third sister, LeAnn, she marries this rich older guy and soon he's dead."

"Heart attack?"

"Yep."

Larson changed his position from leaning back in his chair. Glen finally caught his attention. He leaned forward with his elbows on the desk to listen more intently.

"This other woman, the one you're living with. Has she ever been married?"

"She's a widow."

Larson stopped chewing on the end of his pencil.

"Heart attack, huh?"

"Coincidence?" asked Glen.

"Could be, but then maybe not. Any of these guys have autopsies done?"

"Not to my knowledge. I was hoping that would be something you could look into for me."

"For you? Do you want to consult on the case?"

"I'd sure like to get involved if you'd let me. I kinda have an inside line."

"That could prove extremely valuable. Like before, with your Denver case, we'll keep each other posted. Just don't go shooting anyone. Let us handle that."

"I'm okay with that," said Glen. "One more thing, the girl's mother died recently."

"Correct me if I'm wrong in assuming cause of death was a heart attack."

"No need to correct you."

"You know, it's hell to have something like this happening right under my nose and not have a clue. I wonder how often this really happens?"

"Exactly." Glen stood and shook hands with Larson.

"We'll keep in touch," said Larson. "And take care of that arm."

Glen walked out of the office massaging his arm, hoping to ease the cutting pain. He wondered if his face expressed his pain or if Larson had first hand experience of a gunshot wound.

Paula's small economy car added to the discomfort. He had to squeeze in, then reach across his chest with his right arm to close the door. He needed bourbon in the worst way.

Paula tried to calm Carla who remained furious at LeAnn. She watched and listened to her as she fumed about the crystal incident. Maybe it was not all bad, it seemed to take her mind of off Anthony.

Paula opened her purse to search for her cell phone; she found the tin of tea from LeAnn. She removed the black tin painted with an intricate Oriental design.

"I see you have the tea LeAnn and I found for you. We were shopping at a holistic store and found all these marvelous dried leaves of tea. You could make your own blend. They had books sitting around on the tables to browse for the medicinal value of different teas. The lady ensured us they were all 100% organic."

"Thanks, but it really tastes bad," said Paula.

"The woman there told us it would. She said it's fresher than what you buy in the stores. They're supposed to have more essential oils in them and the taste might be a bit weedy because they've not been dried completely down."

"Great. I'm drinking weed tea."

Glen walked in. He hung his coat over the back of one of the dining room chairs.

"How'd things go downtown?" asked Paula.

"Fine. They said Anthony had a heart attack." He watched their faces for signs of anything out of the ordinary.

"Just like Andy," said Paula, feeling sad. She placed her hand on her belly.

"Was he on any medication that you were aware of, Carla?" asked Glen.

"No, he took lots of vitamins, but had no medical problem that I was aware of."

"That sounds too weird, a lot like Andy," Paula pointed out.

"You don't look so good, Glen," said Carla.

"I don't feel too good."

"Let me make a sandwich for you and I'll pour you a glass of your preferred medicine," said Paula.

"No, thanks. I can make my own sandwich."

"Yeah right. You go lie down and we'll bring you something in a few minutes."

"I'm not one to argue with two beautiful women."

He went to his room to lie down. He preferred the solitude to the guestroom upstairs.

LeAnn and Carla made up at Anthony's funeral. Glen accompanied Paula so he could check out the guests--a detective is always on duty. The pain in his arm eased with each passing day. The decision to stay or go weighed heavily on his mind.

The day before the doctor's deadline to give Glen back his freedom to drive, Paula became ill.

Glen noticed her face grew more pale each day.

"Are you feeling okay?" he asked.

"I guess. I've never been pregnant before so I don't know what's normal and what's not."

"What's your doctor say?"

"He says the vomiting and diarrhea are common and I shouldn't worry unless it becomes too frequent."

"Is there anything I can do for you? I'm feeling more mobile."

"I could use a cup of tea."

"Sure, I can handle that. What flavor?"

"Try the one in the black tin. I've been trying to drink some every day. It's organic and supposed to be healthier for me and the baby."

Glen opened the tin and the strong spearmint smell irritated his sinuses.

"Wow. This is nasty stuff. You actually drink this?"

"It gets easier each time. You should try some."

"Ain't happenin'. I'll stick with black coffee, has to be safer than this."

Paula's condition worsened. Glen waited on her with tea and crackers for two days. He tried to get her to eat something but she refused.

"You know, I think you should go to the doctor. He might want to put you in the hospital to hook you up to an IV."

"No, thank you. That's the perfect reason to not call him."

She went into the bathroom. Glen contemplated calling her sisters to see if they could be more persuasive than he.

"Glen!" she called out. "Hurry!"

He rushed to her side.

"I'm having really bad cramps. I don't want to lose my baby."

"You stay here." He laid her on the floor in the bathroom with rolled towels under her head and knees. "I'm calling an ambulance."

Chapter 16

Paula's doctor walked into the visitor's lounge. Glen, LeAnn and Carla waited impatiently for word of her condition.

"She's severely dehydrated from the diarrhea and vomiting she's experienced this last week. We're hydrating her with an IV. Once her stomach settles and she can hold food down she should be able to go home. The cramping has us confused. At this point, the baby is fine and she shows no signs of premature labor. All of her vitals are strong."

"What caused all the vomiting in the first place?" asked Glen.

"I'm guessing the pregnancy itself caused your wife to be nauseated. It's more common in the first trimester than in the second but it can happen that way. I'd make sure she gets plenty of rest and keeps eating. Your baby is going to need all the nutrition he can get."

"He?" asked Carla.

"I'm sorry, Paula said you already knew it was a boy," said the doctor.

"Not for sure," said Carla.

The doctor excused himself, leaving them to discuss Paula's situation.

"It was a slip of the tongue about *your wife*, wasn't it?" asked LeAnn.

"Of course it was. I'm telling you we're not married. Hell, I'm not even divorced. I saw no reason to confuse things. She'll be leaving here soon," said Glen.

LeAnn and Carla went in to see Paula. Glen waited in the lounge. He wanted the sisters to have their privacy. He thought it strange how quickly he found himself involved with the family when all he intended to do was rent a room.

He called Jennifer to inform her of the sex of the baby.

"Hey Jennifer, Glen."

"How's Paula?" she asked.

"She's fine. How did you know she was in the hospital?"

"I didn't. I knew something was wrong, but I didn't know what. Tell me what happened."

"She's been sick for about a week. You know that pregnancy puking your guts out stuff. She started to dehydrate and had cramps. We thought she was losing the baby so I called an ambulance. The doc says she'll be fine once they can get some fluid and food into her. He says it's not uncommon."

"Glen, there's a black cloud over her. There's more to it than pregnancy symptoms. Either she or someone tried to get rid of that baby."

"I thought of that but tried to ignore it? She's thrilled to be having this baby and she's been around no one except her sisters and me. Oh, by the way, Anthony died."

"Oh dear. How did that happen? Was he in an accident?"

"No. Right as you guys pulled away from the curb Paula's phone rang. It was one of her sisters. Carla found him dead in his house. He had a heart attack."

"That's not right, Glen. Had he been ill or experiencing a problem with his heart I would've picked up on it spending the evening with him. That man was perfectly healthy at the party. Glen, I think you might be dealing with a homicide. I think if you can find out who killed Anthony, you will also find out who poisoned Paula."

"Poison? Who said anything about poison?" asked Glen.

"I guess I just did. You need to look into this. Can you think of any food or medicine she's been taking that no one else has?"

"I've been eating every day with her since my arm makes it difficult to drive. She either fixes something or drives to pick up some fast food. We don't always order the same food but we've been eating together."

"I suppose she could have had food poisoning from the fast food, that's not uncommon. That's one reason I'm so opposed to eating it. But I really feel that's not the case. It'll come to you. I'm sure of it."

"How's Maggi doing?"

"She's getting better every day. If you didn't know what she's been through you'd never know her slow speech is abnormal. She went with Bill to pick up her dogs. They should be back any minute."

"I told her not to leave. I don't want anyone knowing she's in Denver," he fumed.

"Calm down, Glen. She promised to stay hidden in the car while Bill loaded the dogs. Between the two of them I'm confident she'll be safe. I feel no danger for her today."

"I hope you're right."

"Oh, wait the car is pulling into the driveway right now. Uh oh, something's wrong. Maggi's crying."

Maggi burst into the door in tears. "My dogs! She took my dogs!"

Glen heard Maggi.

"Put her on the phone."

"It's Glen." She handed the phone to Maggi.

"Glen, they're gone. My dogs are gone and there's no sign of them."

"Calm down, Maggi. Maybe she took them out for a walk or to a dog park. I'm sure she'll be home later."

"No Glen. There's a pile of newspapers on her front step. Her mailbox was bulging with mail. I thought maybe something happened to her. I told Bill where her spare key was. He unlocked the door and went in to look for her. I followed him. Glen, they're gone."

"Let me talk to Bill."

"Hey Glen, how's the arm? I heard you were quite the hero at the hospital."

"I'm fine. What'd you see at Jean's?"

"Maggi's right. Looks like she took out of there in a hurry. Dishes in the sink, old coffee drying up in the pot and clothes tossed around the bedroom like someone packed in a hurry."

"Any sign of an intruder?"

"Nah. The scene doesn't leave you with that feeling. I'd say she rushed out in a hurry. I did see her phone book opened to boarding kennels. I called to see if she took the dogs there. Yours are fine, but no sign of Jean's dogs or Maggi's."

"What the hell are my dogs doing in a kennel? Where's Debbie?"

"Can't answer that for you. Want me to get your dogs out of jail and keep them at my place?"

"Yeah, that'd be great. Thanks."

Maggi took the phone from Bill.

"Are you coming home soon? You have to help me find my dogs," she cried.

Maggi put Glen in an uncomfortable position. He desperately wanted to help her. If what Jennifer said about Paula had an ounce of truth to it, he had to stay behind to finish this case he unknowingly became involved in.

"Maggi, I can't"

"What do you mean you can't? You have to come home and help me."

"Maggi, let Bill help you. Paula's in the hospital, Anthony's dead. I think I'm right in the middle of a multiple homicide. I can't walk away now. I have to see this through. I'm not going to leave you hanging, kiddo. Bill and I will work together and we'll find Jean and your babies. I just have to be here for now."

"So it's true. There is something going on with you and Paula. Fine, stay there."

She slammed the phone down.

Glen's head began to swim. He had the group of unexplained heart attacks, he had a possible attempt on Paula's life, he had Maggi's missing dogs and his missing wife. Even for a detective with as keen a mind as his, trying to focus on all of them at once proved difficult.

He had no choice but to prioritize the problems and solve them one by one. The first on his list was Paula. He felt responsible knowing someone managed to harm her right under his nose. Glen took situations like that personally.

He tapped on the door to her room before entering.

"How're ya doing?" he asked.

"I've been better. At least the baby's okay. Doc says if I can keep food and liquids down they'll get rid of this." She raised her arm connected to the IV.

"Don't rush it. You stay here as long as they think you should. Don't argue with them. You have to think of the baby."

The nurse brought in her tray. She had a bland diet of rice, dry toast and applesauce. Paula dipped the tea bag in the cup of hot water while she and her sisters talked about the baby boy.

Glen stared out of the window. His mind worked like a computer analyzing the data he gathered since he first met Paula and her family. He reran his conversation with Anthony about the deaths in the family. He looked across the room at Paula with sadness. He wanted to tell her of her danger but she'd been through too much. She squeezed her teabag.

The tea, he thought. That's it.

"Gotta go. I'll see you three later."

"What's the rush?" asked LeAnn.

"Maggi called. Her dogs are missing. I need to call her back."

His pace quickened as he walked to the elevator. Out in the parking lot he jogged to his truck. The jogging brought an ache to his arm that he chose to ignore. He struggled to make the tight turns with one arm. He managed to get out of the parking lot and into the flow of traffic. His mind replayed the previous week's meals. Paula had that tea with almost every meal. When she quit eating she still consumed the tea with crackers to calm her stomach.

He unlocked the house and searched the kitchen cabinets for the tin. He opened the phone book to look for herbal stores. No luck. He found the phone number for the county extension office. His upbringing as a small town country boy came in handy. Most city people would not even know what a county extension agent was.

He dialed the number.

"Yes, I have a plant that I'd like to have identified."

"Bring it in and we'll have a look at it," said the secretary.

"It's been dried and crumbled. Will that be a problem?"

"I'm sure it will. We would have no way to identify it if we can't see the leaves."

Glen thought for a minute. "It's probably an herb. Can you tell from the color and the smell?"

"That's a different story. That might be possible."

Glen got directions then drove to the extension office.

Dr. Lamont shook hands with Glen.

"What can I do for you?" she asked.

"Can you tell me what plants are contained in this tea?"

She poured the contents onto a sheet of white paper on her desk. With her pen she sorted the leaves into piles of the same shade of green. When she accumulated at least a half-teaspoon of three different varieties, she picked them up one at a time between her thumb and forefinger to sniff. She poured them into the palm of her hand and rolled the leaves around crushing them even more to release the aroma individual to each plant.

"This is peppermint," she said, pointing to the first pile. "This is pennyroyal and this last one is spearmint."

She poured more tea from the tin. Upon closer inspection she noted the most prevalent ingredient was pennyroyal.

"What's this mixture used for?" she asked.

"It's the tea a friend of mine's been drinking."

"Is there a problem? Why are you wanting to know the ingredients?"

"She's not been feeling well and I wondered if there was something in the tea that might not agree with her."

"The mint teas are used to calm the digestive system. Pennyroyal, although it has a minty aroma, is not generally used in teas. When it is, the amount is usually minimal."

"Why's that?" asked Glen.

"This herb was used in the 1800's to induce abortion. Unfortunately, the amount needed to actually induce the abortion was so close to a lethal dose that, too often, the women died as well. As a precaution, herbalists don't recommend a pregnant woman drink or handle the tea. One never knows if someone with sensitivity could have adverse reactions. This blend has an unpalatable amount of pennyroyal in it. I'm surprised your friend actually drank it."

"I don't know anything about teas and herbs. Are the effects of pennyroyal common knowledge for most women?"

"I suppose if one is a gardener or into health foods they might know the history. It's not difficult to find the history in any herb book."

Glen shook her hand and thanked her.

Someone definitely tried to stop Paula from having her baby. Paula and her mother were avid gardeners. Maybe Paula herself decided having the baby was too overwhelming. Maybe she was completely aware of the tea she was drinking. No way, he concluded.

He returned to the hospital to check on her.

"The doctor says I'm doing great and can go home tomorrow. I've been able to keep my food down the whole day."

"That's great," said Glen. "Where are your sisters?"

"They had to leave. LeAnn got a call from her office. An auditor needed to look over some of her files. Carla went home to clean her house. She wants me to stay with her for a couple of days."

The mention of Paula being out of his sight and in the presence of her sisters made him uncomfortable. He did not know how to stop that from happening without raising suspicion.

"So you don't feel comfortable having me take care of you?" he teased.

"That's not it. You've been great. But I thought you were in a hurry to head back to Denver."

"I decided to stay on a few more days to be sure you were going to be okay."

"That's really sweet, Glen. I'm going to be fine."

He sniffed her cup of tea. "Still can't do the coffee thing?"

"No, especially now that I'm pregnant. No way am I going to drink that vile drink," she teased.

"Maybe I should try to find out what you and Jennifer see in all the tea you two drink. I think you two are addicted to the stuff. What's your favorite?"

"Oh, gosh. I don't know. I like so many. Orange pekoe, chamomile, peppermint."

"Peppermint, is that the kind in the tin you've been drinking?"

"I wish. No, it's some blend LeAnn and Carla got for me at a health food store. They thought since it was organic I might prefer it."

"So it's not something you bought or grew yourself?"

"No, why?"

"Well, it was in a tin, not a box or bag, so I thought it was your own private blend."

"If I were going to make my own tea, I'd find something that tastes better."

Glen checked his watch. "I'd better go. You could use your rest. I'll stop by Carla's tomorrow to see how you're doing."

That night Glen did not sleep well. He worried about Paula. He now believed one of her sisters could be dangerous. But which one? He would never forgive himself if something happened to Paula while she stayed at Carla's. He thought of the obsession the two sisters had, one for money and the other for insurance. Paula had no money to speak of and with her modest income she was probably under insured. He tossed and turned trying, to come up with a motive. There was none. He debated telling her about the tea but he did not want to let anything slip to the killer. He wondered if he could get the doctor to order her off of it for some medical reason.

Then he thought about Anna. She could have died from her bad heart or one of the girls could have killed her. They all had opportunity. Motive? That could be as simple as, she was a nasty thorn that they grew tired of.

It was nearly four in the morning before Glen drifted off to sleep. His alarm went off at six. Too tired to even consider getting up, he fumbled for the button on the alarm to turn off the blaring sound. He knocked his pill bottle and magazine onto the floor, but he successfully quieted the room and drifted back to sleep.

Carla arrived at the hospital as soon as Paula called her to tell her she had been released. She gathered her things and waited for the nurse to arrive with the wheelchair. No one brought her flowers, both sisters hated to part with the money when her stay was to be so short. Glen normally would have but his mind was more on saving her life than on flowers. Besides flowers are a great reason to visit her at Carla's.

Soon the nurse had them out on the curb assisting Paula from the wheelchair into the front seat of Carla's car. She felt great, the best she had felt in days.

Carla fixed lunch. She walked her to the guestroom where Paula settled in to rest and watch television. The doorbell rang. Carla went to the door. It was LeAnn.

"What're you doing here?" she asked.

LeAnn shoved past her.

"You bitch! I can't believe you did it!"

"Did what?"

"Don't play innocent with me. You know exactly what you did."

"Oh, do you mean the auditor?"

"Yes, I mean the auditor. What else could I mean? Why did you do it?"

"It was Mom's dying wish to have her accounts with you audited. I simply followed through. Amazing what he found, wasn't it. You've been screwing Mom out of her money all along. The money she and Lawrence invested mysteriously ended up in your name. Why, even most of Anthony's money ended up in your name. I had his mother sign for the auditor to check his accounts, too."

"You did what? How could you?"

"I had to. Mom's right, you can't be trusted."

"Me? What about you? Isn't it odd that all of Mom's insurance policies had you as the only beneficiary? Talk about not being trustworthy. When were you going to tell us about that?

"Shhh. Paula's resting. No need to drag her into this. Let's talk downstairs."

LeAnn looked in the direction of the guestroom. She debated whether or not to wake Paula so she could find out about the insurance scam Carla was pulling. But then she would also find out about the audit. She decided to follow Carla into the basement.

The ringing sound of Glen's cell phone startled him awake. He forgot where he was for a moment. The dark basement kept the sunlight out of his room allowing him to catch up on the hours he lost during the night, while he worried about Paula.

His phone was on the dresser across the room from the bed. He jumped up to answer it. As he darted across the floor he hopped and danced as he stepped on his pills that had spilled on the floor when he turned off his alarm clock.

"Hello."

"Glen, Larson here."

Glen sat on the bed picking the tiny yellow pills from his foot.

"Yeah, Larson. Did you find anything?"

"You bet we did. Glen, your hunch was right. The autopsy showed a high level of digitalis in this guy's bloodstream."

"Enough to kill him?"

"Enough to kill an elephant."

Glen turned on the light and sat on the floor to gather the rest of the pills.

"What exactly does digitalis do to the body?"

"It makes you sick as hell to begin with, sorta mimics food poisoning. Most people just puke their guts out and get rid of it. But if enough of it is masked in food, you might get rid of it. If that's the case, after about six hours or so your heart starts to flutter. It gets worse and finally it stops cold."

"Like a heart attack?"

"Exactly."

"So your guess is someone slipped it to him in his food?"

"That'd be my first guess."

"Any idea what the drug looks like?"

"I checked that out with my lab guys. It's a relatively small yellow tablet. Guess it doesn't take much to be lethal."

Glen looked at the small yellow tablets in his hand more closely.

"Do they have any distinguishable marks on them?"

"Yeah, they do."

Larson checked his notes and read the description to Glen.

"Holy shit! I gotta go."

The pills he had in his hand were not the pain pills prescribed by his doctor. They were digitalis. Someone had exchanged them. That explained why the bottle was not tightly closed and the pills spilled out when he knocked it over. Whoever had made the switch was too hasty returning the lid. Rather than worry about fingerprints his thoughts turned to Paula.

He pulled on his socks and shoes and headed out the door. He drove frantically to Carla's house when no one answered the phone.

The argument between Carla and LeAnn escalated when they reached the basement. Carla's desk had files labeled with LeAnn's name, Anthony's name and Paula's name. LeAnn picked up her own folder. Inside she found a two million dollar policy on herself with Carla as the beneficiary.

"I didn't authorize this. I know I didn't buy this insurance."

She grabbed Paula's folder and found the same. Anthony's folder policy was for ten million.

When she looked up at Carla to confront her, she was shocked to see Carla with a gun pointed at her.

"Carla, are you nuts? What's the gun for?"

"I can't let you get away now. I planned to do away with Paula today but you have ruined my little plan."

"What? You're crazy! What plan?"

"Mom told me a long time ago to always watch out for yourself because no one else would. She said Daddy was ruining our family and drinking away our grocery money. She had to kill him. She said it was easy. She slipped a little of her digitalis in his beer. His heart stopped while we were off enjoying a birthday dinner. Daddy didn't have any insurance. Mom said she'd never make that mistake again. She intentionally married a man who sold insurance. Lawrence was no accident. When I told Mom about his girlfriend, she had to take care of him before he left her penniless.

"Reed was easy. No one was surprised when he had a heart attack at his age. Andy was a little more difficult."

"Mom killed them all?"

"Of course not. I came up with the idea for Reed and Andy all by myself. I wrote up nice big policies on them. When the checks came in, I forged your signatures and cashed them myself."

"What about Anthony?"

"The fool. I can't believe he planned to leave me. You know, I really hated to get rid of him so soon. He was really entertaining and the sex, well, the sex was great."

"Why Paula?"

"I need to finish her off then you and I can retire into the lifestyle you've always pressured me to live. So you, see big sister, I'm only doing what you and Mom taught me. I'm taking care of myself and doing it with money."

"You'll never get away with it. How's it gonna look when Paula and I show up dead in your house? Glen won't let it rest."

"Oh yes, our friendly police detective. Damn him for getting involved. Fortunately, for me he got shot. Did you notice his pain pills look exactly like Mom's digitalis? It wasn't exactly a stroke of genius to exchange the pills. That job had to be the easiest of them all. My guess is by now; poor Detective Karst is lying on his bed dead in Paula's house. I couldn't very well let her go home and find him, now could I?"

LeAnn lunged for the gun in Carla's hand. Carla fired one shot but the wayward bullet careened harmless off the floor and lodged in the wall.

"Now you did it. I'm sure Paula's gonna be here any minute to find out where the gunshot came from. You can't fight us both off."

"Don't worry about Paula. I slipped a sedative in her cranberry juice at lunch. If you wouldn't have shown up, the house would already be up in flames."

LeAnn saw the cans of lighter fluid stacked on the floor next to wall with a box of matches.

"You wouldn't burn down your own home?"

"Sure I would. It's heavily insured."

"You're sick. You need help."

"Yes, I do. I need someone to keep you quiet while I finish what I set out to do."

Carla held the gun on LeAnn while she walked around the room lighting candles. She placed them on every table and shelf in her family room and office. She planned to start the fire in the basement, giving her plenty of time to set it and leave. The candles would burn down to the crumpled paper she set next to them. She began to squirt lighter fluid along the walls and on the furniture.

She stopped and looked at LeAnn.

"You seem to be a problem. If I shoot you and they recover your burned body, a bullet hole will show it wasn't an accident."

She sat on the corner of her desk contemplating how to get rid of LeAnn.

LeAnn watched the candles burning down closer to the paper that leaned against them. She looked at her sister who obviously had gone insane. If she did not move quickly they could all perish in the fire. She raced for the stairs. Carla ran after her. She grabbed her leg, pulling her back down the stairs. They struggled on the floor rolling around in the lighter fluid.

As the struggle continued, the first candle ignited the paper up against it. Carla grabbed the iron pig door holder on the floor next to them and began hitting LeAnn in the head with it. She hoped to knock her out to avoid turning an accident into a homicide.

Carla, with LeAnn pinned to the floor, set the gun down as she raised both hands over her head to bring the pig down with one hard blow, hoping to render her unconscious as the flames inched dangerously close.

LeAnn, with only seconds to spare, reached for the gun, fired it and rolled out from under Carla's strike in one swift move. Carla fell over and the fire now consumed the entire lower level. The fumes and smoke made it difficult for LeAnn to breathe. Her vision blurred from being struck on the head, she tried to climb the stairs but as she reached the top step, the flames and smoke had risen.

Glen squealed his tires as he turned the corner into the driveway. He saw smoke and flames in the basement windows of the house. The front door was locked. He picked up a flower stand from the porch and put it through the picture window. He climbed in. Smoke filled the main level now. He searched for a way into the basement to see if the girls were down there. He found LeAnn unconscious at the top of the stairs. He tried to pick her up. The pain in his arm was unbearable; he threw her over his shoulder and out onto the lawn. He went back inside, the flames had made their way up the stairs so he could no longer go into the basement. He covered his mouth with his shirt and crawled through the house checking the other rooms.

He found Paula in one of the bedrooms. The smoke was thinner at that end of the house. He took a deep breath then pulled Paula from the bed and over his shoulder. Once outside he set her down then collapsed next to them. He lay on his back choking and gasping for air. Blood oozed from his arm.

Soon the yard swarmed with firemen and police. When Larson checked the address on the call, he recognized it from the report he and Glen worked up on the three sisters. He arrived on the scene after the paramedics.

"Are you okay, Karst?"

Glen, charred and exhausted, sat in the back of an ambulance drawing in breaths of oxygen. An EMT worked on his arm.

"I'm fine."

"How're the girls?"

"I missed one. I couldn't get to her. I think she was in the basement."

"Don't worry about it. You did the best you could under the circumstances."

"You know, Karst, you're either gonna have to let me put you on as a detective here or get the hell back to Denver so Omaha can return to a quiet little city."

Now it's time to test "*your*" ability as a detective. Can you find the "Elusive Clue"?
It's a word puzzle hidden within the story.
The answer to the puzzle will spell out the name of the killer.
To solve the puzzle:

A. You must locate the page or pages containing the puzzle.
B. Locate the letters you will need to unscramble the name of the killer.

I hope you enjoyed this book. If you haven't already read them, try "Tryst with Dolphins", the sequel "Dolphins' Echo", "Death Foreshadowed" and "Victim Wanted" for more exciting mysteries and once again the challenge of finding that "elusive clue".

Patricia A. Bremmer